TWENTIETH CENTURY VIEWS

The aim of this series is to present the best in contemporary critical opinion on major authors, providing a twentieth century perspective on their changing status in an era of profound revaluation.

Maynard Mack, *Series Editor*
Yale University

PASTERNAK

PASTERNAK,

A COLLECTION OF CRITICAL ESSAYS

Edited by

Victor Erlich, 1914 –

Prentice-Hall, Inc. *Englewood Cliffs, N.J.*

A SPECTRUM BOOK

Library of Congress Cataloging in Publication Data
Main entry under title:

PASTERNAK.

   (Twentieth century views) (A Spectrum Book).
   Bibliography: p.
   1. Pasternak, Boris Leonidovich, 1890-1960.
Criticism and interpretation—Addresses, essays,
lectures. I. Erlich, Victor (date).
PG3476.P27Z747   891.7'1'42   77-21223
ISBN 0-13-652834-1
ISBN 0-13-652826-0 pbk.

Z 891.73
P
475834

10 9 8 7 6 5 4 3 2 1

PRENTICE-HALL INTERNATIONAL, INC. *(London)*
PRENTICE-HALL OF AUSTRALIA PTY. LIMITED *(Sydney)*
PRENTICE-HALL OF CANADA, LTD. *(Toronto)*
PRENTICE-HALL OF INDIA PRIVATE LIMITED *(New Delhi)*
PRENTICE-HALL OF JAPAN, INC. *(Tokyo)*
PRENTICE-HALL OF SOUTHEAST ASIA PTE. LTD. *(Singapore)*
WHITEHALL BOOKS LIMITED *(Wellington, New Zealand)*

Acknowledgments

Quotations from *Modern Russian Poetry* by Vladimir Markov and Merrill Spacks are used by kind permission of The Bobbs-Merrill Co., Inc. and MacGibbon and Kee Limited/ Granada Publishing Limited. Copyright© 1966, 1967 by MacGibbon and Kee Limited.

Quotations from *In the Interlude: Poems 1945-1960* by Boris Pasternak, translated by Henry Kamen, are used by kind permission of A. D. Peters & Co., Ltd.

Quotations from *The Poetry of Boris Pasternak,* translated by George Reavey, are used by kind permission of G. P. Putnam's Sons. © 1959 G. P. Putnam's Sons.

The quotation from "Hamlet" by Boris Pasternak from *The Penguin Book of Russian Verse,* edited and translated by Dimitri Obolensky (1965), pp. 335-36, is used by kind permission of Penguin Books Ltd. Copyright © Dimitri Obolensky, 1962, 1965.

Quotations from Boris Pasternak, *Poems,* 2nd ed., and for scattered quotes of poetry from "The Poems of Doctor Zhivago," by Dimitri Obolensky, are used by kind permission of the Estate of Eugene M. Kayden. Mr. Kayden translated these works.

Quotations from Dale L. Plank, *Pasternak's Lyric* are used by kind permission of Mouton Publishers, The Hague.

Quotations from the Pantheon Books version of *Doctor Zhivago,* by Boris Pasternak, translated by Max Hayward and Manya Harari, are used by kind permission of the publisher. Copyright © 1958 by Pantheon Books, Inc. Pantheon is a division of Random House, Inc.

Quotations from Boris Pasternak, *Poems 1955-1959,* translated by Michael Harari, are used by kind permission of Collins Publishers.

Quotations from the Russian edition of Boris Pasternak, *Doktor Zhivago* (Ann Arbor: The University of Michigan Press, 1958) are used by kind permission of Giangiacomo Feltrinelli, Milan. Copyright © Giangiacomo Feltrinelli 1961.

Boris Pasternak's "Marburg," translated by Yakov Hornstein, is used by kind permission of Mr. Hornstein.

The quotation from "If Only When I Made My Debut," translated by Babette Deutsch and Maurice Bowra, from Boris Pasternak's *Safe Conduct* is reprinted by permission of New Directions Publishing Corporation. Copyright 1949 by New Directions Publishing Corporation.

Contents

PASTERNAK

Introduction:

Categories of Passion

by Victor Erlich

> Images, that is, miracles wrought in the word, that is, instances of a total and arrowlike submission to the earth. And that means directions which will take their tomorrow's morality, their thrust toward truth.
>
> (BORIS PASTERNAK, "A TALE")

I

Nearly twenty years ago the events which followed the appearance of *Doctor Zhivago* brought belatedly to the attention of the Western reading public the ordeal and the achievement of one of our century's finest poets. Since then many of us have had occasion — due in no small measure to the courage of a remarkable widow[1] — to contemplate the still more harrowing plight and the no less dazzling art of one of Pasternak's most distinguished contemporaries, Osip Mandelstam. In fact, during the last decade, Mandelstam's poetic craft has loomed somewhat larger than Pasternak's in the Western forays into modern Russian poetry. Yet where authentic genius is involved, comparative ranking is futile and presumptuous. Essentially Pasternak's position in Russian literature remains as secure as ever. So does the claim on our imagination and admiration of the Pasternak story, replete as it is with paradoxes that verge on miracles. For it is a story of an inwardly free poet in an increasingly unfree society, of a pure lyricist forced by history to bear witness on some of the crucial public issues of our time, a survivor of one of the darkest eras in his country's history who left behind a body of work as bracing and life-affirming as any found in the annals of modern letters.

Other essays presented in this collection will chart Pasternak's

---

[1] See Nadezhda Mandelstam, *Hope Against Hope: A Memoir,* translated by Max Hayward (New York: Atheneum, 1970); *Hope Abandoned,* translated by Max Hayward (New York: Atheneum, 1974).

complex creative evolution and illuminate various stages and facets of his *oeuvre*. All I propose to do in these introductory remarks is to indicate some of the critical junctures in the poet's fateful encounter with his age, and suggest the ambiance of his poetic universe by pausing before one of his finest and most characteristic poems.[2]

A son of a well-known portrait painter and a concert pianist, he was born into a family where dedication to art and to the life of the mind was taken for granted. Poetry was not his first choice. He opted for it as a vocation and a way of life after a period of adolescent intoxication with music, under the spell of the charismatic turn-of-the-century composer Alexander Skryabin, and a subsequent heady bout with neo-Kantian philosophy at the University of Marburg. He entered the Russian modernist ferment on the eve of the First World War, under the aegis of the most militant grouping among the Russian poetic avant-garde, the Futurists. (True, Centrifugue, the avant-garde faction with which he was briefly affiliated, was by Futurist standards relatively moderate.) Yet this association proved short-lived and, arguably, somewhat fortuitous. While the young Pasternak's proclivity for the bold verbal experimentation which marked Futurist poetics is undeniable, he had little use for literary factionalism. The Bohemian antics and the strident posturing cultivated within the Futurist movement left him cold.[3]

Pasternak's early collections of verse, *Twin in the Clouds* (1914) and *Over the Barriers* (1917) contained, along with much that was immature, disheveled, and strained, some poems and lines of striking effectiveness and originality. *My Sister, Life,* comprised of lyrics written in 1917 but published in 1922, and the immediate sequel to it, *Themes and Variations* (1923), rank among the landmarks of modern Russian poetry. Filled to the brim with lyrical excitement, blending emotional intensity with an impetuous boldness of imagery, these slender volumes earned instant recognition and acclaim among the critics and the fellow poets alike.

[2]I am grateful to John Hopkins Press and the l'Institut des etudes slaves in Paris for giving me permission to incorporate in this introduction portions of my essay, "Life by Verses: Boris Pasternak" in *The Double Image: Concepts of the Poet in Slavic Literatures*, (Baltimore: John Hopkins Press, 1964), pp. 133-54, and of the bulk of my paper "Notes on 'Marburg,'" read at 1975 Pasternak Symposium in Cerisy-la-Salle.

[3]In his brilliant if at times cryptic first autobiography, *Safe Conduct* (1931), Pasternak avers that he could never understand Mayakovsky's apparent need for a "retinue of innovators," his loyalty to the "pygmy projects of his fortuitous coterie, hastily gathered together and always indecently mediocre" (Boris Pasternak, *The Collected Prose Works* [London: Lindsay Drummond Ltd., 1945] , pp. 112-13).

Affectionate and enthusiastic response of the latter is especially noteworthy. One of Pasternak's most richly endowed contemporaries, the brilliant poet Marina Tsvetaeva termed her breathless eulogy not a review but "an attempt to get out so as not to choke"..."This is the only of my peers," she added, "for whom my lungs had not been large enough."[4] Osip Mandelstam, too, saw fit to express his elation in a respiratory metaphor: "To read the poems of Pasternak is to get one's throat clear, to fortify one's breathing, to renovate one's lungs; such poems must be a cure for tuberculosis. At present we have no poetry that is healthier than this."[5]

Though the verses contained in *My Sister, Life* were composed in a kind of trance during the fateful summer of 1917, the theme of the Revolution entered these lyrics—at once nature and love poems— obliquely; it was present only as a pervasive sense of turmoil and renewal. Pasternak's doctrinaire detractors, who kept accusing him of self-centeredness and aloofness, were prompt to seize on the passage in "On These Verses" where the persona, still dazed after an encounter with George Byron and Edgar Allan Poe, looks out of his attic and calls to the children playing in the yard below: "What millenium is there, my dears?" But this moment of unworldly absent— mindedness is not a fair measure of Pasternak's sense of history. Keeping his fine sensibility available to historical experience, he did not fail to respond to the elemental sweep of the events, not with bewilderment, now with sympathetic fascination. As Marina Tsvetaeva put it in the above-quoted essay, "he walked alongside the Revolution and listened to it raptly." He sought to absorb and accept the new realities, but on his own terms and at his own pace, that is, as an uncommitted poet rather than a shrill propagandist. By the mid-twenties he clearly felt the need to engage history more directly and thus to transcend the purely lyrical realm.[6] The interesting, but not entirely successful, longer poems, "The Year Nine-

---

[4]The English translation of this essay, quoted near the end of this volume, by V. Weidlé, appears as "The Downpour of Light: Poetry of Eternal Courage" in the excellent collection of Pasternak criticism, edited by Donald Davie and Angela Livingstone, *Pasternak: Modern Judgments* (London: McMillan, 1969), pp. 42-66. This anthology will be referred to henceforth as Davie and Livingstone, eds., *Pasternak.*

[5]"Notes on Poetry," *op.cit.,* p. 71.

[6]In an early essay, "A Black Goblet" (1916), Pasternak says somewhat cryptically: "Reality disintegrates. In the process it crystallizes around two opposite poles: Lyricism and History. Both are equally absolute and *a priori,"* (Boris Pasternak, *Sochineniya [Works]* , [Ann Arbor, Mich.: University of Michigan Press, 1961] , II, 150-51.)

teen-Five" (1926), "Lieutenant Schmidt" (1927), as well as the unfinished novel in verse *Spektorsky* (1931) were attempts to grasp
the meaning of the Revolution by recreating its antecedents.[7] Yet
he would not be used or rushed. He would not be dragooned into
well-intentioned platitudes. "Hell is paved with good intentions./
A view has prevailed/ That if one paves verses with them/ All sins
will be forgiven" ("A Lofty Malady").[8]

It was not until the early thirties, when Russian literature was
being whipped into conformity, that the sense of grim foreboding
entered the buoyant poetry of Boris Pasternak. At first the note was
sounded with cryptic reticence:

> Why is it that when the great Soviet meets
> And highest passion inundates the hall
> The poet's vacancy has to be filled?
> His seat is dangerous if not unoccupied.[9]

But it became clearer in the following poem of 1932:

> If only when I made my debut
> There might have been a way to tell
> That lines with blood in them can murder.
> That they can flood the throat and kill.
>
> I certainly would have rejected
> A jest on such a sour note.
> So bashful was that early interest,
> The start was something so remote.
>
> But age is pagan Rome demanding
> No balderdash—no measured breadth,
> No fine feigned parody of dying
> But really being done to death.
>
> A line that feeling sternly dictates
>   Sends on the stage a slave and that
>   Means that the task of art is ended
>   And there's a breath of earth and fate.[10]

---

[7] For a more extended discussion of these exercises in the epic mode, see M. Aucouturier, "The Metonymous Hero of the Beginnings of Pasternak the Novelist,"
and Andrey Sinyavsky, "Pasternak's Poetry." Both are included in this volume.

[8] Boris Pasternak, *Sochineniya,* I, 264.

[9] Translated from Boris Pasternak, *Sochineyiya,* I, 223. Another English version
appears in Boris Pasternak, *The Collected Prose Works,* p. 37; Stefan Schimanski
was the translator.

[10] The translation is by Babette Deutsch, with the exception of the last stanza,

"A breath of earth and fate." The obtrusive theme of modern Russian poetry, that of the poet's tragic fate — a theme, let me add, which the author of *My Sister, Life* had hoped to eschew[11] — had finally caught up with Boris Pasternak. Apparently, life "by verses,"[12] was proving increasingly incompatible with the kind of commitment and the style of life fostered by the Russian society of the 1930s. When culture is treated as a weapon and literature as a source of moral edification, poetic detachment smacks of sabotage. When politics is viewed as the highest form of human activity, esthetic contemplation seems an act of political defiance. When dry-as-dust abstractions of an official ideology are increasingly used to displace reality and explain it away, even such politically innocuous qualities as delight in the sensory texture of things are likely to appear as escapism.

Repeatedly accused of subjectivism, estheticism and irrelevance, in a word, of being out of step with his time, Pasternak chose to draw upon his vast knowledge of, and profound affinity for, the Western masters. During the more than two decades of the Stalin era he denoted much of his creative energy to the art of translation, to rendering into Russian Shakespeare, Goethe, Schiller, Keats, Shelley, Verlaine. His translations of eight Shakespeare plays occasionally fall short of the dazzling verbal richness of the originals, but in the main are distinguished dramatic poetry in their own right, undergirded time and again by a perceptive reading of a Shakespeare masterpiece.[13]

What, in retrospect, appears surprising is not that Pasternak was muzzled but that he managed to weather the years of the Great Terror without arrest, exile or any other form of overt harassment. Did he, not unlike his hero Yury Andreyevich Zhivago, have a guardian angel, a mysterious and influential protector who kept intervening in his behalf? We do not know and we may never know. Strangely enough, he seems to have enjoyed the tyrant's bemused

---

which is drawn from Sir Maurice Bowra's version. (See Boris Pasternak, *Selected Writings* [New York: New Directions, 1949], pp. 288 and 271.)

[11] In a much-quoted passage in *Safe Conduct*, Pasternak spoke of his early resolve to abandon the Romantic image of the poet, which he describes as a "notion of biography as spectacle." A crucial consequence of this notion, he suggested, is the tendency to build lyrical cycles around the theme of the poet's plight.

[12] "Thus one begins to live by verses," ends a memorable poem from *Themes and Variations, Sochineniya*, I, 85.

[13] See Boris Pasternak, "Translating Shakespeare," in *I Remember* (New York: Pantheon, 1959), pp. 125-52.

tolerance, if not grudging admiration. Nadezhda Mandelstam and some other eyewitnesses tell the bizarre story of Stalin calling Pasternak in order to elicit his opinion of Osip Mandelstam.[14] Stalin's motivation remains obscure. Was he testing Pasternak's loyalty or was he seriously trying to secure some information on Mandelstram's standing as a poet from someone whom he labeled in his mind an "expert" in the field?

Be that as it may, Pasternak's own poetic voice was not heard again until 1943. The lyrics gathered in a slight volume, *On Early Trains,* composed in the throes of a shared national ordeal, sounded quietly but poignantly the theme of solidarity with one's severely tested countrymen. In 1954, the Soviet literary journal *Znamya (Banner)* published "Ten Poems from a Novel." Four years later the appearance of that novel made Pasternak a celebrity in the West even as it subjected him at home to the most virulent public attack of his entire career.

Doctor Zhivago was not Pasternak's first venture into narrative fiction. He had tried his hand at it in densely textured if somewhat baffling and contrived stories—for example, "Tratto di Apelle" (1915), "Letters from Tula" (1918), and "Aerial Ways" (1925)—and, to greatest effect, in "Childhood of Luvers" (1918-1924), a poetically delicate recreation of a young girl's discovery of the world around her, and "A Tale" (1929), which, as Michel Aucouturier demonstrates in his essay[15] has some points of contact with the novel in verse *Spektorsky* (1931). Sometime in the thirties, Pasternak embarked on his first full-length novel. He seems to have completed it in 1955. An inveterate optimist, he was so encouraged by the loosening of Soviet cultural policy after Stalin's death as to envision the publication of *Doctor Zhivago* in the Soviet Union. However, the editorial board of the relatively liberal journal *Novy Mir (New World)* turned down the novel. Though the statement was moderately phrased, its import was unmistakeable: Yury Zhivago was adjudged an unreconstructed bourgeois individualist and the novel itself a repudiation of the October Revolution.[16] In the meantime a publishing house in Milan, previously authorized by Pasternak to bring out the Italian version of *Doctor Zhivago,* proceeded to do so. The French, German, and English translations promptly followed.

The belated recognition in the West of Pasternak's wide-ranging

[14]See especially Nadezhda Mandelstam, *Hope Against Hope,* pp. 145-49.

[15]See pp. 43-50.

[16]For a more extended discussion of this document see Fyodor Stepun, "Boris Pasternak," which is reprinted in this volume.

achievement, coupled with admiration for his courage and sympathy for his plight, found expression in the Nobel prize for literature which was awarded in October of 1958. Faced by a crescendo of official abuse[17] and such reprisals as expulsion from the Soviet Writers' Union and the threat of banishment from his native land, Pasternak found himself compelled to turn down the award "because of the significance given to it in the society to which I belong." As a result the campaign subsided. But the limited vindication of the beleaguered poet did not occur until after his death in 1960. Five years later the prestigious Poet's Library published an extensive and judicious selection from his verse with an affectionate and illuminating introduction by Andrey Sinyavsky. (The introduction was promptly withdrawn when it became known that the critic Andrey Sinyavsky and the "underground" writer Abram Tertz are one and the same person.)

In the West the official Soviet ban on *Doctor Zhivago* was generally deplored but the critical assessments of the novel diverged widely. Some, notably Edmund Wilson,[18] hailed it "as one of the great books of our time." Others,—for example, Philip Toynbee in England and Lionel Abel in this country—found it diffuse or ill-constructed, in a word, disappointing.

Though Pasternak's only major work of fiction is hardly a flawless performance, it is at least arguable that some of these strictures were an overreaction to extravagant and partly misguided praise. The hasty parallel with *War and Peace,* drawn by the early enthusiasts, may not have been altogether unwarranted or "absurd," as claimed by Stuart Hampshire in his excellent *Encounter* article.[19] Outside of a certain philosophical affinity, Pasternak's novel is akin to the Tolstoyan epic in its intermingling of public events with family and love scenes, of a far-flung and absorbing story with meditations on man and history.[20] But beyond this point the comparison breaks down; in fact, it becomes misleading and counterproductive

---

[17]At a public meeting, held on October 29, 1958 one Semichastny, the First Secretary of the Young Communist League, declared to the applause of the Party hierarchy present that Pasternak was worse than a pig since "he has fouled the spot where he ate and cast filth on those by whose labor he lives and breathes." (Cited in Robert Conquest, *The Pasternak Affair: Courage of Genius* [London: Collins and Havill, 1961] , p. 176.)

[18]Edmund Wilson, "Doctor Life and his Guardian Angel," *New Yorker,* 34, no. 39 (November 15, 1958), 201-6, 206-16, 219-22, 224-26.

[19]See Stuart Hampshire, *"Doctor Zhivago,"* reprinted in this volume.

[20]See Victor Erlich, "A Testimony and a Challenge: Pasternak's *Doctor Zhivago,"* reprinted in this volume.

—not only because it urges a standard no contemporary novel would be able to meet, but, more importantly, since it misrepresents the actual thrust and texture of *Doctor Zhivago*. In spite of its panoramic scope and wide moral relevance, this lyrical novel is above all a poetic biography of a richly endowed individual, the story of his unremitting efforts to maintain his creative integrity amidst the overwhelming pressures of an age of wars and revolutions. As both N. Chiaromonte and F. Stepun have persuasively argued[21] the strength of the genre exemplified by *Doctor Zhivago* lies not in vividness but in evocativeness, not in the mastery of the tridimensional texture of human existence but in the ability to convey a state of mind, to orchestrate an inner experience. It is, perhaps, the crowning paradox of Pasternak's paradox-ridden career that this one "epic" of his should have been in a sense more personal and autobiographical than are many of his lyrics. To be sure, Yury Andreyevich Zhivago cannot be wholly identified with Boris Pasternak. (To confuse a literary character with its creator is always a dubious procedure.) But the kinship between the two is not easily overestimated; and it is nowhere more apparent than in Zhivago's religious reverence for life and love and in his challenge to the Marxist pieties, to the arrogant presumptions of "professional revolutionaries," in behalf of a *sui generis* Christian personalism.[22]

Pasternak's apparent readiness to incur considerable risks in publishing *Doctor Zhivago* is a measure of the importance which he attached to his novel. In a letter to an Uruguyan magazine editor he called it "the most important thing which I have until now succeeded in doing." In the same statement he described his early writings which his addressee had praised highly as mere "trifles."[23] Critics of neoclassical persuasion, who had found Pasternak's early verse intensely interesting but often chaotic and arbitrary, were eager to seize upon verdicts such as this and to proclaim the texture and the tenor of Pasternak's Zhivago period as the ultimate payoff of his early, ultramodernistic experimentation and a realization of the ideals of "unheard-of simplicity" proclaimed by the poet as

---

[21] N. Chiaromonte, "Pasternak's Message," in Davie and Livingstone, eds., *Pasternak*, p. 233; Fyodor Stepun, *op.cit.*, p. 110. See also Victor Erlich, *op.cit.*, p. 131.

[22] Rufus Mathewson states Zhivago's existential choice in terms which both Yury Andreyevich and Boris Pasternak would have found congenial: "life lived against life understood and made ready for reshaping. Life reshaped is life violated." *(The Positive Hero in Russian Literature,* 2nd edition [Stanford, Calif.: Stanford University Press, 1975] , p. 273.)

[23] Quoted from N. Chiaromonte, *op.cit.*, p. 232.

early as 1932 and of "an unnoticeable style" envisioned by Yuri Zhivago in one of his meditations.[24] Conversely, some Pasternakians miss in the poet's last cycle, *When the Weather Clears* (1956-9), the creative vitality and the innovative thrust of *My Sister, Life* or of *Themes and Variations*.[25] I must confess to having some difficulty with both positions. No amount of retrospective self-denigration on Pasternak's part can dislodge my sense of *My Sister, Life* as one of the most vibrant collections of modern verse in any language. Nor is there any question that some of the late lyrics are marred by the aging poet's occasional proclivity for the merely declarative. Yet it appears to me equally true that in the best poems of that period, most notably in the best "poems of Yury Zhivago," the richness and intricacy of the imagery are all the more effective for being brought under stricter control and placed in the service of a clearly articulated moral vision.

In his perceptive introduction to the already mentioned anthology of Pasternak criticism, Donald Davie warns against taking the older Pasternak's impatience with his youthful self too literally. He notes, *inter alia*, that "it was Yury Zhivago who claimed to have worked all his life for an unnoticeable style," and adds: "Boris Pasternak could not have claimed this and did not claim it."[26] If one is to believe an otherwise plausible-sounding memoir of an admiring young Soviet playwright, Alexander Gladkov's *Encounters with Pasternak* (1973), the author of *Doctor Zhivago* did share his hero's aspiration. In talking with Gladkov about his emerging novel in the summer of 1947, he admitted, presumably, to "dreaming about an unnoticeable style where there is no distance between idea and its representation."[27] And yet Donald Davie's residual point remains valid: in dealing with art, especially with an art so intricate and so finely wrought as Pasternak's can be even at this chastened and allegedly straightforward stage, such terms as "unnoticeable style" and "simplicity" are of scant value.

Finally, and more importantly, neither partisan discriminations nor, for that matter, the poet's own overly harsh retrospective judgments should blind the student of Pasternak to the underlying continuity of his *oeuvre*. Throughout his long and arduous career he

[24] The passage is quoted in Vladimir Weidle, "The End of the Journey", the last essay in this book.

[25] The two positions are articulated respectively in Vladimir Weidle, *op.cit.*, and Angela Livingstone, "Pasternak's Last Poetry" (see pp. 176 and 166).

[26] Davie and Livingstone, eds., *Pasternak*, p. 33.

[27] Aleksandr Gladkov, *Vstrechi s Pasternakom* (Paris: YMCA Press, 1973), p. 111.

remained his own man, not so much a rebel as an unreconstructed maverick, striving for absolute freshness of perception and utmost directness of representation,[28] rubbing shoulders affectionately with his "sister, life" and steadfastly refusing to subordinate the dictates of his poetic vision to the strident demands of political or literary dogma.

II

One of the tokens of the "internal unity of Pasternak's work" (Andrey Sinyavsky)[29] is the presence in it of poems to which the author kept returning at various junctures, revising, tightening up, paring down, yet preserving intact the original intent and the nuclear imagery. One such poem is "Marburg." Let us listen to its latest version, in its most recent English rendition:[30]

> I trembled. Caught fire. And shivered with cold.
> Just made a proposal of marriage. Too late:
> I flunked like a schoolboy, she flatly said: No!
> I am grieved with her tears. And more blest than a saint!
>
> I emerged on the square. It seemed, I was born
> For a second time. Each insignificant particle
> Lived, and looking me over with scorn,
> Was raised in importance by the power of parting.
>
> The flagstones burned hot; the dark brow of the street
> Frowned at the sky, and the cobbles looked sullen.
> The wind, like a boatman, rowed over the lindens
> Each thing was a likeness, and all was symbolic.
>
> Be it as it may, I avoided their eyes,
> Ignoring their greetings and cheers.

[28] It seems that such directness was Pasternak's conscious aim already in his early period which he later dubbed excessively mannered. In his 1956 autobiographical sketch he describes thus the intent of his poems "Railway Station" (1913) and "Venice" (1914): "There was nothing I demanded from myself, from my readers, or from the theory of art. All I wanted was that one poem should contain the city of Venice and the other the Brest...railway station." (*I Remember,* p. 78.)

[29] See p. 71.

[30] I am very grateful to my friend Yakov Hornstein for letting me use here the bulk of his translation of "Marburg," which is scheduled to appear in the anthology of 20th-century Russian poetry to be published by Doubleday late in 1978. I have permitted myself to omit several stanzas: the Hornstein rendition is based on the 1915 variant; I have opted for the 1956 version since I consider it both more authoritative and more effective.

For all their abundance I could not care less.
I tore myself free, lest I burst into tears.

A tile floated by. Unblinking and burning,
Noonday stared at the roofs. And in Marburg
Someone, whistling loudly, was making a crossbow.
Others, silent, prepared for the Pentecost Fair.

Devouring the clouds, the sand yellowed and dried.
The gathering storm brushed the brows of the shrubbery.
From the airless expanses, the waterless sky
Fell down on some blood-stilling matter—and curdled.

That day, like the actor who carries his part
And repeats, as he walks, his Shakespearian verse—
From your combs to your feet I knew you by heart,
I carried you whole through the town, and rehearsed.

And then, when I fell on my knees and embraced
The whole of that fog, of that ice, of that surface—
(How splendid you are!)—of that storm, suffocating...
"What is it? Do come to your senses!"—Rejected.

Here lived Martin Luther. There—brothers Grimm.
Gables like talons. Lindens. And gravestones.
And all this remembers and hungers for them.
Everything lives. And is likeness and symbol.

No, I won't. I won't go there tomorrow. Rejection
Is more than farewell. All is clear...We are quits.
Not for us is the hustle of platforms and stations.
O time-honoured stones, what will happen with me?

Hold-alls will be placed on the racks. And a moon
Will be put in each window of every compartment.
Anguish, having selected a book
Will be silently reading, as one of the passengers.

Why am I frightened? As well as my grammar
I know my insomnia. We two are allied.
Then why do I dread, like a call from a madman,
My usual thoughts, so long known, so well tried?

For the nights do sit down and play chess with me here
On the moonlight-checkered parquetry flooring.
There is scent of acacia, the windows wide open,
And passion, like a witness, goes grey in the corner.

And a poplar is king. I play with insomnia.
The queen is a nightingale. I reach for the nightingale.
Night wins the game, each piece moves aside.
White morning advances and is recognized.

The very title of this lyrical narrative calls attention to a pivotal point in the poet's spiritual and creative development when immersion in neo-Kantian philosophy at the University of Marburg and the concurrent infatuation with a "beautiful and charming girl" was followed by a "crossing over into a new faith"[31] — faith in the craft of poetry. The two above quotations from *Safe Conduct* clearly suggest that what is at issue here is not simply the connection between *Dichtung* and *Wahrheit,* between life and art, but also an interplay between two kindred stylizations of the same biographical episode within the framework of the Pasternak canon.

The special position which "Marburg" holds in this canon is pointed up by the history of the text. As already indicated, in the course of over forty years "Marburg" was repeatedly reworked and reprinted. Its first variant goes back to 1915; its last, fifth version, dated 1956, was scheduled to appear in the 1957 selection of Pasternak's verse carefully prepared and edited by the author. The poem must have meant a great deal to Pasternak as he returned to it at nearly every stage of his poetic career, including the one at which his attitude to his early writings became severe to the point of unfairness. Apparently, even when viewed from this ultracritical perspective, "Marburg" was adjudged to be one of these early efforts where, as Pasternak put it in the rough draft of his second autobiography, "amidst much that was deplorable and annoying one finds granules of the essential, the shrewdly detected, the felicitous."[32]

Some of Pasternak's fellow poets were quite emphatic in praising these felicities. Suffice it to mention Vladimir Mayakovsky who, in his interesting article "How Verses Are Made," celebrates the effectiveness of the poem's seventh stanza where the persona's disarray on the eve of the fateful marriage proposal is likened to the provincial tragedian's (in the original the actor is described as *tragik*) quivering in awe before a Shakespearean masterpiece.

> That day, like the actor who carries his part
> And repeats, as he walks, his Shakespearian verse —
> From your combs to your feet I knew you by heart,
> I carried you whole through the town, and rehearsed.

And need one insist that the line "And passion, like a witness, goes gray in the corner" is one of Pasternak's most arresting as well as most characteristic images?

This brings me to another aspect of "Marburg." The images which

---

[31]*Collected Prose Works,* pp. 71, 79.
[32]*Sochineniya,* II, 352.

fill this poem to the brim are not only unforgettably felicitous. They are also quintessentially, unmistakeably Pasternakian. The motif of passion turning gray in the corner is a brilliant example of the tendency acutely observed by Roman Jakobson in his deservedly influential "Marginal Notes on the Prose of the Poet Pasternak" (1935): "Pasternak's poetry is a realm of metonymies awakened to independent life."[33] In the same essay Jakobson postulates a connection between the metonymic thrust of Pasternak's imagery and the relative passivity of his lyrical "I." Actually, I would prefer to speak not about the passivity of the lyrical hero but about his existing on a par with other component parts of the Pasternakian universe, no less active or animate than he is. In "Marburg" all these elements or "particles," be they "flagstones," "cobbles" or lindens, lead an independent life as they scrutinize critically and yet sympathetically the deeply shaken hero.

> I emerged on the square. It seemed, I was born
> For a second time. Each insignificant particle
> Lived, and looking me over with scorn,
> Was raised in importance by the power of parting.

The setting of the poem, the history of the text and its dominant imagery—all these are plausible grounds for the proposition about a special significance or attractiveness of "Marburg" to the student of Pasternak. But I would like to pause now before yet another and, perhaps, still more important facet of the poem—notably, the inextricable bond between the theme and the tenor of "Marburg" and the "very essence" of Pasternak's poetic worldview as articulated in the memorable lines of his metapoetry and the aphoristic formulas of *Safe Conduct*:

> Gardens, ponds, enclosures, the creation
> Seething with a whiteness of our howling
> Are nothing but categories of passion
> That the human heart has been stockpiling.[34]

This is the "definition of creativity" offered in the poem under this title which appears in *My Sister, Life*. Nearly forty years later the motif of "passion" as the driving force of the universe and the central poetic theme is heard in the cycle *When the Weather Clears*:

[33]Davie and Livingstone, eds., *Pasternak*, p. 142.
[34]I have made the translation which appears here. The poem is also included in Maurice Bowra's *The Creative Experiment* (London: Macmillan, 1949), p. 134.

> Oh! If only I could write down
> Even just eight
> Good lines about passion and tell
> Its every trait.
>
> I would deduce its law and find
> Its starting flame.
> I would repeat initials of
> Its every name. ...[35]

In *Safe Conduct*, the word "passion" interlocks with the cognate notions of "love" and "feeling": "We take people as our symbols so to overcast them with weather.... And we take weather, or what is one and the same, nature, so that we may overcast it with our passion...." "Love rushed on more impetuously than anything else. Sometimes appearing at the head of nature, it raced the sun...."[36]

And here is, finally, the often quoted definition of art: "When we imagine that in Tristan, Romeo and Juliet and other memorials powerful passion is portrayed, we undervalue their subject matter. Their theme is wider than that powerful theme. Their theme is the theme of power itself. And it is from this theme that art is born. ... Focused on reality which feeling has displaced, art is a record of this displacement."[37]

Let us return to "Marburg." Its "theme" or, to be exact, its plot, such as it is, is exceedingly simple. A young man in love proposes and is turned down. Yet this not uncommon event acquires an uncommon poignancy as it is mediated through impetuous, "passionate" verse:

> I trembled. Caught fire. And shivered with cold.
> Just made a proposal of marriage. Too late:
> I flunked like a schoolboy, she flatly said: No!
> I am grieved with her tears. And more blest than a saint.

It is hard to decide what is the most striking quality of this opening stanza—the thematic and semantic density of its breathless four lines, broken into nine short, abrupt phrases; its emotional intensity; or the unexpected, indeed incongruous note of "blessedness" in the face of a rebuff. One thing is incontestable: the mundane quality of "just made a proposal of marriage" and, especially, the colloquial vulgarism of "I flunked like a schoolboy" are incom-

---

[35]Quoted from *Modern Russian Poetry*, edited by Vladimir Markov and Merrill Sparks (New York: Bobbs-Merrill Co., Inc., 1966), pp. 614-15.
[36]*Collected Prose Works*, p. 56.
[37]*Ibid.*, p. 81.

mensurate—though within the Pasternakian universe entirely compatible—with the whirlwind of powerful passion that grips the hero and is literally, as the French say, *"plus fort que moi."* When the persona helplessly and breathlessly blurts out his love, we witness not just a marriage proposal, however momentous, but a sacrificial act of self-revelation, an eruption of a pent-up feeling that cannot be contained any longer.

It is this headlong impetuousity of the persona's unsuccessful declaration of love, or, to be exact, the poem's overall orientation toward the impetuosity and intensity of the brief encounter, that may well provide the clue to the strange spiritual uplift which, on the face of it, is not easily reconciled with the stark fact of failure. This hypothesis is fully compatible with the treatment which the Marburg proposal receives in *Safe Conduct:* "After my declaration to V—nothing occurred that would change my position, but it was accompanied by surprises that resembled happiness. I was in despair, she comforted me. But her slightest touch was such a bliss that it washed away in a wave of exultation the unmistakeable bitterness of what I heard so clearly and what could not be revoked."[38]

Let us note the affinity between "was such bliss" and "I am more blest than a saint." To be sure, a "correct" interpretation of "Marburg" must be anchored in the text itself. But the above passage lends a measure of support to one's pre-existing sense of a fundamental ambiguity in the word "blest," which appears to hover between "blessedness"—i.e., spiritual purification as a result of a grievous loss—and "bliss," that is, the joy of gratitude for "her" compassionate tears, for a moment of an unexpectedly vouchsafed and irretrievably lost illusion of intimacy.

That to a romantically infatuated young man the slightest physical contact with the hitherto distant love object can spell momentary bliss is hardly news. What matters more at this point is that to Pasternak the very act of self-opening, a spontaneous release of a long-suppressed "passion" is inherently so precious that its very intensity, preserved by grateful memory, is in some sense more important than any specific consequences of such an act, however "bitter" and irrevocable. In other words, Pasternak's panemotionalism spells primary emphasis on the process of experiencing rather than on its results.

The struggle for supremacy between a sense of the unforgettable and precious privileged moment and a growing awareness of the "power of parting"—a tension between "exultation" and the "un-

[38]*Sochineniya*, II, p. 242.

mistakeable bitteeness of what one heard so clearly"—is the pivot of the second half of "Marburg." When in the eighth-stanza *reprise* the central event reenters our field of vision and we are overwhelmed once again by that "storm suffocating," the unwitting delight in "her" beauty ("how splendid you are!") is harshly cut short by a shout of self-rebuke. The abrupt rhythmicosyntactical design of the last line is a kind of sound-gesture, an acoustic and intonational equivalent of calling oneself to order, of forcing oneself into a recognition of the irreversibility of what has happened:

> And then, when I fell on my knees and embraced
> The whole of that fog, of that ice, of that surface—
> (How splendid you are!)—Of that storm, suffocating...
> "What is it? Do come to your senses!"—Rejected.

The imagery of the following stanzas reveals or, if one will, enacts the inexorable movement from the process to the result, from the omnipotence of passion to its gradual withering away, estrangement, "going gray." This remarkable metonymy which I mentioned before is anticipated in the preceding stanza by another externalization of a state of mind that could be viewed as a personified *genius loci:* "Anguish having selected a book/ Will be silently reading as one of the passengers." Yet the singular dramatic weight of the line "passion, like a witness, goes gray in the corner" rests not only on the act of objectifying the hitherto dominant aspect of the lyrical "I," but also on signaling the demotion of "passion" from the status of the driving force of the *agon* to that of its passive and helpless "witness." From the perspective of the Marburg night, the emotional heat of the Marburg day is gradually relegated to the unrecoverable past.

We will recall that the last word belongs here not to the night but to the morning which comes in its wake. Some readers may be puzzled by the fact that in the final stanza the victory of the night is marked by the advent of the morning. In many poetic, and non-poetic, contexts night is opposed to morning or rather to the day ushered in by morning. But the antithesis which dominates the last two stanzas of "Marburg" is not one of darkness versus light, night versus day but the opposition between reality and the play of imagination (illusion, dreaming, myth making). From this vantage point the moonlight-checkered "parquetry flooring," such lyrical props as "poplar" and "nightingale," and the chess pieces are ranged on the side of play—the last-minute attempt to salvage the subjective illusion of fluidity, vagueness, or open-endedness of the situation.

By the same token, the night which "wins the game" as the pieces move aside and the morning which "advances" *qua* segments of real, objective time dwell on the same plane, that of the reality principle. That is why the "white morning" can be a vehicle or a warrant of the night's victory, a logical, or better, inevitable sequel to it, though a more unequivocal one than the night could be, complicated as it was by the poeticized, elusive, playful moonlight. The starkly white light of the morning leaves no room for illusions or ambiguities. "All is clear...."

Reality, previously "displaced by feeling" and slighted in behalf of that feeling, at long last comes into its own. Does that mean that the finale of "Marburg" spells a total victory of fact over illusion or, to paraphrase Pasternak's already quoted formula, the displacement of feeling by reality? It is fair to assume that things are not as simple as that. Surrender of the self to "reality" as a world existing independently of human consciousness is scarcely compatible with the poetic stance of Boris Pasternak.

Let me shift once more from "Marburg" to *Safe Conduct*—this time to a passage which pithily describes the narrator's state of mind on the day after the traumatic encounter: "I was surrounded by transformed objects. Something never before experienced crept into the substance of reality. Morning recognized my face, and seemed to have come to be with me and never to leave me."[39] One may note, along with the obvious stylistic affinity, essential syntactical and semantic differences between the two versions of the persona's coming to terms with reality. In *Safe Conduct*, "I" is not a subject but the object of the recognition process. (The more literal translation of the "Marburg" line would be "I recognize the white face of the morning.") Moreover, morning, which in "Marburg" "advances" as a stern destroyer of the lyrical illusion in Pasternak's first autobiography, seems to perform a positive, protective function. Though, on second thought, is this not protection from self-delusion, from futile dreams? If so, the burden of the morning's message in the two narratives is essentially the same.

Be that as it may, it is the preceding sentence that strikes me as particularly relevant here. "Something never before experienced crept into the substance of reality." This characteristic phrase points up the complex and organic interrelationship in Pasternak's poetic universe between actuality and what he called in his 1913 lecture on

[39]*Collected Prose Works*, p. 76.

"Symbolism and Immortality" the "generic form of human subjectivity."[40] If coming to terms with reality may necessitate aban-
doning, however reluctantly, a feeling proved unviable, the hot
breath of that emotion makes an imprint on reality, imbuing it with
the freshness of the "never before experienced."

In one of Gogol's St. Petersburg tales, "Nevsky Avenue," the
painter-dreamer Piskaryov whose delusions have just been cruelly
shattered exclaims in disgust: "Oh! how revolting is reality! What
is it compared to a dream?" This ultraromantic dichotomy was
always alien to the author of *Doctor Zhivago*, for whom the "omnipotent God of love" and "the omnipotent God of details" are one.[41]
Clearly, reality in all its minute concreteness is indispensable and
precious to the poet. But, in his view, poetry is no less essential to
reality, to a heightened, vibrant sense of the actual. Without the
transforming and articulating impact of poetry, without the "passion
of creative contemplation"[42] and the "wonder-working might of
creative genius,"[43] the "universe," as Pasternak said in his early
"Definition of Poetry," "is a dumb place".[44]

The vast scope of Pasternak's achievement and the wide range of
critical response to it over the last half-century confront the antho-
logist with problems which defy easy solution. In selecting for inclusion in this volume some of the highlights of Pasternak criticism
I was trying to achieve a reasonable balance between the early and
the late Pasternak, between Western and Russian contributions and,
finally, between various critical approaches. A deliberate effort
was made to steer clear of the material available to the English-

[40]"In my paper I argued that this subjectivity [of our perceptions] was not the
attribute of every individual human being, but was a generic and suprapersonal
quality, that it was the subjectivity of humanity at large." (*I Remember*, p. 63.) On
the notion of human emotionality as a suprapersonal force which "melts the bar-
rier between personal experience and brute creation," see Isaiah Berlin, "The Energy of Pasternak," in this volume, and Victor Erlich, "Life by Verses: Boris Pasternak," *op.cit.*, pp. 138-39.

[41]In a lyric which appears toward the end of the *My Sister, Life* cycle, the persona, speaking to his beloved, identifies the force which rules the universe they
share as the "omnipotent God of detail — the omnipotent God of love." (*Sochineniya*,
I, p. 50.)

[42]Significantly enough, this phrase occurs in a passage of *I Remember* where
Pasternak attempts to define the distinctive quality of Leo Tolstoy (p. 69).

[43]A slight paraphrase of the concluding line of "August," one of the "poems of
Yury Zhivago." (See Boris Pasternak, *In the Interlude. Poems 1945-1960*, translated by Henry Kamen [London: Oxford University Press, 1962], p. 51.)

[44]Boris Pasternak, *Sochineniya* [Works], I, p. 22.

speaking reader in collections such as *Pasternak. Modern Judgments*. Two departures from the nonduplication principle seemed to me eminently desirable. I chose to include Yury Tynyanov's 1924 essay, which appears here in a new translation and under a different title, not only because it is one of the most perceptive early critical assessments of Pasternak's poetry but also because its juxtaposition with the more recent article by Yury Lotman points out, in spite of a considerable difference in style, the essential continuity of the Formalist-Structuralist strand in Pasternak studies. As for the longest and the most comprehensive essay in our collection, "Pasternak's Poetry" by Andrey Sinyavsky, I found it too important a landmark to be bypassed. I was especially pleased to be able to present a recently revised and updated version of this by now justly famous introduction to the 1965 Pasternak volume.[45] The introductory essay was written in Moscow; the revision was made in Paris. No longer constrained by the official Soviet taboos, Sinyavsky felt free to comment explicitly on the religioethical tenor of Pasternak's late writings.

It is testimony to the vitality of Pasternak's art, as well as to the precarious status of some of the concepts germane to its appreciation, that the essays presented here should feature occasional discrepancy as well as frequent convergence. Though this collection does not contain any direct polemic,[46] a careful reader we will find several areas of substantial disagreement among the contributors. One of these iş the question of Pasternak's position vis-a-vis the literary cross-currents of his time. If Yury Lotman associates him with the Futurists, Fyodor Stepun discourages any such notion and insists on Pasternak's "philosophical affinity for the Symbolists." That in each case the critic's judgment is visibly affected by his own aesthetic bias is undeniable. Yet another divisive factor here is an apparent lack of agreement about the scope and nature of "Russian Futurism." What matters most to Lotman is the Futurist's attitude to poetic language. What concerns, and repels, Stepun is the sociocultural stance of the Futurist movement. Elsewhere Robert L. Jackson calls *Doctor Zhivago* the *"Liebestod* of the Russian intelligentsia," while F. Stepun emphatically denies the *intelligent* label to Pasternak, and by implication, to Yury Zhivago. Once again we are dealing here with two widely disparate interpretations of the key term.

[45]See above, p. 7.
[46]For an important instance of such polemic see the exchange on *Doctor Zhivago* between Isaac Deutscher and Irving Howe in Davie and Livingstone, eds., *Pasternak*, pp. 240-68.

Robert Jackson speaks of an erosion of a way of life and a system of values dear to the heart of many a pre-1917 educated Russian as a major theme in *Doctor Zhivago;* F. Stepun celebrates Pasternak's aloofness from an influential radical-secular strain in the Russian intelligentsia tradition.

Probably the most controversial issue in Pasternak studies has been that of the relative importance and worth of what might be called the *Doctor Zhivago* period. Two essays which conclude the volume provide contrasting perspectives on the matter. As indicated above, I am not ready to espouse either position, but I thought it essential that within the polyphony of Pasternak criticism both voices be heard clearly.

Language and Reality in the Early Pasternak

by Yury Lotman

An analysis of the drafts of Pasternak's early verse takes us into the laboratory where a new attitude toward poetic language was forged. Insistence on the subjectivity of Pasternak's poetic universe has become a cliche in Pasternak's criticism. Yet viewing this universe at close range one is impressed by the concrete, objective quality of his "poetic household"[1] and by the intensity of his search for the latent connections between the objects and the essences of outer reality. Sketches and landscapes loom larger in his designs and rough drafts than do purely lyrical themes. What is often perceived here as subjective is not so much a matter of the poet's plunging into the depths of his inner experience as that of the total unexpectedness of the world which he portrays. One of the drafts casts a revealing light on this process.

Among the manuscripts made available by E. V. Pasternak there are two sheets of paper which allow a hypothetical reconstruction of the successive stages of a fragment whose theme is reading by the light of a candle. First there are two stabs at the prelude,

> How can I read? The words guttered.
> Oh! Whence, whence do I blow?

and

"Language and Reality in the Early Pasternak" (editor's title) by Yury Lotman. A significantly abridged version of Lotman's article "Poems of the Early Pasternak and Some Problems of Structural Analysis of Texts," which appeared in the University of Tartu publication, *Trudy po znakovym sistemam (Studies in Semiotic Systems),* IV (April 1969), 460-77. Translated from the Russian by Victor Erlich. The drafts to which Lotman keeps referring are those of the early Pasternak lyrics, dated 1911-1913, drawn from the Pasternak archive and made available to *Trudy* by the poet's nephew, E. V. Pasternak. They appear in the appendix to Lotman's article.

[1][Reference to *Poeticheskoe khozyaystvo Pushkina [The Poetic Household of Pushkin]* by V. Khodasevich, a well-known study by a Russian emigre poet-scholar of Pushkin's recurring images and turns of phrase.—Ed.]

> Words run over, run down
> In the guttering book.

And here is an apparent attempt at synthesis:

> Words gutter, burn
> Because I'm blown like this...

The first variant prevailed, but its second line and the concluding hemistich of the first line changed places. Accordingly, the motif of "guttering" was contracted and the motif of "draught" expanded via the image of "blown pages":

> How can I read? The words guttered.
> Oh! Whence, whence do I blow?
> In the lampions of lines I can scarcely decipher
> The alien page I have chased away...

An analysis of the rather limited vocabulary of these variants allows us to define the range of the referents which determine the content of this text. The first group consists of the book and the objects of the real world associated with it—"page," "line"; the second group embraces "candle" and "lampion"; the third points toward "draught" or "wind," which is never mentioned here in the nominal form. The fourth group is made up of "I," and "pain" as it relates to the persona. Each sphere of reality has its counterpart in the text in the form of a definite semantic cluster. Moreover, along with nouns we find here properly distributed predicates which describe the conduct of the referents.

Apparently, the poet's proximate task was to describe an actual situation produced jointly by the nature of these referents, their actions, and interrelationships. Were one to express this contingency in customary linguistic-semantic relations, the resultant text would be something like "I have considerable trouble reading: the candle guttered and the wind scattered the pages." Yet for Pasternak such a text would have had little correspondence with reality. In order to break through toward the latter he had to explode the routine of habitual notions and of the semantic relations which dominate ordinary language. The struggle against linguistic fictions in behalf of reality rests above all on the assumption that separateness of objects is produced by the linguistic schemata. For reality is a blend and what appears in language as an object delimited from other objects is, in fact, one of the representations of a single, indivisible world. Its properties are complex and interdependent like colors in an Impressionist painting rather than separate like planes done by house painters in different hues. At the same time such characteristics as "being a subject," "being a predicate," "being an attribute [of a subject or a predicate]" are perceived here as pertaining to language rather than to reality. That is why the text emerges as a deliberate shift from a predictable set of referents to another, unexpected one and a parallel mutual substitution of linguistic functions. Thus, instead of "the candle gutters" we find "the print gutters," "the words gutter" or a "guttering book." Such lines as "the burning book gutters," or "the words gutter, burn" obliterate the separateness of "book" and "candle." From separate objects they are transformed into facets of a unified whole. At the same time the poet's "I" and the wind merge. Thus, such word combinations as "Whence do I blow?" and "The alien page I have chased away" become possible.

In the struggle with the "normal" distribution of semantic values there emerged two semantic foci—"I"="the wind" and "candle"= "book." If each group is marked by complete semantic equality— this becomes apparent in the process of mutual substitution—this relationship between the groups is properly characterized by the only epithet in the text, "alien." "I," which equals the wind, chases away the page and blows out the candle. The entire text is concerned with the impossibility of contact between the two semantic centers (the impossibility of reading, of the merging of "I" with the book). "I," on the other hand, is made akin to "distance." A reference to movement and disjunction injects the motif of space:

> By which blowy distance am I pierced?

Words which connote space serve as synonyms of words expressing spiritual anguish. The sequence "I am pierced by the distance" is interchangeable with "I am pierced by sadness" and "I am pierced by pain."

One ought to emphasize, however, that the semantic clusters which shape the world of Pasternak in ways different from those of ordinary language are not symbols. Losing sight of this essential fact may lead one to interpret the early Pasternak poetics as a Symbolist one and this would be a gross misconception. In Pasternak the contrast between the real world and the trivial one is not a matter of pitting abstract essences against crass, tangible materiality. Here the real world, too, bears the marks of visibility and perceptibility; it is an empirical, in fact, the only truly empirical realm. For it is world *actually seen and experienced,* in contradistinction to the world of words, phrases, of routine-like, conventional ways of putting it. One of the recurrent motifs in Pasternak is the opposition between the truth of feeling and the untruth of the phrase. That is why the essential relations that organize the world of Pasternak, the world that does away with the habits of ordinary language, are almost invariably relations that have been *sighted*. Thus, Marina Tsvetaeva[2] in a letter to a friend: "In his verse Pasternak *sees* and I *hear*" [author's italics]. One of the fragments published by E. V. Pasternak — the third stanza of the poem "By the buzzing ashes of braziers" [*Zhuzhzhashchei zoloi zharoven'*] read as follows:

> Where the tide of the heavily treading mystery
> Among the ashen apple trees,
> Where you rise above everything like a bridge on stilts
> And even the sky is lower than you.

At its later stage the text took the following shape:

> Where the pond is like a revealed mystery
> Where the apple tree tide whispers.
> Where the garden hangs like a construction on stilts
> And holds the sky in its arms.[3]

In order to grasp the logic of this substitution it is necessary to reconstruct the visual images which can be said to embody the underlying intent of the text. That the Pasternak text is oriented toward the object, the prevalent opinion notwithstanding, is clearly demonstrated by the precision with which the extra-textual realia can be reconstructed on the basis of its poetic representation. To identify those Moscow streets and houses, those railroad stations and railroad tracks, those suburban landscapes that lie behind the text of this or that poem is an entirely feasible task — indeed, given adequate biographical information, a relatively easy one. The "pond" mentioned in the second variant seems absent from the first. However, its latent existence can be inferred unequivocally from a visual reconstruction of the image.

> Where you rise above everything like a bridge on stilts
> And even the sky is lower than you.

The extratextual determinant of the text or of its "correct" reading is the visual perspective available to an observer who looks at the pond from the bridge — the starry sky reflected in the water turns out to lie under him. With the vantage point of the poetic text lifted

[2][See Introduction, p. 3, in this volume. — Ed.]

[3]Boris Pasternak, *Stikhotvoreniya i poemy* [*Verses and Poems*] (Moscow-Leningrad: Sovetskii pisatel, 1965), p. 66.

above the ground, this configuration is projected unto the garden — the tide of apple trees in bloom is placed below. What in a different artistic system would have been a purely speculative elevation of the author above the universe becomes in Pasternak a projection of a visualizable image unto the cosmos.[4]

A revision of this stanza was necessitated by the shifts in the text's underlying visual intent. What was previously seen as a bridge over the water has become a hamlet on stilts, built on the shore. The notion of the garden as a hamlet on stilts at the sky's edge injected into the picture of the universe an element of archaic semantics. (The modern mind associates building on stilts with antiquity, with the roots of our civilization.) In this modified world-picture the sky appears in front of, rather than underneath, the poet. Thus in Pasternak the general idea is always a visualized idea. Recoil from verbal cliches, which are equated by Pasternak's critics with reality, was, for him, not an escape from the empirical but a reaching toward it. In this lay Pasternak's challenge to Symbolism, with its notion of fact as a mere surface of a deeper meaning and to Acmeism,[5] which proclaimed a return to actuality but equated the latter with the extant linguistic consciousness. The fundamental conflict with ordinary language — a stance which Pasternak shared with the Futurists — was alien to the Acmeists.

A salient trait of several early twentieth-century poetic currents was a refusal to treat the linguistic patterns as the embodiment of reality and the semantic system of language as a structure of the world. As a corollary the purely verbal texture of verse now was being reshaped by semantic shifts and the text was being organized by an additional principle which varied depending on the changes in the very notion of reality. Thus the primary material which determines the type of semantic construction is no longer provided by natural language; the latter now performs this role in conjunction with some other components. One might posit the following types of systems whose impact modifies the semantics of ordinary language in a poetic text.

[4] It is difficult to say whether this vantage point was provided by the second-floor window opening to the garden or those boughs of a birch tree about which the poet was to write later: "The green tangle of its branches represented an airy arbor. In their firm interwining one could settle in a sitting or a half-prone position. It is here that I set up my poetic shop" (B. Pasternak, *Verses and Poems*, p. 620).

[5] [Acmeism was a short-lived school of post-Symbolist Russian poetry, marked by a strong neoclassical bias. Its most eminent representatives were Anna Akhmatova, Nikolay Gumilyov, and Osip Mandelstam. — Ed.]

Type of Poetic Text	*Semantic Base*	*Semantic Shifts*
Symbolism	Ordinary Language	Language of Relations (music, mathematics)
Futurism	Ordinary Language	Language of Objects (visual image of the word, painting)
Acmeism	Ordinary Language	Language of Culture (extant ordinary language texts)

It is easy to see that in Acmeism, culture, a secondary system, assumes the function of a primary one as material for stylization, for the construction of a new culture. This kind of semantic structure is the more interesting since at times Acmeists were not averse at the secondary-system level to an emphatic repudiation of culture. Some of the texts which they produced imitate the precultural, the primitive, to be sure, as perceived by a cultivated early twentieth-century person.[6] But the crucial matter here is not what was being imitated but the very fact of imitation, the demotion of a secondary text to the status of a primary one.

Whatever the poet's attitude to language, he is doomed to fashion his world out of words. This dilemma is inseparable from the poetic act. But each school of poetry, each master, resolves it differently. To Pasternak, as to the Futurists, the word has two facets. On the one hand, it is a substitute for an element of reality with regard to which it serves as a pure, dematerialized convention. This word is "deaf." It is a lie. Yet at the same time the word itself has a sensory texture in its graphic and phonic aspects; it is available to sensory perception. Viewed in this way, the word does not substitute for anything nor can it have a substitute. As an object among objects it can only be genuine since it is part of the genuine empirical world. The "right" word combination is called forth by the laws that link the actual phenomena rather than by those that link speech units into syntagms. From this point of view the recurrence of phonemes is only superficially reminiscent of traditional poetic euphony. Such recurrence is designed

[6][Lotman's point has no visible application to either Akhmatova or Mandelstam; he may be referring to the "primitivist" or exotic strain in Nikolay Gumilyov. — Ed.]

to reveal the precariousness of dividing the text into phonetic words just as the semantic structure of the text challenges the practice of dividing the world in line with lexical subdivisions of ordinary language. That is why the marked text is necessarily one whose phonological repetitions project a structure of a special supralexical unity. With the text shaped in consonance with the visible aspect of the world, in line with the ideas generated by the nontrivial—i.e., noncommonsensical juxtapostion of the images of a freshly seen and experienced world—and, finally, in response to the need for an intergrated phonological structure, all these organizing principles compensate for the doing away with customary, everyday ways of putting it, for the elimination of automatic semantic relations and the weakening of rhythmical automatism. Pasternak himself stated these principles with some precision in 1957, in characterizing his verses of 1921: "I was not seeking a clear-cut rhythmical pattern, be it one of dance or of song, under whose impact, regardless of the words used, arms and legs almost automatically come into motion. ... My persistent concern was always with the content, my ardent wish was that the poem contain a new idea or a new picture. That with all its properties it be engraved within the book and that it speak from its pages by its silence...."[7]

The force which brings words together in a Pasternak text turns out to be the lifting of certain taboos operative in ordinary language. However, such an act can be meaningful only when it is perceptible, i.e., whenever the text is projected simultaneously unto two dimensions—a system in which a certain sequence is construed as the only possible one and another system which introduces other kinds of predictability. In this instance both the adherence to a certain pattern and its violation turn out to be—in various systems respectively—vehicles of meanings.

The semantic structure of the early Pasternak poem often rests on the principle of juxtaposing heterogeneous semantic units. However, such a juxtaposition presupposes not only a difference which assures a high degree of nonpredictability but also a definite semantic affinity. Not only semantic disparity per se but also the degree of such disparity is thus invested with meaning:

---

[7][From Pasternak's autobiographical introduction to a 1957 collection of his poems which reached the galley-proof stage but never materialized. The above passage is quoted here from the editor's notes to Boris Pasternak, *Verses and Poems*, p. 620.—Ed.]

Gardens, ponds, enclosures, the creation
Seething with a whiteness of our howling
Are nothing but categories of passion
That the human heart has been stockpiling.[8]

The sequence "gardens-ponds-palings-creation-categories of passion" does not merely bring together meanings drawn from different realms; it also modulates the degree of dissimilarity. "Gardens," "ponds," and "palings" are homogeneous as designations of material notions, as elements of an empirically given landscape. Their co-occurrence within a single sequence corresponds to the linguistic norm and to the habits of everyday perception, and produces the inertia of "familiarity." The differences in meaning activated within the line are differences between various objects existing on the same plane of reality. "Creation" introduces the antithesis of the whole versus the part. However, by ushering in the "categories of passion," Pasternak supplants this opposition by yet another one — "man versus the world," "objective reality versus human feeling." Thus each new element undercuts some expectation and gives a rise to a new one which is cancelled in turn by yet another accretion. The injected clause ["seething with a whiteness of our howling" (see above)] is constructed differently. The words do not form here any such chain of functionally equivalent elements. However, if the syntactic structure of the clause does not feature parallelism, the semantic affect is one of co-occurence. "Seething" is a notion which belongs to the realm of motor sensations — what is suggested is the quality of foaminess; "white" is a visual-color concept, "howl" an auditory one. Bringing them together within one line produces an inertia of sensoriness even while it highlights the diversity of modes of perception and thus suggests a sense of fullness.

The possibility of violating customary and predictable semantic relations disautomatizes the text and projects the image of a disautomatized world.[9] However, the early verses contained in the present collection are merely a significant step in that direction.

The principle of juxtaposing heterogeneous elements performs

[8]Boris Pasternak, *op. cit.*, p. 128. [Translation by the editor. This poem also appears on page 134 of *The Creative Experiment* by Maurice Bowra (London: Macmillan, 1949).]

[9]In this sense the "traditional" quality of the late Pasternak's poetry does not represent a repudiation of the structure of his early verses: though the reader confronts here familiar linguistic constructions he knows that they can be violated and that they are not used by the poet as a matter of linguistic automatism. The everyday, "plausible" world is not the only possibility. Though it is this world that is being portrayed, the reader is mindful of alternate options.

yet another function in the building of semantic models. It equalizes in that it both brings out and cancels certain semantic oppositions, most notably, the opposition "animate-inanimate." Pasternak's early verses are very revealing in this respect. Critics insistently accuse Pasternak of subjectivism, of having lost interest in the outside world. However, in Pasternak the very distinction between the outer and inner world is discarded. The former is invested here with human energy, the latter with vividness and concreteness. The boundary between "I" and "non-I," very pronounced within any subjectivist system, is emphatically obliterated in a Pasternak text. This is laid bare in such poems as "To Feel Like a Field — First a Winter Crop...," "I am Found at the Source of My Cheeks," "With Each Step I Clutch at My Head."

The humanization of the world thus achieved was a significant act. If for the Symbolists everything was meaningful, post-Symbolist culture had to contend with a problem of the meaningfulness of a reality which was no longer seen as an external sign yet was expected to retain its cultural status. The thrust now was toward vindicating life as such. However, it would be erroneous to assume that the philosophical antithesis "subjective versus objective" has no place in the early Pasternak's model of the world. Though neutralized where the relationship between "I" and nature is concerned, it remains fully operative as an opposition of "I" versus the "others." Hence the pervasive motive of a psychic "border" which separates man from man. This border is at once a source of anguish and testimony to the richness of personality. (The angels, claims Pasternak, have a flaw, "their souls lack a border)." We observe here the emergence of the essential themes of Pasternak's poetry. The poet's attitude toward others appears here under three guises: notably, as themes of love, of the people, or of another human being who performs a heroic deed and earns thereby admiration, awe, and compassion.

In the materials made available by E. V. Pasternak the theme of the people is represented by two interesting drafts: "No, I am not yours, of the light-headed mob/ I am a carefree and bold brother": "Oh! to become like those/ who through the night race on wild horses!" As for the third theme, very important for Pasternak — later it will give rise to the theme of the Revolution — in the present draft it begins to be associated with the image of a heroic woman ("Is it the crowing of the hurdy-gurdy or the Tatar shouts...?" and "Who will summon the Amazon into battle?"). The emerging theme of the woman's plight ("And I was a child, when the sunset...") is located at the crossing of the first and second themes.

One can conclude from the above that in Pasternak's poetry all the essential facets of the social issue are embedded in various plot structures reducible to three basic components—"I," "nature," "woman." These elements suffice for the construction of any social or cosmic model. Therefore, devising a grammar of Pasternak's lyrical plots appears an entirely feasible task. However, since the materials under discussion are, in the main, fragments, to undertake this task would require extensive forays into the poet's later works.

The repudiation of the world picture created by "common sense" and by the ordinary language is neither a world view nor an esthetic system. It is a language of the culture of an era. That is precisely why it can lie at the core of various, even conflicting, ideational-aesthetic structures. Twentieth-century art provides many instances of this.

Pasternak was a man of a thoroughly professional philosophical culture. Understandably, he was often impelled to state his own position in terms of a philosophical metalanguage. Yet such definitions of his own consciousness exerted a demonstrable influence on Pasternak's poetic stance. The two aspects of the problem ought not to be equated. The cycle featured in the appendix casts an interesting light on the history of Pasternak's attempts at philosophical self-determination. We can easily discern within it a cluster of poems and poetic fragments whose explicit subject is philosophy. These poems share a few characteristics. For one thing, all of them are couched in the humorous or satirical vein. For another, the semantic texture of Pasternak's early poetic experimentation is conspicuously absent here. There is no room in the cycle for semantic juxtapositions such as those featured in the following lines:

> Clouds were painted by autumn
> Into white crusty furs,
> On highways chaos was robbing
> Last night's departed dreams.

What we find here instead are puns and humorous nonsense—a traditional phenomenon in ironic verse; e.g., the following ditty:

> In the candidate's belly round
> Polycrates's ring was found.
> [*V zhivote u kandidata*
> *nayden persten'Polikrata*].

Let us note another curious fact: in the nineteenth century such genres as humorous poetry, intimate album verse, and satire or parody featured in journals often served as a laboratory in which new modes of poetic expression were forged, be they the punning rhyme or colloquial turns of phrase. When this kind of poetry was granted equal rights with "high" lyric verse and came to share with the latter its characteristic devices, it ceased being a revolutionary force in genre hierarchy and turned into a conservative one. Verse oriented toward facetiousness became considerably less experimental than lyrical poetry. This is apparent in Mayakovsky's *Satyricon* cycle[10] and in Pasternak's satirical verse.

Finally, the poems of this cycle are marked by an ironic attitude to the very brand of philosophy whose influence on the young Pasternak is amply documented. The language of philosophy is contrasted with the language of poetry as verbiage with life. The incompatibility of these two poles of reality generates a special kind of humor akin to Romantic irony and to the satire of Andrey Bely:[11]

> And letting go in a folk dance
> In a boundless expense of a blind alley,
> In front of a tavern a chorus of substances
> Prances about lustily.

Romantic oxymorons as "the boundless expense of a blind alley" or the coexistence of "substance" with "prancing about" are of a different order than the semantic juxtapositions of the Pasternak lyric. It is significant that satire should draw on more archaic stylistic strata.

Eschewing the customary modes of perception is here not an end in itself nor is it the only salient stylistic proclivity of the early Pasternak. No less characteristic is his attraction to everyday forms of thought and speech. The essential point is that from the matrix of the authorial language they become the object of representation. Throughout Pasternak's career the everyday world was one of his most persistent poetic themes. However, the quotidian relations are not transferred automatically from the realm of ordinary language and of daily routine but are recreated out of poetic materials where any conventional sequence is subject to substitution and thus becomes a matter of free poetic choice, of knowledge and awareness.

---

[10]The *Satyricon* was a Russian journal of humor and satire which flourished from 1906 to 1917. Mayakovsky was for a short time a contributor to this magazine. — Ed.]

[11][Andrey Bely (1880-1934), a novelist, poet and critic, was a leading Russian Symbolist and one of the most versatile and influential men of letters in early twentieth-century Russia. — Ed.]

Words and Things in Pasternak

by Yury Tynyanov

The rebellion of Khlebnikov[1] and Mayakovsky gave the literary language a jolt, revealing in it the possibility of a new coloring. At the same time this rebellion pushed the word away quite a distance. In Khlebnikov things make themselves felt mainly as essences. The insurgent word tears itself loose from the thing. (Thus, Khlebnikov's "self-valuable [*"samovitoe"*] word" converges with the "hyperbolic word" of Mayakovsky). The word became free, but it became too free, it ceased to brush against things. Hence the hankering of the leading former Futurists for things, for the unadorned, everyday object; hence their "negation of verse" as a logical solution. (Too logical, in fact, for the more impeccable is the logic brought to bear on things that are not static—and literature is such a thing—the more straightforward and correct it is, the less right it turns out to be.)

Hence, too, another pull—the desire to aim the word straight at the thing, and somehow to turn around both words and things so that the word be not left hanging in midair and the thing not left naked, an urge to reconcile words and things, to entangle them fraternally. There is also a natural recoil from the hyperbole, the thirst of one who has reached a new tier of poetic culture to use the nineteenth century as material without construing it as a norm but without being ashamed, either, of kinship with one's fathers.

Therein lies the mission of Pasternak.

"Words and Things in Pasternak" (editor's title) by Yury Tynyanov. A section from an essay "Promezhutok" ("Interlude") in *Arkhaisty i novatory* [*Archaists and Innovators*] (Leningrad, 1929), pp. 562-68; first published in 1924. Translated from the Russian by Victor Erlich.

[1][Velemir Khlebnikov (1885-1921) was one of the leading Russian Futurists and, more broadly, one of the most original and seminal twentieth-century Russian poets. — Ed.]

Though he has been writing for a long time now, he stepped into the front ranks only in the last two years. He was sorely needed. Pasternak presents us with a new literary object. Hence the remarkable obligatoriness of his themes. His theme does not protrude; it is motivated so strongly that somehow there is no need to speak of it.

What are the themes that bring verse and thing into collision? First, there is the very roaming about, the very birth, of the verse amongst things.

> Offshoots of downpour make muddy clusters
> And long, long until the dawn,
> They drip from roofs their acrostics
> Blowing bubble rhymes as they go along.

Here the words get entangled with the downpour ("downpour" is Pasternak's favorite image and setting); the verse is intertwined with the surrounding scenery through the medium of images interlinked by sound. This comes close to "meaningless sound-speech" *("zvukorech")* and yet it is inexorably logical—what we find there seems an illusory imitation of syntax, and yet the syntax is impeccable. And as a result of this alchemical-poetic operation, the downpour becomes a poem, and "the March night and the author" walk along together, shifting to the right along a square "like a three-tiered hexameter"—and the thing begins to come to life:

> The slantwise images, flying soaked in rain
> From a highway that extinguished my candle
> I cannot prevent from falling rhythmically
> And tearing toward rhyme from hook and wall.
>
> What if the universe has a mark on?
> What if there are no expanses such
> That someone wouldn't volunteer
> To staff their mouth with putty for the winter?
>
> But things tear off their masks,
> They lose control and shed their honor,
> When they have a reason to sing,
> Where's an occasion for a shower.[2]

Here things not only rip off their masks but also "shed their honor."

[2][From a 1922 poem which appeared in the collection *Themes and Variations.* The translation of the last two stanzas are quoted from Dale L. Plank, *Pasternak's Lyric* (The Hague: Mouton and Co., 1966), p. 107.—Ed.]

This is how Pasternak's "Pushkin Variations"[3] came to be written. The "swarthy lad" who had become a cliche was supplanted by a "flat-lipped hamite" roaming about among sounds.

> But breaking into the rustling of clusters
> Some thundering peal was dying painfully.

Pasternak's Pushkin, like all the objects in his verse, like the garret which "will break into recitation [of poetry] ,"[4] rips off his mask, begins to ferment with sounds.

Which themes are the best springboard for the act of leaping at the thing and arousing it? Illness, childhood, more broadly, those accidental and therefore intimately personal angles of vision which are usually varnished over and forgotten.

> So life begins! When almost two
> They leave the nurse for malady,
> They chirp, they babble—and then words
> Will soon appear before they're three.
>
> So oceans, sudden like a sigh
> Hover above the fences where
>   The houses are supposed to be.
> And so—iambics begin there.
> …So they begin to live by verses.[5]

The strangest definition of poetry ever offered becomes comprehensible;

> Poetry, I will swear
> By you, and finish hoarsely,
> You are not the bearing of the honeyvoiced,
> You are summer in a third-class seat,
> You are a suburb, and not a refrain.[6]

Among Pasternak's fellow poets, perhaps, only Verlaine with his vague hankering after the material object could have provided such a definition.

Childhood, not the childhood of high school anthologies, but childhood as a turning around of vision, confounds thing and verse so that

---

[3][A cluster of five poems in *Themes and Variations.* — Ed.]

[4][The line is drawn from the much-quoted poem in *My Sister, Life,* "About These Verses."—Ed.]

[5][From another poem in *Themes and Variations.* The translation, with the exception of the last line, is quoted from *Modern Russian Poetry,* edited by V. Markov and M. Sparks (New York: Bobbs-Merrill, 1967), p. 601.—Ed.]

[6][From "Poeziya"["Poetry"] , *Themes and Variations.* — Ed.]

things are brought onto a level with us and verses can be felt with our very hands. Childhood justifies, indeed necessitates, images which bring together the most incongruous and disparate objects.

Christmas will look up like a young daw.

The distinctiveness of Pasternak's language lies in that it combines difficulty with supreme precision: it is an intimate conversation, a conversation in the nursery. (Pasternak needs the nursery in his verse for the same reason that Lev Tolstoy needed it in his prose.) No wonder his book *My Sister, Life* is essentially a diary with dutiful indications of place (Balashov) and with notes at the end of each section of the volume, such as "These diversions came to an end when, on going away, she relinquished her mission to a substitute" or "That summer the trains in that direction left from Paveletsky station." This is the source of that prosaic quality one finds in Pasternak, of the homely matter-of-factness of his language; it comes from the nursery.

> The sky in a heap of reasons
> For mischief making.

His linguistic exaggerations too stem from children's language:

> Storm instantaneous for ever.

From here, too, derives his strange visual perspective, characteristic of a sick man, with its attentiveness to things close at hand and a sense of boundless space extending immediately beyond them.

> (A yard or so from the window
> plucking the woolen threads of a bournous[7]
> He swore by the peaks' glaciers
> Sleep, my love, I'll return as avalanche!)

The same is true of illness that projects "love" through the "eyes of medicinal phials" and, finally, every chance angle of vision.

> A steamy cup of cocoa in a pier-glass,
> Tule sways and down the garden walk
> Into the windfallen trees and chaos
> Toward the swing the pier glass races.

Pasternak's stock of images is an unusual one; their selection is governed by fortuitous criteria. In his verse things are linked rather tenuously; they are merely neighbors, close only by virtue of con-

---

[7][Bedouin cloak.—Ed.]

tiguity (the second term in an image is invariably both humdrum and abstract); yet the fortuitous turns out to be a firmer link than the strongest logical connection.

> The small rain shuffled uneasily at the door.
> There was a smell of wine corks.
> So smelled the dust. So smelled the weeds.
> And if you look at it closely
> That was the smell of the gentry's screeds
> About equality and brotherhood.

(These half-abstract "screeds" are of a piece with a whole repertory of such abstractions to be found in Pasternak, e.g., "pretext," "right," "discharge." Curiously enough, Pasternak converges here with Fet,[8] in whose poetry "pretext," "right" and "honor" occur in the most unexpected juxtapositions with the most concrete objects.)

There is a phenomenon that we call "false memory." Someone talks to you and you have a feeling that it has all happened before, that once before you sat in this very same place while your interlocutor was saying these very same things, and you know in advance what he is going to say. And the person who talks to you really says what he is supposed to say. (In fact, of course, it is the other way around: your interlocutor talks and while he talks you are under the impression you have heard all this before.)

Something like this happens with Pasternak's imagery. The link which joins things in his universe is not available to you, it is fortuitous, yet once it is provided, you seem to remember it as if it had already been there somewhere — and the image becomes an obligatory one.

Now what makes both the image and the subject obligatory is that they do not obtrude: they are the poem's consequence rather than its cause. The subject cannot be extracted — it is inseparable from the cavernous bodies, from the rugged textures of the verse. (Roughness, cavernousness suggest a youthful tissue; old age has the smoothness of a billiard ball.)

The subject is not left suspended in midair. There is a key to the poet's words — to the "fortuitous" vocabulary, the "monstrous syntax":

> Of careful drops
> Youth swam in happiness as might
> In quiet childish snoring
> A pillowslip much slept upon.

[8][Afanasy Fet (1820-92) was one of the finest nineteenth-century Russian lyric poets. — Ed.]

Nor is the "free word" itself left suspended in midair; it stirs the thing up. To do this it has to collide with it, and collide it does — on the plane of emotion. Not the naked "real-life" emotion of Esenin,[9] posited from the start as the poem's ostensible subject. What we confront here is a vague emotion which seems to resolve itself toward the end, a musical emotion quivering in all the words, in all the things, akin to that of Afanasy Fet.

This is why Pasternak's tradition or, more exactly, the points of reference which he signalizes are the poets of emotion — *My Sister, Life* is dedicated to Lermontov, the epigraphs are drawn here from Lenau and Verlaine.[10] This is why Pasternak's "variations"[11] feature the themes of the Demon, Ophelia, Gretchen, Desdemona.

But above all he echoes Fet:

> A boat throbs in the sleeping breast.
> Willows overhang, kiss collarbones,
> Elbows and rowlocks — O, wait,
> After all, this could happen to anyone![12]

One hesitates to attach historical labels to living persons. Mayakovsky has been compared to Nekrasov. (I myself committed a more serious offense by comparing him to Derzhavin and Khlebnikov to Lermontov.)[13]

Mea culpa, but this bad habit stems from the fact that, while prediction is difficult, some retrospective orientation is necessary.

For this we have Pasternak's authority — and, as it happens, also Hegel's:

> Once, inadvertently,
> And, one suspects, at random,
> Hegel called the historian
> A prophet who predicts backwards.

I shall refrain from predicting Pasternak's future. We live in an answerable age, and I do not know which way he will go. (And this is

[9][Sergey Esenin (1895-1925) was a wayward and self-dramatizing lyricist; he claimed to be the "last village poet." — Ed.]

[10][Mikhail Lermontov (1814-41), a major poet and one of the pioneers of Russian artistic prose, was the leading Russian Romantic. Nicolaus Lenau (1802-50) was an Austrian Romantic poet. — Ed.]

[11][Reference to several poetic cycles contained in *Themes and Variations.* — Ed.]

[12][See "Life as Ecstasy and Sacrifice," footnote 1, in this volume. — Ed.]

[13][Nikolay Nekrasov (1821-78) was an influential mid-nineteenth-century Russian poet; his verse had a strong sociohumanitarian bent. Gavrila Derzhavin (1743-1816), a sonorous and grandiloquent lyricist, was the key figure in eighteenth-century Russian poetry. — Ed.]

good. It is bad when the critic knows which way a poet is heading.)
Pasternak ferments and his fermentation rubs off on others—it is
significant that no other poet is encountered so often in the other
poet's poems as he is, he not only ferments, but he is himself the
ferment, the leaven.

The Energy of Pasternak

by Isaiah Berlin

Boris Leonidovich Pasternak was born in Moscow in 1890. His father was a well-known painter, his mother a musician. He published his earliest poems during the First World War towards the end of the renaissance of Russian poetry which began in the nineties and ended with the death of Esenin.[1] By 1919 Pasternak's poetry began to be read beyond the literary coteries of Moscow and Petrograd and today, at the age of 60, he is recognized as a poet of genius upon the quality of which no serious critic has ventured to cast any doubt. Although attention was drawn to his work by D. S. Mirsky, who admired his gifts and wrote about him with great understanding (in English) in the twenties, it was not until recent events stimulated a new wave of interest in Russia that any systematic translation of his work into English was attempted. Verse translations by Professor C. M. Bowra and by Miss Babette Deutsch (which form the last section of this book),[2] — in particular the former — convey something of the heavily charged and twisting rhythms, the tormented yet luminous vision of the orginal; in particular, of the depth and unity of his world in which men, things, relationships, emotions, ideas, sensations, situations are conceived within a kind of universal biological category. Within this orbit the force of nature flows with a violent almost self-conscious energy, at many interpenetrating levels; sometimes it flows in rich, enormous overwhelming waves of feeling moving freely and in many dimensions. Sometimes the stream is arrested or compressed into narrow defiles, in which it forms knots and gathers into violently condensed globules of extreme intensity; Pasternak's verse is in the first place a vehicle of metaphysical emotion which

"The Energy of Pasternak" by Isaiah Berlin. From *Partisan Review*, 7 (1950), 748-51; reprinted by permission of the author and *Partisan Review*.

[1][See footnote 9 in "Words and Things in Pasternak," which is reprinted in this volume. — Ed.]

[2][Boris Pasternak, *Selected Writings* (New York: New Directions), 1949. — Ed.]

melts the barriers between personal experience and "brute" creation. The poet himself remarked somewhere that poetry or art is the natural object informed by, or seen under, the aspect of energy—the all pervasive *vis vivida* whose flow, at times broken and intermittent, is the world of things and persons, forces and states, acts and sensations. To attempt to give more precise significance to this kind of vision may be perilous and foolish, save by discrimination from what it is not: it is neither a pathetic fallacy whereby human experience is projected into inanimate objects, nor yet is it the inversion of this, to be found, for example, in the novels of Virginia Woolf, where the fixed structure of human beings and material objects is dissolved into the life and the properties of the shifting patterns of the data of the inner and the outer senses, sounds, smells, colors, real, imagined, and recollected. There is, on the contrary, a sense of unity induced by the sense of the pervasiveness of cosmic categories (perhaps derived from the poet's neo-Kantian days in Marburg) which integrate all the orders of creation into a single, biologically and physiologically, emotionally and intellectually, interrelated universe; this world in which clouds and flowers, the earth and the sky, the actively burning rays of the sun and the cold mountain water and the shape of a sound or a human limb or a continent, or a half articulated movement— physical or mental—and the stresses and pressures of inanimate objects and of human sensations, emotions, perceptions, images, and passions, all penetrate one another and strain against one another, both act and suffer; the words communicate this by means of a kind of violent and unexpected modulation to which Pasternak is as prone as Donne or Hopkins. Nor is this a consciously bold device or technical method of juxtaposing opposites to secure a spark or an explosion; it conveys a directly experienced vision of a single world-wide, world-long system of tensions and stresses, a perpetual ebb and flow of energy, rising to a climax in the painful frustration, but in the end, triumphant agony of individual centers of consciousness—the life of personalities, solid men and women, vis-a-vis solid material objects. Both persons and things are related to each other by real and not symbolic relationships heightened and transfigured by an extreme concentration of a vision which reveals the inner outline—the permanent bony structure—and does not transmute them into elements of an other worldly language, or become attenuated into a succession of vaguely relevant emotions of verbal patterns. As always with great poetry, these systems of tensions resolve themselves at their greatest height into passages of noble simplicity and repose, moments of serenity and harmony towards which the discords inevitably tend and in terms of which alone they acquire their significance and purpose.

Pasternak grew up during the Symbolist phase of Russian poetry, when problems of philosophy and theology dominated the thoughts of some among his most gifted contemporaries. He originally set out to be a composer, was a pupil of Scryabin, but became a poet profoundly influenced by Andrey Bely and the other writers of the Moscow circle. Between 1915 and 1924 he composed half a dozen short stories, and in 1930 his autobiography appeared. The stories, to be properly assessed, must be understood in the historical context of his life. His prose is of that painfully over-elaborated and euphuistic kind in which the maximum and sometimes more is squeezed out of every word; and owes much to the precious, sometimes unsuccessful, at other times dazzlingly brilliant technical method of Bely,[3] a great innovator of language, who before Joyce invented new methods of using words, and generated a world of his own, filled with the fitful memories of half understood German metaphysics, choc a bloc with treasured mysteries drawn from Baudelaire, Nietzsche, Wagner, French and Belgian Symbolist poets, the anthroposophy of Rudolph Steiner—a queer amalgam of profound inspiration, insight, and astonishing flights of imaginative virtuosity, in which moments of tranquility, beauty and innocence mingle with mere neurosis, extravagance, hysteria, genuine madness, and at times a particularly false and irritating aesthetic exhibitionism.

The prose style which Pasternak created during the period of literary and spiritual turmoil, is, to say the least, not easy to convey into another language, and it is almost at its most obscure and artificial in his autobiography, which he called *Safe Conduct*. Hence the translator, Mrs. Beatrice Scott, was clearly most courageous to have attempted it at all; courageous or blind, for, more often than not, she gives the impression of having surrendered the resources of the English language without a struggle to the untranslatable Russian original, and we get strange collocations of words which leave the reader perplexed.

Nor do Pasternak's stories fare better in Mr. Robert Payne's renderings. And although the heroic martydom of these translators may entitle them to our respect, the author remains unlucky. The selection of stories seems open to question. "The Childhood of Luvers" is a masterpiece and well worth inclusion, but "Aerial Ways" and "Letters from Tula" are so intimately connected with a particular period and manner and literary atmosphere that their value to the untutored

[3][See "Language and Reality in Early Pasternak," in this volume.—Ed.]

reader without an apparatus of commentary may be doubted. The editing is slovenly to a degree; Mr. Schimansky's references to his introductory essay published in the original English edition are left intact in his Preface, although the essay in question has been omitted from the American compilation. Of the two-score or so translations of the author's poetry, five at least are somewhat surprisingly given in the versions both of Professor Bowra and Miss Deutsch — as if the translations had been independently chosen and carelessly allowed to overlap. And why does the second part of "Luvers" appear as a completely separate story under the title, "The Stranger" (this is only a chapter-heading in the original and is given quite correctly in the English edition)?

Nevertheless one should not cavil too much; everything which throws light upon the creative activities of an artist of rare genius about whom too little is known (and all facts are valuable) is to be welcomed. Mr. Lindsay Drummond (who has published these works in England), and the editors of New Directions, as well as Mr. Schimansky, have performed a service to literature by this act of homage to a noble poet and one of the few men of authentic genius of our time.

The Metonymous Hero or
the Beginnings of Pasternak the Novelist

by Michel Aucouturier

It is generally believed that *Doctor Zhivago* is Pasternak's first novel. Strictly speaking, it is his third. The novella *The Childhood of Luvers*, published in 1922, constituted already the beginning of a novel, the manuscript of which was lost in the course of the civil war, and only the first part of which was reconstructed by the poet. One of the first works which he tackles in the aftermath of the Revolution is the "novel in verse" *Spektorsky* begun in 1924, concluded in 1929, completed in 1930 by an introduction, and revised in 1931 for a separate edition.

In comparison with *Doctor Zhivago*, both of these works have something of the fragmentary and incomplete about them which is not simply accidental. One may think that Pasternak with good reason did not reconstruct in its entirety the novel of which *The Childhood of Luvers* is the remnant. As to *Spektorsky,* it is remarkable that even before having finished it, he felt the need to complete it by a novella in prose, the *Tale* where one encounters again the hero and some of the secondary characters of the novel. Otherwise, even considered jointly, *Spektorsky* and the *Tale* do not give the impression of a completed whole; they appear more like fragments of a larger work of which they are only the toothing stones.

This impression of incompleteness is intentional: it is on purpose that in a work such as the *Tale*, the most cleverly structured of his stories, narration breaks off on an inconsequential remark which refers to a marginal character and offers a nearly superfluous explanation of an unimportant misunderstanding. This faulty con-

From "The Metonymous Hero or the Beginnings of Pasternak the Novelist," by Michel Aucouturier, *World Literature Today* (formerly *Books Abroad*), 44, no. 2, 222-26. Copyright © 1970 by the University of Oklahoma Press. Translated from the French by Ivar Ivask. Reprinted by permission of the author, the publisher, and the translator.

clusion is neither clumsiness nor negligence; it is a structural trait
of Pasternak's narrative prose and proceeds from the very nature of
its central character.

Spektorsky marks the first appearance in the work of Pasternak of
what may be called the "metonymous hero."

We are basing ourselves here on the terminology of Roman Jakobson who, in his article of 1935,[1] has strongly urged the fundamental
opposition which separates Pasternak from Mayakovsky. The poetic
language of the latter, he claimed, is founded on the metaphor which,
by analogy or opposition, connects the entire universe to the "I"
of the poet, while the art of Pasternak, founded upon metonymy, on
the contrary dissolves the "I," and generally any kind of conscious
or deliberate agent, in the image of a world where the "subject" is
nothing but a grammatical fiction because there exists only one single
real subject, life, whose essence is supra-individual. In the figure
of speech which Jakobson calls metonymy one recognizes what Pasternak himself called, in a polemical article of 1914,[2] the "metaphor
of contiguity" *(po smezhnosti)*, which he opposed to the metaphor
based on analogy *(po skhodstvu)*, the latter being too rational for his
taste. To give just one example, let us see how the approach of Christmas in a big city is depicted in *Spektorsky:* "The crunching dusk was
buying up toys." A double metonymy substitutes here the image of
the winter dusk for that of the crowds (who buy toys) and for that of
the snow (crunching under the steps of the crowds) which are associated
with the dusk through the medium of "contiguity" and not "analogy."
The metaphor for reasons of contiguity, which associates and substitutes certain objects, notions, images for others not by virtue of
an abstract relationship of resemblance, but by a virtue of a concrete
connection between elements of the same sensory experience, actually
results in an image of a world where the actions and attributes can
be but indifferently related to the interchangeable subjects, and thus
underline the illusory character of all individual subjects.

It is the growing awareness of the aesthetic, moral, and philo-
sophic implications of this poetics of metonymy which explains the
evolution of Pasternak from his Futurist beginnings to the collection
My Sister, Life, where his originality is fully realized. The "Romantic manner"[3] which he denies himself after his encounter with May-

[1]"Randbemerkungen zur Prosa des Dichters Pasternak," *Slavische Rundschau,*
VII, 6 (1935). [The English translation of this essay is "Marginal Notes of the Prose
of the Poet Pasternak," in Davie and Livingstone, eds., *Pasternak,* pp. 134-51.]

[2]"Vassermanova reaktsiya" ["Wasserman Reaction"], Rukonog, Moscow, 1914.

[3]*Okhrannaya gramota [Safe Conduct]* in B. Pasternak, *Sochineniya [Works],* vol.
2, Ann Arbor, 1961, pp. 281-82.

akovsky in order to free himself of what brings them together is precisely this poetics of the metaphor (in the restricted sense given this word by Jakobson) which places on the first plane the "I" of the lyrical poet and which still dominates the first collection of Pasternak, "*Twin in the Clouds*." And the very year of *My Sister, Life*, Pasternak writes a novella "Letters from Tula" which is in reality a kind of literary confession where he repudiates the character of the poet who is preoccupied with his "I" and with that which distinguishes him from the others, and proposes instead as the ideal that of a theater actor who finds the "physical silence" indispensable for creation in "making someone else speak through his mouth."

This effacement of the subject which Pasternak attempts and which is inscribed in the very nature of his poetic version of things—is not a depersonalization. This is so because for him personality is not found on the level of the conscious and active "I," but beyond it, in the pure spontaneity of the élan vital to which both conscience and will should always remain open. Personality is not defined by activity, but by receptivity: "Modernist movements have imagined," he wrote in 1922,[4] "that art is similar to a fountain while it is more similar to a sponge. They decided that it should gush forth when really it should absorb and soak up." This definition of art is obviously also a definition of the personality.

The view of the world expressed by metonymy implies a definite conception of the personality and imposes on Pasternak also a definite type of hero. It is not astonishing that this type should have been incarnated for the first time in the figure of a small girl. Child and woman, Zhenya Luvers unites in herself all the ideal conditions for a receptive attitude toward the world: a child who perceives things directly without the screen of words, solidified concepts, habits; a woman who is in her very body sensitive to the mysteries of life and creation. However, precisely because these are generic and not individual qualities which mark her for the incarnation of the Pasternakian concept of the personality, one cannot consider her as the first metonymous hero of the poet.

It is Sergey Spektorsky who is entitled to this honor. In his case, actually for the first time, a childlike spontaneity and a feminine receptivity appear as traits of an individual character.[5]

---

[4]"Neskolko polozheniy" ["Several Propositions"] , in B. Pasternak, *Sochineniya* [*Works*] , vol. 3, p. 152.

[5]It is true that one can discern these same traits already in the character of Heinrich Heine in "Tratto di Apelle," written in 1915. But this character presents altogether different traits as well.

To tell the truth this character is not described except in a negative fashion ("a man without qualities," says the author in his introduction), or indirectly because he himself or other characters make brief allusions to his artistic talents, his dilettantism, his passivity, and a certain irresponsibility. Nor is he more "shown-up" by his words or revealing actions; Spektorsky speaks little and does not act. As a matter of fact, his character develops from the inherent structure of the narrative to the point of appearing an emanation of it

Two traits, shared by the poetry of *Spektorsky* and the prose of the *Tale*, strike one in this narrative structure. First is the absence of a real plot. The events are interconnected not by threads of causality, but by those of contiguity. Thus in *Spektorsky* nothing connects the affair of the hero with Olga Bukhteyeva, a married woman who helps him discover carnal love, to his idyll with a young poet Marya Ilyina — nothing except their proximity in time. Nothing, except their simultaneity, connects (in the *Tale*) the adventure of Sergey with a young prostitute Sasha, who emerges from the pathetic world of urban poverty, to the amorous intensity which turns him to the young Danish widow Anna Arild Tornskjold, forced by her poverty to take employment with the Frestelns, a parvenu family where Sergey is tutor.

The succession of these four encounters, all of them taking place between the winter 1912-13 and the summer 1914, could constitute a dramatic plot, a psychological study, a theme of a light novel. Yet Pasternak will have none of this. "The word 'drama,'" the author will say of his hero, "was not part of his vocabulary." Spektorsky's sister Natasha, just as Marya Ilyina or Arild, knows that "there is no room in his character for escapades or pranks," and that he is neither a Don Juan nor a fop. As for psychology, Pasternak tells us in *The Childhood of Luvers* that he considers it one of our illusions that life fosters in order to deflect our attention from its real work; one will look in vain for a psychology of love in *Spektorsky* or in the *Tale*.

The second remarkable aspect of the narrative structure in these two works is that all that which makes up the woof of events — the plain facts, the objective identity of the characters, the spatial and temporal references, the casual relationships — all this is but suggested in an allusive and often obscure fashion, as if on the margin of a tale constituted essentially by sensations. The latter are organized into a succession of pictures at once plastic and dynamic, inspired by the spectacle of the hours and the seasons, of nature and city, of life at home and in the streets, where "things" are nothing but the witnesses of a lyrical surge without subject which indissolubly merges the spectacle and the spectator. Not even the presence of the hero is always explicit: thus, for example, in the first chapter of *Spektorsky* where a night of thaw in Moscow is depicted at the hour when the revelers return home, just two scraps of monologue suggest to us vaguely the silhouette of the hero who comes home from a nocturnal walk. Nevertheless, it is he who constitutes implicitly the connecting link of all the episodes. He is the privileged one for whom the universe unfolds all its spectacles; he is the sponge avidly absorbing them. He has no other function, no other character than this.

It is thus that the structure of these "love stories," dispensing as they do with dramatic situations and psychological analyses, expresses very faithfully the character of a protagonist for whom love, though clearly the central event, is not an involvement of will, but rather a perpetual and total readiness of mind and heart to respond to the ever-new call of life.

An organ of marvelously sensitive reception, but bereft of will and incapable of acting, such is the "metonymous hero" whom Pasternak submits in *Spektorsky* to the judgment of history. For this is precisely the meaning of a work undertaken in the aftermath of the Revolution—to confront, across ten years of violent events, the certainties of yesterday with the realities of today. The last two chapters of the novel are in opposition to the first seven, where history is almost totally absent, a kind of allegorical vision of the Revolution, and paint the hero against the background of hungry, haggard, and chaotic Moscow during the civil war. Six years have passed. The year is 1919. Accidentally, in the course of one and the same day, Spektorsky suddenly recalls Marya Ilyina and meets again Olga Bukhteyeva in person. His past is revived, yet depreciated by the present: it is in a warehouse for storing abandoned furniture and household goods, amidst intimate nicknacks profaned by a stranger's glances, that he finds his own photograph in an album which once belonged to Marie. As for Olga, whose leather jacket and revolver mark her as an important figure in the new regime, she looks upon Sergey with somewhat disdainful pity. A speaker for the revolutionary tradition of the Russian intelligentsia ("I am the daughter of the *narodovoltsy*,"[6] she proudly proclaims), she embodies, as she confronts the hero, the historical legitimacy of the Revolution.

Nevertheless the elliptical conclusion of *Spektorsky* leaves in doubt the nature of the conflict which opposes the "metonymous hero" to the Revolution. It seems that to clarify this, Pasternak wrote the *Tale* even before formulating in the two chapters of the novel the

[6]Members of a terrorist organization in the 1870's called "The People's Will."

pitiless verdict of history. The *Tale,* actually, was conceived in 1929 as a "direct continuation of the *Spektorsky* chapters which have been published to date [the chapters 1-7, M. A.] and as an intermediary link between the novel and its conclusion in verse. ..." "When I have finished it," Pasternak adds, "I will be able to take up the final chapter of *Spektorsky.*"[7] The same note contains an interesting explanation of the specific functions of prose and verse in the development of the subject matter shared by both works: "I have confided to prose," Pasternak literally writes, "that part which is connected with the years of war and revolution because the characteristics and formulas which in this part are most necessary and obvious surpass the possibilities of verse." This somewhat obscure formula perhaps simply means that prose is better than verse for articulating the social and historical aspect of his characters.

The comparison of the two works seems to confirm this. In both, the personality of Natasha, the sister of Spektorsky, brings out by contrast the negative aspect of the hero's political attitude. However, in the novel, only some fleeting allusions permit us to guess that she is a typical representative of the leftist intelligentsia before the Revolution (when she, for example, reproaches Sergey for being "cut-off from his generation"). The description of the workers' suburbs, which Sergey crosses after having accompanied her to the railroad station, and where one feels that the city "had paid for its comfort with a prison" and where "one expects something all the time," makes us understand that he is, in the receptive and intuitive manner of a poet, closer than his sister to the social and historical reality. It is only in the *Tale* that Natasha's personality, her university years, her circle of friends in Moscow, her provincial milieu in Usolye in the Urals, her manner of awaiting the Revolution are drawn with indisputable sharpness. Yet it is above all the positive aspect of Sergey's historical and social personality which becomes evident in the *Tale.*

The novella has more unity than the novel in verse. It owes its title to a "tale within the tale" which forms a nucleus that expresses its essential meaning. This tale is the first narrative work by Sergey, a kind of symbolical story the hero of which is designated by the algebraic formula of Y3, thus underlining the schematic nature of the narrative. The action is also reduced to the scheme of an auction, where Y3 proposes himself as a slave to the highest bidder. He does this after having demonstrated his astonishing talents as poet and

---

[7]Note published in the section "Writers Speaking of Themselves," of the journal *Na literaturnom postu* [*On Literary Guard*], 1929, Nos. 4-5, See B. Pasternak, *Verses and Poems,* p. 671.

musician. Before handing himself over to his owner, an immensely rich Maecenas, he distributes the proceeds from the sale in the workers' suburbs.

This tale is of capital significance. For the first time we see Spektorsky expressing himself as a writer, in other words, acting. For the first time, the "metonymous hero" is not only passive receptivity, but also action. To be sure, this action remains true to his character:hardly an expression of will, it is completely inefficacious. The tale of Sergey actually is presented like an immediate and spontaneous reaction of the hero to the confessions of Sasha and Arild who have opened up before him the abyss of human anguish; the naive and clumsy schematism of his tale underlines precisely the spontaneity of his reaction. But it is remarkable that artistic creation should be thus connected to the social sensibility of the hero. On the other hand, his reaction has no practical value whatsoever though he also thinks, quite naively, about all the good that he could do with the money obtained from his writings. As a matter of fact, his response to the challenge of human suffering is purely symbolical: it resides in the idea of sacrifice just as it spontaneously is embodied, almost against his will, in the character of Y3, the projection of his secret dreams. Thus for the first time the social mission of the poet is evoked here in terms of sacrifice, and redeeming sacrifice being associated by Sergey himself with "that which happened in Galilee." The image of Zhivago-Hamlet-Jesus Christ is already outlined against the horizon of the *Tale*.

The adventures of Sergey with Arild and Sasha which provide the frame of the story about Y3 are in turn framed in the *Tale* by a series of scenes where we see Sergey arriving at the home of his sister Natasha in the small industrial town of Usolye in the Urals early in 1916. This setting of the novella seems above all intended to put the central episode in a historical perspective by attaching it to the war and Revolution, and perhaps to insert it in the design of a much larger narrative. This seems to be the sole function of an episode where we see a sailor on leave coming to visit a comrade at the factory in Usolye, an episode which nothing but the location attaches to the rest of the story. This seems likewise to be the reason for the insistence with which the character of Lemokh is evoked, whom we see for a moment in *Spektorsky*, then on the last pages of the *Tale*, but who plays no role whatsoever in the story. Both vaguely suggest by their unexplained presence the approaching Revolution and the role they possibly could be called upon to play in it.

Nevertheless the character of Lemokh has a more specific function than that. Seeing him for the first time, Sergey immediately guesses in him "a rebel, that is to say, a despot." When he sees him again in the *Tale*, he has the feeling of having before him "something elevated and strange which depreciated him, Sergey, altogether from head to foot. It was the masculine spirit of matter-of-factness, the most modest and most terrible of all spirits." In the character of the revolutionary (Lemokh prefigures in this respect the character of Pavel Antipov in *Doctor Zhivago*), the "metonymous hero" clashes with his opposite.

However, there exists a mysterious link between Lemokh and Sergey which is underlined by the insistence with which destiny places one on the path of the other, and the secret connivance which establishes itself between them at the end of the *Tale*, over the heads of mediocre intellectuals such as Natasha and her husband. We guess that this link, which makes for the thematic unity of the *Tale*, resides in a common sensibility and a common feeling of responsibility in the face of human misery. But only the revolutionary possesses at this moment an effective response to this metaphysical and historical challenge of evil. The response of the poet, as we have seen, belongs to the realm of fantasy, myth, and legend. Hence his feeling of inferiority before the revolutionary. We are still far from the moral victory of Zhivago over Antipov. To attain it the poetic work itself would have to become that total gift of oneself which is prefigured here under the guise of fiction.

And yet the idea of sacrifice is already there, marking for the Pasternakian hero the path on which he can find his social and historical vindication.

Life as Ecstasy and Sacrifice:
Two Poems by Boris Pasternak

By Nils Ake Nilsson

"Oars at Rest"

A boat throbs in the sleeping breast.
Willows overhang, kiss collarbones,
Elbows and rowlocks — O, wait,
After all, this could happen to anyone!

For everyone is amused by this in a song.
For this implies — the ash of a lilac,
Largest of chopped camomile in dew,
Lips and lips got in trade for stars.

For this implies — embracing the sky
Entwining huge Hercules in your arms,
For this implies — for ages on end
Squandering nights on the thrilling of warblers![1]

This poem by Boris Pasternak is from his book *My Sister, Life*, written in 1917 but published in 1922. It cannot be said that it is difficult to understand — already the title offers a clue to what it is a- bout — but even so, it demands a considerable amount of care in reading if one is to grasp the subtlety and complexity of its imagery, structure and sound patterns. It is a poem in which various devices co-operate in the creation of a striking poetical density, a poem which is in many ways characteristic of Pasternak's earlier period.

Let me first try to reconstruct what I think its content to be. One summer night the poet and his beloved are out rowing. The oars are drawn in and they let themselves drift along the banks. They do not see the ripples that lap the sides of the boat: they are only aware of them through the tremors of the boat. The impelling, rhythmical

"Life as Ecstasy and Sacrifice: Two Poems by Boris Pasternak" by Nils Ake Nilsson. This essay, which first appeared in *Scando-Slavica* (Copenhagen: Munksgard, 5, 1959), pp. 180-98, has been revised by the author for inclusion in this collection.

[1]Quoted from Dale L. Plank, *Pasternak's Lyric*, p. 55.

slaps against the boat reverberate in their breasts, become as one with their heartbeats. Finally it is as if it were not the heart but the boat that is throbbing in the breast. "The boat throbs in the sleeping breast."

This is a characteristic example of Pasternak's concentrated poetic style. First of all, the image is based on a concrete observation. It is one of those metaphors which, in Pasternak's words, are not invented by the poet but "given to him" by nature itself. When they realize what it means many readers will probably say: "I never thought of it but, of course, one may get such an impression." The image is further given a startling, concentrated form (cf. the long discursive explanation above). And finally, it does not just stand there by itself as an original and puzzling image. It is made to work as part of a particular view of life, stressing a connection between man and the reality surrounding him, a relationship of man to life in all its manifestations. There is no border line between living things and dead things. All is life, everything is part of Life. The same idea returns in the following line: the willows kiss collarbones (*"klyuchitsy"*) and rowlocks (*"uklyuchiny"*), both the boat and those in the boat, and here are used words which sound very much like each other, suggesting by paronomastic means a close relationship between man and the world of objects.

The poetic atmosphere built up here is suddenly broken at the end of the third line by a prosaic "wait a moment" (*"pogodi"*). This is a typical way Pasternak has of suddenly changing a mood, upsetting the balance of an emotional atmosphere before it has had time to set. His fondness for ellipse is also prominent here: certain parts of the situation are skipped over, and these the reader has to fill in for himself. Consequently, it is quite possible to imagine that the poet's beloved, filled with the harmony and fullness of the moment, speaks of no one ever before having experienced such a feeling, no one ever before having loved so. It is this that leads the poet to his deflating reply. No, they are not the first to have loved, they are not alone in experiencing such awareness of the fullness and happiness of life. They are not the only people on earth; it happens to everyone, and if not in just this way, people are able to experience it in verse and song.

The next two stanzas form a kind of monologue: the poet tries to define the powerful emotion pervading him and his beloved, an emotion which is love and human happiness and something still more, the generous, active energy of life itself, the creative meditation of poetry. This emotion is so rich that it is impossible to drain it.

It can only be presented metonymically. It does not really matter which aspects of it are brought out, because in Pasternak's poetic world "each detail can be replaced by another. All this is precious. Any one of them chosen at random serves as evidence of the state which envelops the whole of transposed reality."

This reconstruction of the content of the first stanza points to yet another of Pasternak's characteristics. The poem, it seems, is a-bout two people, the poet and his beloved. They live in the poem and yet somehow are not there. They are never described, and no verb refers to any action they perform. They are presented metonymically. What is to be found of them is in pieces: the breast drunk with sleep, the collarbones and elbows brushed by the willows. This method gives sparkle to a situation which is by no means unknown to the romantic poets of the time: the lovers out rowing on a summer evening.[2]

The motif was popular in Russian poetry. When comparing Pasternak's poem with this tradition (Fet, for instance),[3] we will notice that he has weeded out or altered all the cliches and simplified the situation to the utmost, to something which resembles a rebus or pieces from a jugsaw puzzle. Instead of a picture of sentimental romance or soft impressionism we are given a cubist painting.

The ecstatic lust for life bubbling over in the lovers does not make them any different from others, then. On the contrary, it couples them to others, to nature, to the stars and the universe, to the gods, to all that bears the mark of life. Everything is permeated with life, with feeling. The poet turns first to nature. The lilacs—especially the withered blossoms—suggest something mild, soft and melancholy, something which is also embodied in this feeling. The next line, "the wealth of a crumbled camomile in the dew" with its associations of freshness, light-heartedness and generous giving, comes as a contrast.

A typical Pasternak crescendo follows. We suddenly find ourselves among the stars: "to exchange lips and lips for stars." Lips, which are something human, warm and time-bound, are exchanged for something remote, silent, timeless. While the previous lines described short moments of melancholy and happiness, here the perspective of eternity is introduced. This cosmic perspective is retained in the two lines that follow. "It is like embracing the roof of heaven" interprets the all-embracing span and power of emotion, the challenge to Hercules to fight. After this intensification there is a return to the

---

[2]The part played by metonymies in Pasternak's verse was pointed out by Roman Jakobson in his "Randbemerkungen zur Prosa des Dichters Pasternak," *Slavische Rundschau*, 7 (6, 1935), [For English translation, see Introduction, p. 13.—Ed.]

[3][See "Words and Things in Pasternak," footnote 8 in this volume.—Ed.]

peaceful contemplation of the first line: loving, composing, living, nights whiled away listening to the singing of the birds. The poem has come full cycle.

"Oars at Rest" shows several very characteristic features of Pasternak's early poetic style: the use of ellipse, dislocation and metonymy, of sharp contrasts and sudden intonational changes. In the poem there is both rest and movement; there is softness and passivity, but also expansion and strength. What holds these opposites together, what gives the poem life, is its emotionality, its intensive personal diction full of exclamations and repetitions, as if out of breath.

"Passion" is one of the key words to Pasternak's verse, but in his case it ought not to be understood in the narrow sense. It is more than love, it is more than sensual passion. "When we imagine that in Tristan, Romeo and Juliet and other memorials powerful passion is portrayed, we undervalue the subject matter. Their theme is wider than that powerful theme. Their theme is the theme of power itself."[4] This "power" is the boundless, ecstatic sense of life that flows through the universe, the same power which "Oars at Rest" deals with. All nature is vibrating and throbbing with it; it gives Pasternak's poetic world its strange balance between rest and movement. Everything he describes — scenery, interiors, inanimate objects — appear both quietly resting and at the same time in a state of inner movement, of revolt, overwhelmed by this powerful feeling of life.

Man's most concentrated experience of this power lies in love and artistic creation. These are the two subjects that dominate in *My Sister, Life*. In his earlier prose, too, Pasternak often stresses the connection between these two manifestations of life, and his interpretation of this connection is often that poetry is born out of an intense experience of love.

This sounds like a well-known and rather trivial idea, but Pasternak gives it a special twist. Love as an experience of the "power" makes him see a new and transformed world. Its close connection with man is suddenly revealed. It begins to speak to him in concentrated allegories and in metonymies dislodged from their usual contexts. This experience is described in his autobiographical book *Safe Conduct*, when, after an unsuccessful love affair, he suddenly notices that the world is changed: "I was surrounded by transformed objects. Something never before experienced crept into the substance of reality. Morning recognized my face and seemed to have come to be with me and never to leave me. The mist dissolved, promising a hot day.

---

[4][*Safe Conduct, The Collected Prose Works* (London, 1945), p. 81. — Ed.]

Gradually the town began to move. Carts, bicycles, vans and trains began slithering in all directions. Above them like invisible plumes serpentined human plans and designs. They wreathed and moved with the compression of very close allegories which are understood without explanations. Birds, houses and dogs, trees and horses, tulips and people became shorter and more disconnected than when childhood had known them. The laconic freshness of life was revealed to me, it crossed the street, took me by the hand and led me along the pavement."[5]

But feeling alone does not make a poet, even though it may appear so to the young. The passion that leads the artist is something deeper and more mature than just youth's mere youthful, unreasoning intoxication with life, something which is at the same time passively receptive and actively recreative. This realization is expressed in some pages devoted to Tolstoy in Pasternak's later autobiography. There he calls the passion which must guide the eye of the poet "the passion of creative contemplation." Tolstoy had this, and it was in its very light that he could see everything "as if in original freshness, from a new angle, as if for the first time."

The passion described in "Oars at Rest" is of a similar kind. The poem begins and ends with passiveness: the poet as a listener. In between there is plenty of energy and activity. But the poet's listening attitude does not exclude activity either: reality is transformed by metaphor ("the heart"—"the boat"), time by hyperbole ("to squander the nights listening to songbirds").

Thus, passion has a double connection with art. It is both the origin of artistic creation and the only content of the art itself ("Art concerns itself with life as a ray of power passes through it"). Now, how is the poet able to reproduce his new, fresh vision of reality? Can language cope with this? The poet has his special means of describing reality—the image. Pasternak often speaks of this in his prose and verse, speaks of it with great enthusiasm: "Images, that is, miracles wrought in the word," he writes in a typical passage from his story "*A Tale.*" It is obvious that he was living and writing at a time when poets in Russia as elsewhere were intoxicated by the infinite possibilities of imagery. Some of his statements concerning this connect him to both Futurists and Imagists.[6]

---

[5][*Ibid.*, pp. 76-77.—Ed.]

[6]["Imagism" ("imazhinizm") was a short-lived school in modern Russian poetry. Its chief spokesmen were Vadim Shershenevich and Anatoly Mariegof. The most prominent figure to be associated with the movement was Sergey Esenin.—Ed.]

As we know, these two schools were interested in the speed with which the image is capable of connecting two separate points in our sphere of experience, thereby creating a message full of concentration and associative tension. They spoke of a "telegram language" working in time with the fast tempo of the period and its technical advances; they spoke of "the unexpected meeting" between disparate and remote things. "Outside personalities," says Pasternak in "Translating Shakespeare," use metaphor as a shorthand of the spirit. The poet disseminates his thoughts "in momentary flashes." "Just as if someone were by turns showing him the world and hiding it up his sleeve," he says in "*A Tale.*"

These attempts at defining imagery agree well, for instance, with Ezra Pound's well-known definition from 1912, that "an image is that which presents an intellectual and emotional complex in an instant of time" or his emphasizing of "that feeling of sudden light which the works of art should and must convey." It would be easy to find several other parallels between Pasternak and the Imagists (T. E. Hulme's theoretical "Speculations," for example).[7] It shows that similar thoughts leading towards a new poetry of imagery occupied the minds of poets over the whole of Europe during the 1910's.

This is not the right place to probe deeper into Pasternak's use of imagery in comparison with that of the Russian Futurists and Imagists, but it might be of value to point out just one thing in this connection. When Pasternak uses the word "image" ("*obraz*") it is not usually the poetical tropes such as metonymy or metaphor that he is getting at but rather the segment of concrete reality that is transmitted by the poem (Compare the Imagists' "hard, clear patterns of words, interpreting moods by 'images,' i.e., by pictures, not similes," or Ezra Pound's theory of "images" and "Image.").

In the later autobiography, Pasternak emphasizes that the difference between himself and the more program-minded of his contemporaries lay in the fact that it was his dream that the poem contain a new thought or a new image. An image was enough in itself to justify a poem, but by this he did not mean — as the Imagists sometimes did — that a single successful or original metaphor was sufficient to give it life. When speaking of his early pieces "Venice" ["*Venetsiya*"] and "The Station" ["*Vokzal*"] he says that "all I wanted was that one poem should contain the city of Venice and the other the Brest railway station."[8] The poem should encompass the poet's vision,

---

[7][Reference to Anglo-American Imagism championed by Ezra Pound, Amy Lowell, and the English poet and philosopher T. E. Hulme. — Ed.]

[8][*I Remember.* (New York: Pantheon, 1959), p. 78. — Ed.]

his personal experience of certain fragments of reality, and this vision should be original enough to justify a poem and general enough to include the reader.

This is also true of a poem like "Oars at Rest." Here the different metonymies do not fall apart, do not clash with each other. It is not only his emotional diction—I have spoken of this earlier—that holds it together, but also the fact that they are associatively capable of forming a whole, forming a concrete picture: lilac, camomiles, stars, the heavens, song-birds, boat, waves, willows, a pair of lovers. The various metonymies in the poem thus resolve themselves into a picture of summer, a fragment of visual reality, at the same time that the emotion, to use the words of T. S. Eliot, finds its objective correlative in them.

In this analysis of the structure of the poem "Oars at Rest" one important thing has been missing: its "orchestration." Like French Symbolists, Russian Symbolists were also greatly interested in the "musicality" of poetry. Not only did they work with alliteration, assonance, consonance, internal rhymes and other types of sound repetitions; they also formulated whole theories concerning the "magic meaning" of vowels and consonants.

In his later autobiography, Pasternak stresses that he was not interested in these speculations. Nor could he accept the attempts of the Symbolists to overemphasize rhythm, to allow their poems to sound like gypsy dances, Russian folk dances or military marches. He did not wish the different devices of orchestration to become ends in themselves; their job was to support and sustain the poet's new idea or picture.

Such a statement may seem surprising, for orchestration quite obviously plays a most important part in Pasternak's earlier verse. However, on closer inspection one soon finds that he handles it both less dogmatically and in a more intricate way than many of the Symbolists. Above all, one is aware that it is not just "musicality" in the Symbolist sense that Pasternak is after. His poetry is orchestrated according to principles similar to those already encountered in the construction of his poem: contrast, sudden breaks, rest and movement, softness and explosive power.

The three first lines of "Oars at Rest" create, as we have seen, an atmosphere of a summer evening, of rest and harmony. Each phase introduced in these lines is marked by the repetition of a certain vowel. Thus, the first line describing the movement of the boat and the lovers drunk with sleep is dominated by one particular phoneme in stressed position: *"Lodka kolotitsya v sonnoy grudi."* Three stres-

sed "o's" lead to and culminate in the word *"sonny"* ("sleepy").
The next phase of the picture, the hanging branches of the willows,
is built on *"i"*: *"Ivy navisli."* In the third phase, the willows kissing
the boat and the lovers in it, we find a dominance of *"u"*: *"tselvyut
v klyuchitsy, v lokti, v uklyuchiny."*

Why this sound pattern? Is it just to show that the resources of
the Russian language were much richer than the Symbolists ever
imagined? Or an allusion to the Futurist *"concert bruitiste"*? Or
rather an attempt to seek new connections between the words via
phonetics, that semanticization of phonetics which is a characteristic
feature of modern poetry?

The Russian Symbolists often allowed a certain vowel to dominate
a line, a pair of lines or even a whole stanza. But they would never,
as Pasternak does here, switch so abruptly from one vowel to another.
This calls for a quick change of the center of articulation: *o-i-u*.
Such examples of "speech mime" (*"rechevaya mimika"*), letting the
articulation itself contribute to the expressiveness of the lines, were,
however, not uncommon in post-Symbolist poetry, in Akhmatova, for
instance, as pointed out by [the Russian Formalist critic Boris]
Eikhenbaum.

And if Pasternak is using this common device of vowel dominance,
he also knows how to make the sound pattern richer and more tension-
ridden by introducing dissonant consonants. This is what happens
here. In the first line the dreamy atmosphere suggested by the dactylic
rhythm and the dominating *"o"* in the stressed positions is chal-
lenged by a dissonant repetition of consonants: *"Lo-dka ko-lotitsya."*
"Tka-ka" (reminiscent of blows) together with the rhythmical repetition *"lot"*—*"lot"* create associations of both the rhythm of the
waves and their lapping knocks on the sides of the boat. We also encounter something similar in the line describing how the willows
caress the boat and those in the boat. The dominance of *"i"* and *"u"*
is enriched by a series of consonant repetitions inserted into each
other: /ts/ /kts/ /ch/ /ts/ /kt/ /kl/ /ch/.

This seems to create an incongruity between the planes of content
and expression. Should such a romantic scene really be described
with so many harsh consonants and with so much articulatory energy?
The function of the elaborate orchestration of the stanza, as of the
poem as a whole, is apparently to challenge the traditional romantic
clichés describing a situation which, in the poet's view, "can happen
to everyone." There is also another function: to express the "power"
the poem is speaking of. What syntax, vocabulary or intonation can

only partly do is better achieved by phonetics: to illustrate the dynamic, vital, complex energy of the power of life.

There is something else in this poem to which I wish to draw attention, something which is also of importance for a complete understanding of Pasternak as a poet, and that is his vocabulary. Here, too, the reaction against earlier poetry is as clearly marked as it was already shown to be in connection with orchestration and structure. It would not be true to say that Pasternak avoids traditional "poetic" words (such as "kiss," "willow," "lilac," "stars"), but he does place them in a setting of very ordinary colloquialisms. The result is an exchange of associative tension: the formality of the "poetic" words is broken, and at the same time they transfer some of their poetic tension to the everyday words. "Kiss" in the second line appears in conjunction with the objects of the willows' caresses: such prosaic things as collarbones, elbows and rowlocks. "lilacs" in the second line of stanza 2 is balanced by the much simpler camomile and in the last stanza the romantic nightingale (*"solovey"*) is transformed into the more humble and unusual (in poetry) "warbler" (*"slavka"*).

In an article entitled "The Music of Poetry," T. S. Eliot writes that each poetic revolution tends to become a turning back to the spoken language. Such reactions must occur at regular intervals, because the spoken language is always moving, while the poetic language lags behind, weighed down by the inertia of tradition and the example of the great masters. One such revolution in European verse occurred just about 1910.

In Russia the Futurists led this campaign for a new poetic language. Pasternak was, no doubt, influenced by it. He belonged for a while to a Futurist group, and he has several times stated his admiration for the young Mayakovsky. But in his renewal of the language of poetry he never went as far as the Futurists. They introduced slang and jargon and took special interest in shocking and vulgar expressions. But Pasternak's poetry was no "slap in the face of public taste" in the Futurist sense. In his poems, traditional poetic vocabulary exists side by side with colloquialisms and words considered to be "unpoetic." His poetry is both romantic and unromantic in a very personal and special way. "Oars at Rest" is a fine example of how it works.

"Hamlet"

The hum has died down. I have come out on
the stage. Leaning against the door-frame, I
seek to grasp in the distant echo what will happen
during my life.

The penumbra of night is focused upon me through
a thousand opera-glasses. If only it be possible,
Abba, Father, take away this cup from me.
I love your stubborn design, and am content
to play this part. But now another drama is being
acted, so this time let me be.
But the order of the scenes has been thought
out, and the end of the road is inevitable. I
am alone, everything is sinking in Pharisaism.
To go through life is not the same as to walk
a field.[9]

"Hamlet" is one of the poems in *Doctor Zhivago*. It was written right after the end of the World War II, which means that some thirty years lie between it and the previous poem. During this time Pasternak's verse underwent a marked development and change.

What characterizes his earlier period is, as we have seen, a close connection with the Russian poetic tradition and at the same time an openness to post-Symbolist avant-garde trends. The verse form is traditional, but rhyme and rhythm are combined with daring imagery and expressive sound patterns to make a poetry of unusual density. There were two possible ways in which his poetry could develop. The first would have meant a continued emancipation from traditional verse forms toward free verse lying close to that of most modern European poets'. The other possibility, a firmer alliance with the poetic heritage of Pushkin, Lermontov, Tyutchev[10] and Blok, could be realized only at the expense of the modernistic modes of expression.

Pasternak's verse took the second path. There are several conceivable reasons for his choice. Isolation from modern European poetry was probably no mean factor. An ever-increasing attachment to things national, to the life and future of his countrymen, was perhaps even more decisive. And most important of all, as it seems, was the development of his own personality, a maturity which was attained in a very special personal and historic situation, which discarded many poetic devices as unnecessary. A striving toward simplicity, content, and essentials. This development is clearly felt already in his poems from the early 30's. His collection of verse dated 1932 had a significant title, *The Second Birth (Vtoroye rozhdenye)*. It apparently hints at various

---

[9]Quoted from D. Obolensky, ed., *The Penguin Book of Russian Verse* Baltimore; Penguin Books, (1962), pp. 335-36.

[10][Fyodor Tyutchev (1803-73) was one of Russia's most remarkable lyric poets.— Ed.]

things, one of them being a reconsideration of his earlier views on the function of poetry and the role of the poet.

There is a similarity between the poem we have already looked at and "Hamlet." In both the poet is trying to define an emotional situation, but in "Oars at Rest" it is a question of a feeling which is infinite, knows no bounds, which can only be hinted at by allowing some of its parts to speak for themselves. In "Hamlet," on the other hand, there is a clearly defined situation which can be described by reference to direct parallels. This is not "something that happens to everyone"; it is something that only a few people experience, the chosen few. There are also several other differences. "Oars at Rest" is composed of simple phrases, but this simplicity is superficial: the intermediate links have been removed and the poem consists of a series of concentrated, allusive, richly associative images. "Hamlet" begins with two short, syntactically very simple sentences which state directly both circumstance and location. The whole poem is built up in this simple way. It moves logically from verse to verse without ellipse. It is more straightforward than "Oars at Rest," but even so, its simplicity, as we shall soon see, is, like all poetic simplicity, full of associative tension. Further, one sees that a clearly marked "I" immediately makes itself felt, and thereafter the whole poem is continued in the first person; in *My Sister, Life,* where it is "the image that speaks,"[11] one has to hunt for the word. Euphonic devices are less important in "Hamlet," which has none of the rich orchestration found in "Oars at Rest." It is thus clear that one must approach this poem differently from the first.

The name "Hamlet" and the poem's use of the first person is naturally a convenient starting point. The poet apparently wishes to identify himself with Hamlet. But which Hamlet? To what in this character does the poet feel kinship? The situation is not quite as simple as this, however. It is not Hamlet himself who speaks in the poem, but the actor who is going to play his part. This is by no means unimportant. A well-known poetic image is introduced: the poet as an actor and the world as a stage.

The curtain rises and the player enters. "I seek to grasp in the distant echo what will happen during my life." The sentence intimates a double perspective: behind the player we see the poet scanning the world with eyes and ears. Now the eyes of the binoculars are turned on him. It is not just the groundlings, it is the general public, it is the world. The poet is both outside of what is happening, in his art, and

[11]["In art the man is silent and the image speaks" (*Safe Conduct*, p. 74).—Ed.]

at the same time out front in full limelight. Is this what scares him? Yes, in part, but it is not the most important thing: the subject and the key element of the sentence is the simple, suggestive "darkness of night" *("sumrak nochi")*. The following sentence with its allusion to a well-known biblical phrase explains what this means.

An unexpected parallel is introduced: Christ and Gethsemane. Christ, sent by his Father, is aware of the night of darkness that awaits him, he sees his own death. For a moment he is afraid and prays that the cup might pass him by. Hamlet is also sent by his father. Weighted down by his sense of duty, he becomes aware of his fate and hesitates. Finally the poet: even he has a calling. He too has been sent by some-one or Someone. There are times when even he must hesitate when he realizes that the path he has to follow is a path of sacrifice. He turns to this Someone (we might call him God, Fatherland, Poetry, Time) and prays to him to free him from his difficult task, although he is the whole time quite aware that there is no turning back. His fate is already decided. He stands alone, like Hamlet, like Christ. At this point a shadow of fatalism appears, but this is made less noticeable by the Russian proverb in the last line. What is suggested here not exactly resignation or despair, but rather a recognition of how grave and full of meaning life is: "To go through life is not the same as to walk across a field."

The poem "Hamlet" has close connections with an essay Pasternak wrote on his translations of Shakespeare which was published shortly after the war. In it there are some interesting lines which deal spec-ifically with Hamlet and have an obvious connection with this poem. Here Pasternak opposes the usual view of Shakespeare's Hamlet as a tragedy of will. He sees something else in the play: "From the moment the ghost appears Hamlet denies himself in order to do the will of him who sent him. Hamlet is not a drama of a weak-willed character, but of duty and self-abnegation. When it is discovered that appear-ances and reality are irreconcilable, that there is a gulf between them, it is of no moment that the reminder of falseness of the world comes in a supernatural form, and that the ghost calls for revenge. It is far more important that chance has so willed that Hamlet be chosen as the judge of his own time and the servant of a more distant time. Hamlet is a play of a high destiny, the drama of a vocation."

This is what connects him with the two others in the poem, with Christ and with the poet. But there is something further. The poem apparently refers to a certain situation in Shakespeare's play: Ham-let in the "To be or not to be" soliloquy. The chosen one, the one who has received the call and hesitates under the press of duty, loneliness, the realization of what must be. The essay contains some lines about the soliloquy which are of importance for an understanding of the poem: "These are the most heartfelt and frenzied lines ever written on the anguish of the unknown at the gates of death, in strength of feeling they rise to the bitterness of Gethsemane."

Compared with his early poetry it appears that the poem "Hamlet" shows a change in Pasternak's view of the poet and his work. In *My Sister, Life* the man was silent and the images spoke. In the *Doctor Zhivago* poems the poet speaks and the images support what he has to say. He has reached a state of maturity and inner assurance which gives him the right to speak in his own name and directly to his readers.

There is a passage in *Safe Conduct* where Pasternak describes the romantic view of the role and importance of the poet that dominated literature at the beginning of this century. "This was the conception of life as the life of the poet."[12] It was a cult, an overrating of the ego which knew no bounds. The Symbolists had borrowed it from the Romantics and developed it further. Poets such as Mayakovsky and Esenin carried it further and paid for it with their lives.

Pasternak admits that he, like all poets at that time, could not avoid being influenced by this conception, and it is also possible to see traces of it in his earliest verse, but he was finally able to free himself of it. He chose another form of poetry, where this exaggeration of the poet's own life had no place. There was apparently another reason for his retraction as well. According to this view, he writes, the poet was inconceivable without the nonpoet. It drew a line between the poet and other people. In order that he, the great one, the godlike, might appear in relief, a background of mediocrity was necessary, an insistence of the inferiority of the nonpoet.

Instead, Pasternak developed the idea that a poem or a book, once it is written, no longer belongs to its author. It lives its own life, and if it is a good book then it is far more important than the author himself. "When *My Sister, Life* appeared and was found to contain expressions not in the least contemporary, which were revealed to me during the summer of the revolution, I became entirely indifferent as to the identity of the power which had brought the book into being because it was immeasurable greater than myself and the poetical conceptions surrounding me."[13]

Similar thoughts on the impersonality and individuality of poetry

[12][*Ibid.*, p. 115.—Ed.]

[13][*Ibid.*, p. 116.—Ed.] On Pasternak's views on the role of the poet see V. Erlich, *The Double Image. Concepts of the Poet in Slavic Literatures* (Baltimore: Johns Hopkins Press, 1964), pp. 133-54.

can be encountered in the English Imagists of the same period; they are to be found in the neo-Kantian view of the function of art and were also to be included in the new Formalist criticism which emerged during these years. But what is perhaps most striking here is the connection with Rainer Maria Rilke, a poet for whom Pasternak held a great admiration. *"Das Kunstwerk,"* Rilke writes, *"möchte man also erklären: als ein tief inneres Gestandnis, das unter dem Vorwand einer Erinnerung, einer Erfahrung oder eines Ereignisses sich ausgibt und, losgelöst von seninem Urheber, allein bestehen kann."*[14] In his younger days Mayakovsky wrote a play which he called *Vladimir Mayakovsky*, but, as Pasternak writes in *Safe Conduct*, it was no autobiography: "The title contained the simple discovery of genius, that a poet is not an author, but the subject of a lyric, facing the world in the first person. The title was not the name of the composer but the surname of the composition." This also carries one's thoughts to Rilke, to his article on Rodin. For Rilke, Rodin is not the name of a man, but a content, a term for works of creation (*"der Name unzähliger Dinge"*).

This view of the connection between the poet and his work followed Pasternak through the years. It is fairly clear that it dictated the reserved attitude which always was one of his more prominent characteristics. But nevertheless, certain important changes later occurred which can be seen both in the poem "Hamlet" and in *Doctor Zhivago*. There is a passage in this novel where Dr. Zhivago is working at night in the cottage in the Urals: "At such moments Yury felt that the main part of his work was not being done by him but by something which was above him and controlling him: the thought and poetry of the world as it was at that moment and as it would be in the future. He was controlled by the next step it was to take in order of his historical development; and he felt himself to be only the pretext and the pivot setting it in motion."

Anyone familiar with Russian literature will be reminded of the well-known words Nikolay Gogol wrote while he was working on *Dead Souls*. Preoccupied with the thought of his calling as a poet, he felt himself a tool in the service of some higher divine power: "Someone unseen is writing before me with a mighty rod." This was a concept of the poet's task which was typical of the Romantics.

[14]["Thus, the work of art could be explained as a deep, inward confession which emerges under the guise of a memory, recollection, an experience or an event, and which, disengaged from its creator, can stand alone."] D. F. Bolinow, *Rilke*, 2nd ed., (Stuttgart, 1956), p. 115.

Pasternak has obviously gone in this direction. In his work, however, it is not the divine power that leads the poet, but rather the
events of his age and the poetry living and developing around him.
The poet is not standing outside of or above his age; he is living at
its center; he is shaping its thoughts and ideas, its language and its
attitude toward art. So inseparable is he from this reality that it is
as if it spoke through him rather then being expressed and formed
by him.

The poet's dependence on his age may be difficult to bear, but he
is unable to escape it. To quote one of Pasternak's poems "Night"
["Noch"] , written after *Doctor Zhivago*, he is "in time's captivity."
But at the same time the poem emphasizes that the poet has the possibility of rising above his age, he is "eternity's hostage." In his
art, he attains something which is denied most people—eternity,
immortality. He lifts himself above time and place. It is a thought
which has occupied Pasternak ever since his first years as a poet,
even, for that matter, before he began to write seriously. The talk
which he gave in 1910 to a group of poets on Symbolism and immortality deals with just this. The manuscript has been lost, but he quotes
it in *I Remember.* He regards the poet's way of understanding reality
as a "generic property of man." It is something both subjective and
all-human. His subjective understanding is to be found in the history
of human existence and can be appreciated and experienced anew
by future generations. He himself will die, but his experience of
this life will remain.

Thus, the poem lies above and is greater than its maker, but this
does not mean that the role of the poet is unimportant. It may quite
rightly appear that such a conclusion is the logical sequel to the first
statement, that the poet is just a middleman, a player playing a part
set down for him but by no means everyone is called upon for such
work. When all is said and done, he is one of the chosen few. "Hamlet" is a poem about the poet's call, his election, his responsibility.
As a person, as an individual life, the poet is of no interest. His daily
actions and utterances are no different from other people's. They are
of no interest to anyone and he wishes above all to keep them to himself. But in his role as poet he is someone else. This is a view that
Pasternak shares with many poets. Rilke has formulated it in his
often cited words: *"Wo ich schaffe bin ich wahr."* Actually, we do not
need to go outside of Russian literature to find confirmation of this
thought. Pushkin expresses it in his poem "Poet" (1827).

Pasternak's opposition to the ego cult of the Symbolists was thus mainly directed at the way in which they confounded the poet and the private individual. Otherwise his view of the poet's task and importance lies undoubtedly close to theirs, and this similarity has become more apparent with the years. At one time Pasternak accused the Symbolists of placing the poet and nonpoet in opposition to one another, but later he reached a way of thinking which is reminiscent of theirs: in "Hamlet" the poet stands alone, surrounded by a sea of falsehood and hypocrisy. And yet this is not exactly the same thing. With Pasternak it is not the poet who has removed himself from the others; on the contrary, it is the others who have broken away. They have moved apart from him, left him standing alone. But he does not hesitate, he must complete his task and play his part to the end, even if the action has suddenly changed and the play is now different from the original. He has not changed, but they have. He is still true to his course when the others fail.

Both Hamlet and Christ were set tasks by their fathers. What, then, is the task of the poet? Has he come to save mankind or to set the time in joint again? The poem says nothing about this. The poet is certainly surrounded by falsehood, just as Hamlet was, but nothing is said to intimate that his task and duty is to fight it. What the poem has to say about the poet's task must be sought in the last line with its tone of contemplation and gravity: "Living life is no easy matter." Life is the poet's task.

This can also be said of *My Sister, Life,* but much has changed since then. Life is no longer the ecstatic intoxication of youth. Fortune and experience have taught him that it is something deeper, full of meaning and responsibility. Faced with this task, he feels humility and gratitude, and further, the natural dignity that the chosen man must possess. He may despair under the burden of his responsibility, but at the same time he is fully conscious that this is a duty he must fulfill, he must be prepared to offer his life as an individual.

The poet's task, as he sees it now, is not only to reproduce life in new, unexpected images, to rediscover reality for those who are incapable of seeing and experiencing for themselves. Now something else is emphasized—it appears in the last line of the first stanza—something which we had seen before in the Romantic and Symbolist poets. The poet's eyes are no longer fixed only on the present or the past, but also on the future. In *Safe Conduct* Pasternak says that "it was in this gazing back that what is called inspiration consisted." He has now discovered that poetic inspiration is also to be found in a looking forward. Poetry is also prophetic. It walks in front of life, shows the way. Looking out on the world, listening to the hum of life, the poet tries to apprehend with all his senses "what will happen during [his] life." He is "chosen as the judge of his own time and the servant of a more distant time."

Pasternak's Poetry[1]

by Andrey Sinyavsky

Pasternak's work was for a long time known only to a relatively small circle of connoisseurs and poetry lovers. Over many years, critics have noted Pasternak's literary isolation and loneliness, and explained these in part by the difficulties that confronted the reader opening Pasternak's books for the first time. "Readers encountered a poet of a very special stamp," wrote one of these critics at the end of the twenties. "To understand him one had to force oneself in a sense to overhaul one's habitual mode of apprehension. His manner of perceiving and the very words he used seemed, at first, unacceptable, surprising, and for a long time obtrusive complaints about "unintelligibility" and questions "how is this possible"[1] accompanied the appearance of each book."[2]

Often the densely metaphorical quality of Pasternak's early poetry was treated as a formal affectation, beneath which the content was only vaguely divined. Moreover, his first books gave the impression of almost total aloofness from contemporary life. Pasternak acquired the reputation of a poet distant from social problems, locked in a world of utterly private experiences.

But while this sharply negative, at time intolerant, attitude towards Pasternak persisted, in the early twenties Mayakovsky named Pasternak's works among the model of "the new poetry that has a splendid sense of the contemporary."[3] At the same time Valery Bryusov noted: "Pasternak has no individual poems about the revolution, but his verses, perhaps without the author's knowing it, are imbued with the spirit of the present; Pasternak's psychology is not

---

[1]This article is a revised version of my introduction to Boris Pasternak, *Verses and Poems* (Moscow-Leningrad, The Poet's Library, 1965). Since a number of Pasternak's late poems were not included in that edition, I have found it necessary to expand the introduction somewhat in order to highlight the previously excluded material. [Translated by Elizabeth Henderson.]

[2]K. Liks, "Boris Pasternak, *Over the Barriers,*" Gosizdat (1929), *Literary Gazette,* October 28, 1929.

[3]*Teatralnaya Moskva,* 8, (1921), 6.

borrowed from old books; it expresses his own being and could have been formed only in the conditions of our life."[4]

While fully contemporary, Pasternak did not, of course, belong to the tribunes and heralds of the revolution. He was drawn to spiritual and moral transformations. His approach to reality was shaped by lofty ideals of moral perfection and rejection of cruelty. In his poetry life is seen primarily from the vantage point of the eternal categories of good, love, and universal justice. But in Pasternak "eternity" and "heaven" appear to descend to earth and acquire all the climatic peculiarities of the earth's atmosphere. Many of his poems leave the impression of having spoken of nothing else than what today's or yesterday's weather was like. Strange as it may sound, Pasternak's special place in the literary process and in society is linked with his depiction of weather and his partiality for weather.

In the Party press Pasternak was censured very early for, supposedly, writing only about the weather and nature instead of responding to the burning issues of contemporary Soviet life. In the 30's critics dubbed Pasternak a "vacationer of genius," an epithet which many people at the time took for deadly mockery.

But "faithfulness to the weather" was for Pasternak not only a means of defending his independence in art and avoiding participation in politics which repelled him increasingly. It was also a form of active opposition to the world of official lying and violence. "Faithfulness to the weather" ultimately proved to be faithfulness to his fellow humans and their moral core.

In the novel *Doctor Zhivago* Pasternak draws the following analogy: during the Civil War people competed with one another in cruelty in such a way that human history seemed no longer to be the history of the earth but of some other monstrous planet. Only nature preserved her faithfulness to human beings in their true meaning and purpose.

It is possible to apply this analogy to Pasternak's own poetry. In serious 20th-century lyric verse the tragic world-view clearly predominates and the poet's *oeuvre* is often colored in somber hues. The tenor of Pasternak's poetry, taken as a whole, stands out against this background as an exception. Among great Russian lyric poets of our century, Pasternak is the brightest, the most bracing and life-affirming. It was as if he remained untouched by his time and managed to

[4]V. Bryusov, "The Yesterday, Today and Tomorrow of Russian Poetry," *Pechat i revolyutsiya (Press and Revolution)*, 7 (1922), 57. [A leading Russian Symbolist, an influential and versatile man of letters, Valery Bryusov (1873-1924) remained active as a poet and pundit through the first years of the Soviet era.]

keep his faith with nature, and preserve his spiritual stamina. In reality things were somewhat different. Pasternak experiences the tragic events of his epoch with extreme difficulty, anguish and pain. This would bring on sometimes long interruptions in his work; there were periods when he would disappear from literature, subsisting by means of translations. But the terrifying visions of history, imprinted in his soul, were ground anew and transformed into the soil from which later grew verses full of love and trust in life. In this sense Pasternak's poetry is a living plant, which, using history as its soil, serves as the accumulator of goodness and humanity, drawing life-giving juices from death itself.

Towards the end of his life Pasternak tackled this theme in the poem "Soul," which offers an insight into the nature of his creative process and its relation to the contemporary era. The poet compares his soul with the earth of a cemetery where for forty years now innocently murdered people have been buried. Extending Pasternak's thought, we may say that the fraternal grave of history becomes the nutritive medium for the poet who transforms human sufferings and sacrifices into enduring moral values.

Let us refrain from a survey of Boris Pasternak's life. Suffice it to sketch in provisionally some of the most important events in his evolution.

His childhood years were spent in an atmosphere of art, music and literature. The many-sided cultural interests and connections of his family (his father was a well-known painter, his mother a pianist) left an early mark. Already during Pasternak's childhood and early youth Rainer-Maria Rilke, Lev Tolstoy and Scryabin made indelible impressions on him. Subsequently, he attributed a decisive significance in the formation of his own cast of mind to these first encounters with artistic genius. Soon these influences were overlaid by an equally personal response to the poetry of Alexander Blok and an acquaintance with Mayakovsky.

Pasternak's first creative preference and enthusiasm unquestionably was music. Strongly influenced by Scryabin, from the age of thirteen Pasternak devoted himself to composition and its theory. After six years of persistent work he left music forever. In 1909 Pasternak entered the historico-philological faculty of Moscow University and began a thorough study of philosophy. To further his philosophical education, he traveled to Germany in 1912 and studied for one semester at the University of Marburg.

Pasternak had become interested in contemporary poetry in 1908-

09, and made friendly connections in that milieu. Not until Marburg did it become clear to him where his true calling lay. Having lost his zest for philosophy, Pasternak gave himself up wholly to the art of poetry, which from 1913 on became the main and permanent business of his life.

The same sudden breaks and impulsive switching from one cluster of ideas and occupations to another (music, philosophy, poetry), the same dissatisfaction with himself, the same readiness to sacrifice years of work in order to experience a "second birth" characterize Pasternak's literary biography as well. As he evolved, he boldly crossed out his past. The early period of his poetic quest was marked by the crisscrossing influences of Symbolism and Futurism (along with Nikolay Aseyev and Sergey Bobrov, he belonged then to the moderate Futurist group "Tsentrifuga"). Later on, he sharply reexamined these beginnings. Much of what he wrote before 1917 he did not include in later editions.

The appearance in 1922 of the book *My Sister, Life* (which took shape in the summer of 1917) placed its author among the most prominent masters of contemporary verse. This book, we might say, marks the emergence of a great and entirely original poetic phenomenon. The books which preceded it — *Twin in the Clouds* (1914) and *Over the Barriers* (1917) — had the character of an experiment, a preparation, a tuning up, and represented a search for one's own voice, one's own place in the motley of literary currents. Many of the poems included in the collections *Twin in the Clouds* and *Over the Barriers*, were later rewritten and appeared in an unrecognizable form. Although in *Over the Barriers* some of Pasternak's important traits and persistent proclivities e.g., his striving for unfettered verbal expression, for impetuous, dynamic imagery, were already in evidence, he found it necessary to rework the collection radically in preparing it for a new edition in 1929. Poetic cliches, stemming from the Symbolists, now disappear, as does the abstractness and deliberate verbal obscurity, and what he was to call later the Futurist "trinkets," which lent his verse an "extraneous cleverness" at the expense of its meaning and content.

If we break down Pasternak's work into periods, we can designate the period from 1912 to 1916 as the time of apprenticeship; his poetics was then barely emerging, it was still not mature, not entirely independent. The major landmark on Pasternak's literary path was the writing of *My Sister, Life*. He worked at this book with a stormy impetuosity which bears witness to the flight of poetic inspiration, to the sudden, powerful pressure of creative energy. Then, after the collection *Themes and Variations,* which was published in 1923 and was in many ways an off-shoot of *My Sister, Life,* begins the period of a quest for the epic (1923-30): work on *"A Lofty Malady, "*the historico-revolutionary poems "1905" and "Lieutenant Schmidt," and the novel in verse *Spektorsky.*

In the 1920's Pasternak was affiliated with the literary grouping "LEF" (The Left Front of the Arts which included Vladimir Mayakovsky, Sergey Tretyakov, Nikolay Aseyev, Osip Brik, Nikolay Chuzhak and others). LEF's aesthetic orientation toward a tendentious, agitational art, their preaching of utilitarianism and technicism were alien to him. Pasternak's temporary and unstable connection with the LEFists derived from a shared striving for poetic innovation, and the forging of a truly modern poetic language. But in the LEF milieu he felt himself to be an outsider. Let us note that Pasternak never had any use for group regimentation, for adherence to a definite literary school or platform. Even in the early period, when he was publicly associating himself with the Futurists of "Tsentrifuga," he reinterpreted Futurism in a different, rather Impressionistic manner and felt constrained by the narrowness of the group to which he belonged.

In the early 30's, after a period of intense involvement with large-scale historical poetry, Pasternak once more turned to lyric verse in his book *Second Birth.* His tone and manner noticeably changed, pointing as they did toward a greater clarity and classical simplicity of language. This process dragged on and was accompanied by a temporary creative slump and by long interruptions in his work. Besides strictly creative difficulties, a series of objective reasons contributed to this—the waves of cruel mass repression and the growing sense of one's isolation and estrangement from both society and literature. The 30's was an extremely painful and critical period for Pasternak. During this time he produced few original works and devoted his main energies to translation; he worked at it regularly from 1934 on and continued to do so until the end of his life. (He translated Georgian poets, Shakespeare, Goethe, Schiller, Kleist, Rilke, Verlaine, and others).

Only at the beginning of 1941, on the eve of the war, did the poet overcome this crisis and enter a new period of upsurge. A number of first-class poems appeared, collected in the book *On Early Trains* (1943). Some of the themes sounded here anticipate Pasternak's later lyrics, his poems from the novel *Doctor Zhivago* and the cycle *When the Weather Clears.* This, the final period of his life (1945-1960) is dominated by the writing of *Doctor Zhivago*, and then, after the publication of the novel in the West and the Nobel Prize award, by the new ordeals that descended upon him at the very end of his journey.

In the poems from the novel and some other verse closely linked with that cycle, the Pasternakian vision scales a new height, comparable to his first "peak," *My Sister, Life*. In these late poems Pasternak reveals himself fully as a religious-ethical poet, whose morality, however, is cast not in the form of doctrine and preaching, but in images of living nature or in unconstrained and unpretentious parables, free from righteousness.

In the 1920's and 1930's, and later till the last years of his life, Pasternak was visibly engaged in continual attempts to review and reevaluate his literary past. His declaration in 1956 that he did not like his style before 1940 is well known. Such self-evaluations, though not always just, are a part of his nature. To Pasternak art means continuous giving of oneself, movement concerned not with balance sheets but with discoveries. The persistent yearning for a renewal of his artistic perspective and style which runs throughout Pasternak's biography does not preclude the internal unity of his work. The continuity of its central spiritual and stylistic thrust is not to be gainsaid. After *My Sister, Life*, Pasternak kept changing, but the basis of his lyric remained intact. He enriched and developed what had taken shape in that book.

Having outlined in the most general way the contours of Pasternak's poetic path, let us attempt to enter into the artist's individual world, an effort which demands great attention to the verbal texture of his works and their imagery pattern. To do this we shall depart somewhat from chronology and turn directly to the poems themselves, which though written at various times and in varying styles, are held together by certain common impulses and resolutions.

I

The pride of place in Pasternak's lyric, as mentioned earlier, belongs to nature. But the scope of these poems is broader than that of the usual landscape description. In telling about springs and winters, about rainfalls and sunrises, Pasternak tells about the nature of life itself and about the existence of the world, and confesses to his faith in life, a faith which, it seems to me, pervades his poetry and constitutes its moral foundation. Life in his interpretation is something unconditional, eternal, absolute; an all-penetrating element and the greatest of miracles. Amazement before the miracle of existence—this is the recurrent stance of the poet in Pasternak, forever astonished and bewitched by his discovery: it is *"spring again."*

His nature poems breathe freshness and health. As Osip Mandelstam has noted, "To read Pasternak's poems is to clean your throat, strengthen your breathing and renew your lungs: such poems should help cure tuberculosis." Day after day, line after line, Pasternak never tires of affirming the salutary, all-conquering vitality of nature. Trees, grasses, clouds and streams assume here the lofty right to speak in the name of life itself, to cure sufferings and set us on the path of truth and goodness ("On earth there is no anguish which snow could not cure.")

Accordingly, the landscape in Pasternak's poems, no longer the depicted object, becomes the subject of the action, the main hero, the mover of events. All the fullness of life in its diverse manifestations fits into a scrap of nature which begins to perform actions, to think, to feel and to speak. The likening of nature to human beings, typical for poetry, goes to the point of a reversal of roles, with the landscape serving as a mentor, guide, model. "The forest drops its crimson attire..."—this is the classical formula for fall, firmly established in Russian poetry.[5] In Pasternak we often encounter the reverse train of thought: "You throw off your dress as a grove throws off its leaves...;" "Your meaning, like air, is unselfish," says the poet to his lover. In a word, human beings are defined through nature and it is in comparison with nature that they gain their place in the world.

The power or, to put it more correctly, the intercession of nature does not debase human beings, for submitting to, and becoming like, nature, humans follow the voice of life which exercises its rights through the mediation of nature. At the same time, nature in Pasternak's poetry is so close to human beings that, pushed aside and displaced by the landscape, they come to life again in it. The degree of humanization of the world is so great that when we stroll through the woods and fields, we have to do, in essence, not with pictures of these woods and fields but with their characters, their psychology.

In *Safe Conduct* Pasternak recalls his stay in Venice: "Thus, I too was touched by this happiness. And I had the good fortune to learn that day after day one can go to a rendezvous with a piece of built-up space as with a living person." In his poetry this kind of rendezvous with the landscape, perceived as a unique and distinctive person, actually takes place:

[5][Reference to a famous poem by Alexander Pushkin, "Autumn."—Ed.]

And now you walk into the birchwood.
You take a good look at one another.

Becoming human, nature acquires all the features of an individual personality. Such fullness of individualization we have not encountered before. We are accustomed to the fact that "rain falls," but now we learn: "Rather from sleep, than from the roofs; rather absentminded than shy, the rain stamped its feet at the door. ..." Pasternak's landscapes have their own mores, sympathies and favorite diversions — clouds play catch, the thunder takes up photography, streams sing a love song. ...

Pasternak's poetry is metaphorical through and through. But we often do not perceive the metaphorical character of all these parallels, so vivid is the action occurring before our eyes. "A garden weeps," "a storm runs" not figuratively but literally ("Metamorphosing and frolicking, in darkness, thunder peals and silver, it runs up the galleries"). Pasternak presents natural phenomena in the full verisimilitude of an authentic, real-life action.

The metaphor in Pasternak's poetry performs first of all a linking role. Instantaneously, dynamically it gathers into a unified whole the scattered parts of reality, embodying thus the great unity of the world, the interaction and interpenetration of phenomena. Pasternak operates on the assumption that two objects, placed next to one another, closely interact with and penetrate one another, and therefore he links them — not by likeness, but by contiguity — using the metaphor as the connection. The world is described "as a whole," and the job of unifying it is done with the help of the figurative meaning of words.

> Spring, I'm from the street, where the poplar is amazed,
> Where the distance is frightened, where a house is scared it
> will fall,
> Where the air is blue-white, like the bundle of laundry
> Of a person just discharged from the hospital.

The last line allows us to understand why "the distance is frightened" and "a house is scared it will fall": they too were just discharged from the hospital — like the person whose bundle has turned the air blue.

The landscape — and more broadly, the world surrounding us — acquires in Pasternak's poems a sort of heightened sensitivity. It sharply and instantly reacts to the changes taking place in a person, not only in correspondence with his feelings, thoughts, and moods (common enough in literature), but becomes his complete likeness, an extension of him, his alter ego. The mechanism of these transformations is laid bare in Pasternak's prose piece "A Tale." The enamoured hero suddenly notices:

> Of course, the entire alley, in its total gloominess, all around and as a whole, was Anna. Here Seryozha was not alone, and he knew it. And in truth, who before him has not experienced that. However, the feeling was even broader and more precise, and here the help of friends and predecessors ended. He saw how painful and hard it was for Anna to be a city morning. ...She silently stood in splendour in his presence and did not call to him for help. And, dying with longing for the real Arild...he watched, as, covered with poplars, like towels of ice, she was swallowed up by clouds and slowly tossed back her brick Gothic towers.

Note: the feeling which gripped Seryozha was *vaster* and *more precise* than similar phenomena experienced by other people—his friends and predecessors. In this passage Pasternak is telling us about himself and of what made him different from his predecessors and contemporaries. His "correspondences" are distinguished from the traditional ones (landscape as accompaniment to human feelings) precisely by the vastness and precision of the resulting image: everything—*all utterly and wholly*—turns into Anna Arild.

In these acts of shifting feelings, persons, things, or nature from one place to another, Pasternak comes closest of all, perhaps, to the metaphoric sprints of Mayakovsky, who likened the world to his own passions and sufferings ("From my weeping and laughter the room's mug screwed up in horror..."). But in Mayakovsky the motivation for a projection of emotions unto reality comes from anxiety, brought to the highest level of tension ("...I cannot be more tranquil"), and from the force and grandeur of the poet's inner experiences. But Pasternak is "more tranquil," "quieter," "more restrained" than Mayakovsky, and this sort of displacement is evoked in him not so much by the exclusiveness of his passion as by the delicacy of his feeling for reflexes and resonances, by the sensitivity of each object in his universe to the neighboring, contiguous one. With Pasternak the responding reaction does not reach such hyperbolic dimensions; all objects, even the most insignificant, influence one another and imitate one another's proclivities. Elsewhere in "A Tale," Seryozha, awakening, discovers this picture:

> On the table in clean formation stood cheerful, well-rested vodka glasses. And the complex assortment of wind and percussion snacks gladdened the eye. Above them like a conductor hung black wine bottles and any minute they were ready to burst into deafening pre-

lude to any laughter and puns. ...In general the entire room seemed to swim in cognac. ...Everything that had edges and was capable of playing was filled with the hot yellowness of the furniture, like lemon brandy.

We confront here several characteristically Pasternakian mutual influences and comparison: the well-rested Seryozha and the vodka glasses; the orchestra of the still-life before a drinking bout; the wine, spilled from the table to the interior of the whole room. Similar solutions of people, things and nature saturate Pasternak's poetry. In his poetry it is impossible to separate a person from his surroundings, live feeling from dead matter. By means of this metaphoric shorthand reality is imaged in the blending of heterogeneous parts, in the intersection of edges and contours as an indivisible unity.

This is the task that fascinated Pasternak: within the limits of a poem to recreate the all-encompassing atmosphere of existence, and to communicate the feeling of intimacy with the universe which gripped the poet. In his verses the lyrical narrative does not develop consecutively from phenomenon to phenomenon, instead it jumps "over the barriers," drawn toward broad sketches, toward sweeping canvases of the whole. With the help of allegories and the figurative meaning of words, things tear themselves loose of their well-worn places and are drawn into violent, chaotic motion, called upon to engrave reality in its natural disorder.

In this draughty, reshuffled world, intersected and united by metaphors, the image of the poet, of the artist, occupies a special place. With the exception of a very few poems he is not marked out or developed as a distinct, fully independent person. In contrast to Blok, Tsvetaeva, Mayakovsky and Esenin, Pasternak's lyrics are seldom couched in the first person. With the other poets, the poet's personality stood at the center and his work, extending as a diary of many years, a tale "about oneself," constituted a sort of life story, a dramatic biography acted out before the reader's eyes and surrounded by an aura of myth or legend. Pasternak moves away from this conception which in *Safe Conduct* he designates as "romantic," "the concept of the poet's biography as spectacle." He tells us little about himself, painstakingly distancing, hiding his "I." In reading his verses one sometimes has the illusion that there is no inkling here of the author, that he is absent even as a storyteller, as a witness who has seen all that is depicted in the poem. Nature speaks in her own voice:

> ...through the open windows the clouds, like doves,
> Settled on their needlework.

> They noticed: the water had thinned
> The fences—noticeably, the crosses—just slightly.

It is not the poet who noticed; the "clouds noticed," just as in another instance it is not the poet who recalls his childhood, but "the snow remembers fleetingly, fleetingly: 'sleepikins' it was called, whispery and syrupy, the day sank beyond the little cradle. ..." In one of Pasternak's late poems, "First Frosts," we again encounter that reversed, or reversible representation in which landscape and viewer change roles and the picture itself examines the person standing in front of it:

> One chilly morning when the sun was dim
> And stood a fiery pillar in the smoke,
> I too was hardly visible to him
> When seen as in a photograph all blurred.

> Until the sun comes striking out of gloom,
> And lights the meadow past the pond,
> The view trees have of me is very dim
> As on the pond's most distant edge I stand.[6]

If Mayakovsky and Tsvetaeva like to speak in their own name for the entire world, Pasternak prefers to let the world speak for him and instead of him: "not I about the spring, but the spring about me," "not I about the garden, but the garden about me."

> ...Near the fence
> Between the damp branches and the pale breeze
> An argument. I froze. About me!

Nature itself appears as the chief lyric hero. And the poet is everywhere and nowhere. He is not one viewing the panorama spread out before him, but its likeness, its double, becoming now the sea, now the forest. In the poem "The Weeping Garden," for example, the usual parallelism—"the garden and I"—turns into an equation, "I am the garden," and Pasternak speaks in the very same words "about it" and "about himself":

> Appalling: It drips and listens:
>   Is it all alone in the world—
> It crumples a branch like lace at the window—
>   Or is there a witness here?

> To my lips I will raise it and listen;
>   Am I alone in the world—

[6][Quoted from *The Poetry of Boris Pasternak,* translated by George Reavey (New York: G. P. Putnam's Sons, 1959), p. 223.—Ed.]

> Prepared for desperate sobs if need be—
> Or is there a witness here?

This union with nature, free from witnesses and spies, lends Pasternak's poems a special intimacy and genuineness and makes them sound like the voice of the scenery itself.

The hero of the well-known poem "The Mirror" is also a garden, but a garden reflected in a pier glass, living, so to speak, a second life espied from the mysterious depths of the mirror: "A huge garden scrambles about in the chamber in the pier glass—without breaking the mirror!" It is curious that in an earlier publication this poem was declaratively entitled "I myself": the story of the pier glass which absorbed the garden was for the poet a story about himself. Pasternak recognizes himself to be precisely such a mirror, related to life, and its equal. And in the poem "The Girl," which echoes the imagery of the "Mirror," the reverse connection is made—the mirror recognizes itself in a branch which has rushed in from the garden; the poet sees in nature a likeness, a repetition of himself:

> My dear, huge, as the garden, but in character-
> Sister! A second mirror!

Pasternak's artistic system crystallized in a book with a title that rings like a poetic manifesto—*My Sister, Life*. The poet's first and fundamental credo—the unity of the poet and nature—was thus affirmed.

> It seemed to be the alpha and omega—
> Life and I are of one cut;
> And the year round, in snow, without snow,
> She lived, like my alter ego,
> And I called her sister.

It was Pasternak's conviction that poetry is the direct consequence of life, its derivative. The artist does not invent images; he comes upon them in the street, assisting nature's creation by never supplanting it by his interference.

> Sometimes the snow boils in a swirl
> Whatever comes into its head.
> At dusk I prime it with
> My house, and canvas and utensils.
> All winter it writes etudes
> And in full sight of passers-by
> I carry them out of there,
> I hide, copy and filch them.

The birth of art in the depths of nature—here is a favorite theme of Pasternak. Though it assumes various forms, it is unchanging in one respect: the source of poetry is life itself; the poet, at best, is a collaborator, a coauthor. Most of the time art comes into being despite the will of the artist and without his slightest participation. The poet does not write the verses—rain, snow, spring, etc., do it. All that remains for the poet is to spy on the literary activity of nature and to wonder at it as he gathers ready-made rhymes into the proffered notebook. Hence, the prevalence of literary terms in Pasternak's landscapes: they write sometimes in prose, sometimes in verse:

> As an epigraph to this book
> The deserts grew hoarse...

> Offshoots of downpour make muddy clusters
> And long, long until the dawn,
> They drip from roofs their acrostics,
> Blowing bubble rhymes as they go along.

> Call it what you will, the forest
> Which lent all things around its dress,
> Ran on, like an unfolding story,
> And thought itself of some interest. ...

This equating of art and life, this demonstrative denial of authorship and transference of author's rights to the landscape, in general, serve a single goal: by offering to our attention verses and stories composed by nature itself, the author appears to assure us of their authenticity. And this authenticity or reliability of the image is for Pasternak the highest criterion of art. His views on literature are dominated by the care "to be able not to distort the voice of life which sounds in us" ("Several Theses," 1922). "Realism," as he interpreted the term (heightened receptivity and conscientiousness of the artist in conveying real being, which, like the human personality, is always whole and always unique), marks any genuine art and manifests itself in the work of Tolstoy and Lermontov, Chopin and Blok, Shakespeare and Verlaine. On the other hand, for Pasternak "Romanticism" is a rather negative notion: it implies proclivity to fantasizing and readiness to neglect faithfulness of representation.

This aspect of his aesthetic views is all the more interesting since for a long time Pasternak was linked with the Futurists and later the LEF group, among whom the so-called Formal method, which treats a work of art as the sum of its technical devices, had wide circulation.

"Contemporary trends," Pasternak wrote in that same piece, "have imagined that art is like a fountain, while it is like a sponge. They have decided that art must spurt forth, when really it must absorb and become saturated. They have concluded that it can be analyzed into the means of representation, when, in fact, it is made up of the organs of perception. It should always stand among the audience watching more purely, sensitively and accurately than anyone else, but in our day it has come to know powder and the dressing room and to display itself from the stage. ... "

Pasternak, who sees heightened receptivity as the decisive feature in his work, develops the same image — "poetry as a sponge" — in one of his early poems:

> Oh, poetry, be in my life like a sponge,
> With a suction pad that cleaves,
> Drinks in, on a wet green bench in the garden
> Alone with gummy young leaves.
>
> Swell splendid with ruffles, lawns, clouds,
> With trilling valleys converse.
> At night I will squeeze your substance out
> On thirsty white paper in verse.[7]

As one gets to know Pasternak's literary views, one is struck by the insistence of these warnings: don't interfere, don't scare away! For the most part he directs these apprehensions against preconceived attitudes to nature, against thinking in ready-made, sterotyped formulas, against the cliche in the broadest sense of the word. Strength, purity, and directness of perception are posited here as the necessary conditions of art, and innovation as a search for the greatest possible naturalness and authenticity of representation. In his article on Chopin (1945) Pasternak noted that his work was "original through and through, not because it was unlike that of his rivals, but because it was like nature, which was his model."

Art conceived thus presupposes a renewed vision of the world, which the artist seems to comprehend for the first time. To Pasternak the creative process sets in when we "cease to recognize reality" (*Safe Conduct*) and attempt to speak about it with the ease and artlessness of the first poem on earth. Hence the emphases and strains characteristic of his poetry — the extraordinary, and fantastic quality of everyday phenomena which he prefers to all fairy-tales and

[7][Quoted from *Boris Pasternak. Poems*, 2nd ed., translated by Eugene M. Kayden, (Yellow Springs, Ohio; The Antioch Press, 1964), p. 108. — Ed.]

fictions, the morning freshness of his vision (his characteristic pose is that of someone who has just awakened—"I am waking up. I am enveloped by the revealed..."), the sense of the primordial, the total newness of all that is occurring around him ("The entire steppe, like before the fall...").

In the striving to look at reality and poetry with new eyes, to re-vivify the aesthetic perception of the world and to transform accordingly the poetic system, Pasternak had much in common with a number of poets who sought to liberate literature from antiquated forms. In this broad movement, embracing all spheres of art in the twentieth century, there were not a few excesses, but there was also that healthy, renewing force without which the development of genuine modern art would have been unthinkable, and the voice of life itself which balks at being described in the language of worn-out canons and cliches that stick in our teeth. Mayakovsky spoke about this:

> And suddenly,
> all things
> rushed,
> straining their voices,
> to throw off the rags of worn out names.

This same cry is heard in Pasternak's poems:

> What if the universe has a mask on?
> What if they are not expanses such,
> That someone wouldn't volunteer,
> To stuff their mouth with putty for winter?

> But things tear off their masks,
> They lose control and drop their honor,
> When they have a reason to sing,
> When there's occasion for a shower.[8]

Characteristically, the renewal of poetry is construed here as liberation of things from the impersonality of words and from the masks of literary cliches.

In his search for new words capable of restoring to the world its individuality, Pasternak turned to living, colloquial speech and thus took part in that momentous democratization of the poetic language which affected many poets in the 1910s and 1920s and which found the most vehement expression in the work of Mayakovsky. But Mayakovsky broadened his vocabulary primarily in order

[8][Quoted from Dale L. Plank, *Pasternak's Lyric* (The Hague: Mouton and Co., 1966), p. 107.—Ed.]

to make room for the language of the street, which had just found its voice, and so as to encompass the larger themes of the city, war, and revolution. Pasternak, on the other hand, remained for a long time within the circle of traditional themes, well worn by poets past and present. However, he talked about traditional springs and sunsets in a new way and spoke about the beauty of nature not in the language of habitual poetic banalities but in the ordinary words of our daily life, in everyday prose. In this way he restored its lost freshness, its aesthetic significance. In his treatment a trite subject turned into a vital event.

In introducing the low language of life and of the modern city into the lofty discourse of poetry, Pasternak does not shun bureaucratic jargon, colloquialisms, or conversational idioms. Forms, worn down in daily use like old coins, acquired a fresh, unexpected ring. Consequently, the colloquial cliche becomes a weapon in the fight against the literary cliche. Pasternak has a tendency to discuss the most lofty themes in a plain, homey language. He conveys the turbulent grandeur of the Caucasus simply, in the tone of a casual everyday conversation—"it [the Caucasus] was out of sorts" or "The Caucasus was all spread out on my palm and was all like an unmade bed. ..." His trademark lies in his ability to poeticize the world by means of prosaisms which instill the truth of life into his verses and thereby transpose them from realm of contrived fiction to that of genuine poetry.

In the story "The Childhood of Luvers,"[9] tracing the development of the heroine in her encounter with reality, Pasternak notes: "Ceasing to be a poetic trifle, life began fermenting like a stern, black fairy tale inasmuch as it became prose and turned into fact." In his work the prose of actual fact serves as a source of the poetic, for it is through this that his images acquire the authenticity of the way things really happen. In this connection Pasternak's paradoxical statement in *Safe Conduct* becomes clear: "We drag the everyday into prose for the sake of poetry. We draw prose into poetry for the sake of music." Later, referring to *Romeo and Juliette* ("Notes to the Translations of Shakespeare's Tragedies"), he again declares that the prose in poetry is the bearer of life. "This is an example of the very highest poetry, the best models of which are always saturated with the simplicity and freshness of prose."

Prosaisms and colloquialisms lend Pasternak's images concreteness; abstract concepts are made palpable and are brought closer to

---

[9][See "Introduction," p. 6 in this volume.—Ed.]

us. The syntactic and rhythmic structure of his verses is subordinated to the same goal: to create a poetic system so supple that its tonality will suggest (of course, only suggest) conversational speech and will make it possible to use the language of poetry as unconstrainedly as we speak in real life. He deploys in the poetic sentence the full panoply of subordinate clauses, interrupts himself, and, just as one would in ordinary speech, omits connecting links; above all, he strives for free, unfettered poetic idiom, possessing long breath and built on the unfolding large and integral intonational periods. The ability to think and speak in verse, not in separate lines but in stanzas, periods or phrases, was a quality which Pasternak especially valued in the work of other poets. He gave high praise in particular to Tsvetaeva's verbal art which in this respect is kindred to his own.

Pasternak did not reduce this problem simply to bringing his verse close to conversational forms. In his practice he correlated naturalness, ease of intonation, with a more general aesthetic demand which he made upon himself—the demand for breadth and integrity of artistic perception, "the impetuous plasticity" of poetic outline, called upon to recreate in verse some unified panorama or atmosphere of life. One can feel this distinctly, for example, in the poem "The Death of a Poet," dedicated to Mayakovsky: the life of the genius in the ages, his sudden death, the chatter and confusion of the witnesses of the catastrophe and the clamorous spring street, presented at once as a fragment of the drama that is unfolding and as its wretched accompaniment—all this gathered into one chunk and set in motion by the irrepressible thrust of the voice that rushes after the event, embraces it, flows around it and orders it in a few powerful intonational periods rolling one after another:

> They did not believe him, said he raved
> But tried to find out now from two
> Then three, then everybody. Then aligned themselves
> As time has suddenly stood still
> The houses of clerks' and merchants' wives,
> Yards, trees and upon them rooks
> That, all inflamed by the sun, screamed
> Heatedly at the fool crows
> To bid them stop their idle chatter
> And be out of trouble from now on.
> All trees showed a damp displacement
> Like creases formed in tattered fishnets.

Pasternak willingly resorts to seeming digressions (for example, the rooks on the trees at the beginning of "The Death of a Poet"), which, in fact, represent a broad sweep of intonation and draw into the action all of the environment, leaving no neutral background in the poems. Not infrequently, he appears to stumble as though going back to what has been said, begins from the beginning in order, after "beating around the bush," to move on, encompassing the full picture in an unfettered flow of speech (In the poem "The Snowstorm" — "Wait, in the settlement, where not a single foot has tread...," etc.). Despite resourcefulness and high craftsmanship, his verses do not create the impression of elegantly finished knickknacks. On the contrary, their language is rather clumsy, sometimes impeded to the point of seeming tongue-tied, with unexpected pauses, repetitions, gasps for breath — a choking, sobbing speech, full of words heaped up and clambering over one another. Later his speech was to become light, winged, transparent, but it would always preserve the same immediacy. In this naive, artless outpouring of words which, at first glance, seem out of the poet's control, indeed appears to sweep him along, Pasternak achieved that naturalness of the live Russian language which he had sought to emulate. What he says of the poetic system of Paul Verlaine (1944) in many ways applies to Pasternak himself:

> ...He gave to the language in which he wrote that unlimited freedom which was his own discovery in lyric poetry and which we encounter only in the masters of prose dialogue of the drama and the novel. The Parisian phrase in all its purity and enchanting precision flew in from the street and lay down whole in his lines, with no sign of constraint, as the melodic material for the composition that was to follow. In this free-flowing ease lies the principal delight of Verlaine. For him the turns of French speech were indivisible. He wrote in idioms and not in words, he did not split them up or transpose them. In comparison with the naturalness of Musset, Verlaine is natural without premeditation, that is, he is simple not so that he will be believed but so as not to disturb the voice of life bursting from him.

In Pasternak's works the organization of sound in verse has particular importance. It is not limited to rhymes, although this aspect of his poetics, too, is extraordinarily novel and varied. (Not without reason did Valery Bryusov consider him, to a greater degree than Mayakovsky, the creator of the new rhyme). In Pasternak's poems not only the end of the lines rhyme, so can virtually any words within the text. In his verse phonetic affinities link both adjacent words and those distant from one another:

> Paris all golden calves, all wheeler-dealers,
> all rains, like vengeance, long awaited....

This phenomenon is broader than euphony and more significant than the melodic ordering of speech endemic in poetry. Phonetic connections arise as a reflection, a reverberation, of customary semantic connections; similarity of sound cements adjacent images, speaking, ultimately of the harmony of various interconnected and interpenetrating aspects of existence. The sound instrumentation aids that transference of meaning from one object to another which is effected by metaphor and spurred by the poet's striving to convey the inner unity of the world. In Pasternak's vivid definition, rime is "not the echoing of lines," but immeasurably more: in it is heard "the roar of roots and bosoms," through it "the discordant noise of the worlds enters our little world as the truth."

This heightened attention to the "acoustic identity" of words and their selection according to phonetic-semantic affinities is reminiscent of Khlebnikov. But Khlebnikov tried to make phonetics logical, connecting each sound with a definite abstract concept, a precise "energy-measuring instrument" by which to calculate the laws for his poetic cosmogony. This a priori approach, the notion that sounds have an inherent meaning, and Khlebnikov's linguistic rationalism, as well as his insistence not on the concrete meaning of a word, but on its latent abstract content, all these are foreign to Pasternak. In his verses the bridges between the phonetically kindred words are not those of abstract logic, but rather of metaphor and association, built as they are upon the contiguity of proximate phenomena or simply upon the accident of a random comparison:

> A boat is beating in my breast
> The willows hang down, kissing my collarbone,
> My elbows, the oarlocks—oh, just wait, rest...
> Really this could happen to anyone:[10]

In this stanza "oarlocks" ("*uklyuchiny*") occur near "collar bones" ("*klyuchitsy*") for the same reason that the willows kiss and the boat throbs in the breast; in Pasternak nature, human beings and things are likened to each other—a likeness which is emphasized here by the sound analogy.

In his poetic idiom frequent consonances occur upremeditatedly and as if involuntarily. They do not violate that everyday conversational intonation which forms the basis of the verse. Like his metaphors, these consonances are not obligatory; they are fortuitous.

In Pasternak's poems, Yuri Tynyanov has observed, "the fortuitous

[10][Quoted from Dale L. Plank, *op.cit.,* p. 55.—Ed.]

turns out to be a firmer link than the strongest logical connection." "The link that joins things in his universe is not available to you, it it fortuitous, yet once it is provided, you seem to remember it as if it had already been there somewhere—and the image becomes an obligatory one."[11]

The explanation of this should be sought in the peculiarities of Pasternak's language. We believe in the connections (metaphoric, acoustic, etc.), that he provides, despite their unexpectedness, precisely because they are expressed in so casual and unemphatic a manner, like something taken for granted. Here randomness merely enhances naturalness. And the naturalness of intonation serves as a pledge of the truthfulness of the unfolding lyrical narrative.

Pasternak's poetic idiom of the 1910's and 20's is often complex and difficult to understand. For one thing, it was oversaturated with images, owing to the author's striving to take account of, and convey in language, all the heterogeneity of life's interconnections. Pasternak knew too well that if two objects are placed next to one another, the combination will produce some third thing. He stubbornly refused to break up the world into pieces and painted the whole, where everything intermingled whimsically and chaotically, where the poet did not forget for a minute "what becomes of the visible, when we begin to see it" (*Safe Conduct*). Thus the complexity was the result of encompassing too many items. At the same time, immersing nature in the torrent of conversational speech, Pasternak tore many concepts out of the rut of our habitual associations and provided them with new ones, which, though borrowed from everyday life, were unfamiliar because they had not been used in such combinations before. The simplest and most natural means of expression becomes thus unintelligible to the ears, grown accustomed to the fact that the poet does not talk the way we actually do.

When, for example, in "The Death of a Poet," Pasternak says of the dead man,

> You lay asleep, cheek pressed to the pillow,
> Asleep—you who, as fast as your legs could carry you,
> Crashed again and again by surprise
> Into the ranks of nascent legends,

Mayakovsky's immorality, which is the subject of this poem, marches into the future really, not figuratively, just as the words used are those of everyday life, of conversation or of a business report. In

---

[11][See "Words and Things in Pasternak," in this volume.—Ed.]

common usage these words have grown cheap and it is very rare and
unexpected to meet them in a poem, all the more so in a solemn,
lofty meter, a form long inclined to verbal pieties. This violation
of the pieties, this noncanonical freshness, may well evoke in the
reader a deceptive sensation of "complexity," although, in fact, the
example cited is not complicated in any formal sense, and the reader
need only set aside literary blinkers, the habitual conventions which
govern our responses to a text, in order to feel its direct, forceful
content.

In one of Edgar Allan Poe's stories the experienced detectives
knock themselves out searching for a stolen document which the
thief has hidden by leaving it in the most obvious place. It is precisely what is most obvious, explains the author, that often escapes
our observation. Something similar happens at times with Pasternak's
images: they are "unintelligible" only because they are too close to
us, too obvious.

II

From the painting of nature, upon which Pasternak bestows his
foremost attention, let us proceed to pictures of contemporary history
insofar as they have a place in his poetic system. For the realization
of this theme he had significant credentials: sensitivity to "the voice
of life" and freedom from the poetic cliches banning the use of the
low language of reality. It is well known that in the first years after
the Revolution many authors, limited as they were to a meager collection of commonly used pretty phrases, experienced difficulties
along these lines. "Nightingale" is allowed, "pulverizer" is forbid-
den—gibed Mayakovsky. At issue was the right of poetry to use
modern vocabulary.

Here Pasternak was on safe ground: for him "nightingale" did not
exclude "pulverizer." On the contrary, he was offering "pulverizer"
as the stylistic confirmation of "nightingale." His difficulty such
as it was, lay in something else—an approach to history and a pre-
disposition to the kind of poetry that, contrary to the persistent
current demand, emphasized the *perception* of life rather than its
decisive, radical transformation. Pasternak's attitude toward art as
an organ of perception, his likening of the artist to an attentive and
sensitive observer (but not a direct participant in the transformations
which had begun) restricted his potential for portraying the contemporary, revolutionary epoch in images that would convey directly

and adequately its shattering stride. In this sense Pasternak presents a total contrast to Mayakovsky, who noted somewhere that he and Pasternak lived in the same house, but in different rooms. The very conception of poetry as an organ of perception and the urge to soak in the colors of living nature are foreign to Mayakovsky. Immersed in the events of contemporary history, in political struggle, he saw nature above all as raw material needing to be processed, and treated it with disdainful condescension ("If even Kazbek gets in the way— raze it"). He compared poetry to tools and weapons, to a bayonette, a factory, to production. Pasternak, for the most part, attributes "natural" qualities to poetry: "It's a whistle's precipitous rise/ it is icicles broken and ringing." Mayakovsky puts the poet alongside the worker, the engineer and the political leader, while Pasternak differentiates and contrasts these realms and professions.

Pasternak had offered a sharp distinction between the functions of poet and social activist as early as 1916 in an article entitled "Black Goblet." Poet and hero, lyric poetry and history, time and eternity, are designated here as categories of different, incompatible planes. "Both are equally a priori and absolute," and, giving their due "to the soldiers of absolute history," the author claims for poetry the right not to deal with time, not to take on "the preparation of history for tomorrow."

In one form or another echoes of these views, expressed at an early, still fairly immature stage, recur in Pasternak's later work. He is capable of bestowing all the lofty titles upon history, the activist, the hero, but he reserves and keeps for himself "the poet's vacancy."

In his relation to history, as to nature, the poet is a receptive sponge, and not a hammer splitting stones. This sponge absorbs the surrounding world, grows heavy with the omens of time, but it does not become part of socio-historical existence in the sense in which it is part of nature. In Pasternak's treatment of contemporary history we sense an outsider's cautious view of things which is totally absent from his depictions of nature. This view can be very penetrating, but it belongs to a keen observer of, rather than a participant in, events. It is as if Pasternak somehow did not trust history.

Pasternak called art "the extremity of an epoch" (and not its resultant force) and saw works of art and great historical events as commensurate phenomena belonging to different realms. Thus, in his book *My Sister, Life* he saw a certain parallel with contemporary revolutionary events ("In it I expressed all that is most fantastic and elusive that can be learned about revolution," he wrote in the afterword to *Safe Conduct*), although the subject was not social storms and sunrises, but the most ordinary natural ones, and an allegorical interpretation of these poems would be very far-fetched.

Nevertheless, history entered Pasternak's work even as he was pointedly refusing to have any truck with it and pretended that he could not remember "what millenium is there outside, dears." Echoes of war and revolution rolled through many of his landscapes; history sets its stamp on his descriptions. Even then, in the years 1915-1917, there appeared "heavens on strike," and traces of cavalry on the ice. In memory of 1905, the spirit of "soldiers' revolts and summer lighting" flashed through the air, and Pasternak likened the clouds to recruits and prisoners of war.

> The clouds passed through the dusty market,
> Like recruits, beyond the farm, in the morning,
> They trudged in endless time,
> Like captive Austrians,
> Like the quiet wheeze,
> Like the wheeze,
> A drink of water,
> Sister, please!

After the revolution these historicized landscapes receive a special treatment in Pasternak's work. Nature adopts alien characteristics, drawing them from the world of social turmoil and conflict. This penetration of historical reality into the kingdom of nature was natural for the poet since he described the landscape as perceived by a contemporary city dweller who, side by side with his everyday concerns, drags along on a stroll a chain of social and political associations, involving the meadows and glades in the circle of events among which he spends his life.

In the chapter intended for an autobiographical sketch (1957), Pasternak recalls:

> Forty years have passed. ... At such a distance in time, the voices of the crowds which day and night conferred on the summer squares under open skies, as at an ancient *veche*,[12] no longer reach us. But even at such a distance I continue to see these meetings, like silent spectacles or like frozen living tableaus. ... Simple people unburdened their hearts and talked about the most important things, about how to live and what to live for and by what means to bring about the only thinkable and worthy way of life. The infectious universality of their

[12][Old Russian equivalent of a town-hall meeting. — Ed.]

elation erased the boundary between human beings and nature. During that celebrated summer of 1917, in the interval between two revolutionary dates, it seemed that along with the people, the roads, trees and stars held meetings and orated too. From end to end the air was gripped by a burning thousand-mile long inspiration and seemed to be a person with a name, clairvoyant and animated.

The cleansing downpours, whirlwinds and snowstorms which dominate Pasternak's descriptions of that turbulent era were called upon to convey the "universal meaning" of the upheaval which had occurred. We sense the theme of revolution in these poems as a powerful force; as emotional intensity of imagery that unites the murmur of the crowd with the meeting of roads and trees. It would be difficult to isolate this theme in Pasternak's verse of that period, to locate it in a special paragraph. It is omnipresent and elusive like the air, whose presence in the verse like the presence of a higher, spiritualizing principle, the meeting place of eternity and time, has always been the artist's main concern.

The poet's direct turning to history in the 1930's is connected with the unexpected awakening of epic tendencies in his work. In 1923 in "*A Lofty Malady*" he sends out "a scout into the epic"; then follow the poems "1905" and "Lieutenant Schmidt" (1925-27); in 1930 Pasternak completes *Spektorsky*. The epic absorbed Pasternak to such a degree at this time that he, until recently the most confirmed of lyric poets, could declare: "I believe that the epic is what the age demands, and therefore in the book "1905" I am turning from lyrical thinking to the epic, although that is very difficult."[13] At the same time he expressed the opinion that "in our era lyric poetry has virtually ceased to be heard. ... "[14]

Along with this growing interest in the epic, we should take into cosideration Pasternak's tendency to work with extreme concentration and purposefulness and to see as his mission the revival of the very genre of the book of poetry as an integral, compact unit. He usually marked out his creative path, not by scattered poems but by books, which would acquire in his biography the significance of fundamental signposts, turning points, often abruptly changing the direction of his work. In the mid-twenties his preference was entirely for the epic.

Initially in "A Lofty Malady," Pasternak "gives us an epic without a plot, as a slow swaying, a growing of a theme — and its realization

[13]*Na literaturnom postu* [*On Literary Guard*], 4 (1927), 74.
[14]*Molodaya gvardiya* [*The Young Guard*], 4 (1928), 74.

towards the end."[15] The poet's speech, deliberately impeded, and slowed down, absorbs into itself the "moving rebus" of events— pictures of revolution, war and destruction, which are not deployed in the form of a consecutive narration, but appear as if dissolved in the unbidden flow of the verse. The epic "cumulates" as the narrator recites his part, "drawls and mumbles," conveying the course of life through the modulations of the flow of speech. "A Lofty Malady" is an attempt to approach the creation of an epic by an essentially verbal route. What we are dealing with here, in essence, is a kind of extended lyrical digression, which, taking certain contemporary facts as its point of departure, tries to encompass that age in a broad epic manner and to reveal its image, without recourse to a plot, by means of metaphoric imagery, syntactical constructions, and varying vocal intensity.

In the long poems which succeeded "A Lofty Malady," Pasternak turns to more distinct forms of epic narration. But he still fails to allot much space to the delineation of human fates and characters. Even in "Lieutenant Schmidt," the attention is focused on the re-creation of the very spirit of the time, on deploying a broad historical panorama. The far-flung sketchiness of the images, the colorful under-glow which unites everything but at the same time washes away the contours of separate characters and which is essential and significant in and of itself—these are the distinguishing features of Pasternak's poetry and prose.

> Can it be that, having dwelt within the scope of that picture,
> He believes in the truth of an individual existence?

the author asks the reader, and continually reminds us in *"Spektorsky"* that:

> There can be no question of personalities,
> We had better dispense with them once and for all,

and that even the protagonist for whom the poem is named, strictly speaking, is of little interest to us:

> I started to write *Spektorsky* in blind
> Obedience to the strength of the object-lens.
>
> I wouldn't give anything for the hero
> And would rather not hasten to discuss him,

[15]Yury. Tynyanov, *Archaists and Innovators,* p. 579. [The quotation is drawn from the essay "Interlude," a section of which appears in this collection as "Words and Things in Pasternak."]

> But I was writing about the spectrum of rays
> Within which he loomed up before me.

What mattered to Pasternak was breadth of scope, general perspective, not Spektorsky, but the spectrum which included him, the piece of history torn from the past by a ray of memory. The flow of memories plays a special role in the structure of the poem, the logic of which links individual figures, episodes and parts so that the vast historical picture is gradually restored.

The broad sweep of the theme is closely bound up with the multiplicity of meanings carried here by the motif of space: it encompasses the wide horizons and distances, both temporal and spatial, and the urge to look around oneself and to embrace all that the eye can see. "Space sleeps, in love with space"—such is the world revealed to the poet, the world of history, projected unto the geometrical dimension. Space becomes the stimulus for creation ("the very surveyability of space wanted poems from me..."), the driving force of the plot ("With visions of infatuated space let us turn the story back a year..."), the hero of the work and the force creating heroes—the chosen ones. Promoted to a hero by it, Schmidt learned "how amorous is homeless space."

Pushing back the frames of the narrative to the limit, Pasternak crowds into the space thus formed images from the most varied levels. He includes people sketched in a few strokes, landscapes that have taken on human passions or the features of the age, whole classes and estates—peasants and factory workers, sailors and students, fathers and children. History, like nature, is set forth whole, all at once, with a kaleidoscopic interaction of flashing parts. The emphasis is laid on the general picture of life. A story at sea spreads over to the uprising on the *Potemkin*, and in the days of the December battles on the Presnya[16] "the sun peers through binoculars and listens to the guns." There are strands that lead from particular details to the destinies of nations. Heterogeneous objects and concepts are brought together under a single characteristic:

> Snow lies on branches,
> On wires,
> On the branchings of parties,
> On the cockades of dragoons,
> And on railroad ties.

Pasternak loves lists, collections, enumerations, in which he com-

---

[16][A district of Moscow which in 1905 was the scene of a workers' uprising.—Ed.]

bines objects pulled from various spheres of life and places them
next to each other. In a few lines there emerges a summary picture,
which at the same time is full of concrete detail and seems created
by a single stroke of the hand; a cursory sketch achieves instantaneous
wholeness of impression.

In his depiction and his very perception of history Pasternak comes
close to Blok. This closeness lies in their ability to capture the fundamental rhythm of the epoch not only in the obvious course of events
lying on a single plane, but in all the spheres of life; in the poet's
urge to seek some common historical equivalent to everything that is
happening around him and to show the world in the integral unity of
its constituent parts, be they revolution, earthquake, or love. In the
preface to "Retribution" Blok juxtaposes such heterogeneous phenomena as the Beilis trial and the heyday of French wrestling in St.
Petersburg circuses, summer heat and strikes in London, the development of aviation and the assassination of Stolypin.[17] "All these facts,
seemingly so diverse," Blok concludes, "have a single musical meaning
for me. I am used to juxtaposing facts drawn from all spheres of life
which my vision can reach at a given time, and I am sure that together
they always create a single musical thrust."

Pasternak has an equally keen eye for the signs of time scattered
everywhere and lending each object a special significance. True,
Pasternak's pictures are both more detail-oriented (down to a micro-
analysis of the living matter of history) and more dynamic and sketchy
in their pictorial design than Blok's panoramas. But Pasternak too
is eager to bring out the common denominator of human actions,
sunsets and city streets. And if "Lieutenant Schmidt" deals with the
time of the Russo-Japanese War, the eve of the revolution, then everything, even the Kiev hippodrome, speaks of the troubled state of the
world. History penetrates all the pores of life, transforming the
pettiest detail of the setting into its own likeness.

> Fields and the distance sprawled in an ellipse.
> The silks of parasols breathed thirst for thunder.
> The parching day aimed its fathomless skies
> At the stands of the racing hippodrome.
>
> The people sweated, like bread *kvass* in an ice box,
> Bewitched by the distances' melting.
> Swirling in a sandstorm of hooves and shin-binders,
> The horses beat space like churning butter.

[17][Pyotr A. Stolypin (1863-1911), a forceful and controversial prime minister under
Nicholas II, was assassinated in 1911. — Ed.]

> And behind the measuredly beating effluence
> Of some underground source
> The year of war reared after the jockeys
> And the horses and the rocking chairs' spokes.

> No matter what they whispered, no matter what they drank,
> It grew up all around and crawled along the crossroads,
> And meddled in the conversation and mixed
> In the waters like a pinch of ashes.

Pasternak's letters to Gorky of that period contain his views of the contemporary epic dedicated to the recent past. In his favorable estimate of the first part of Gorky's novel *The Life of Klim Samgin*, he indicates in passing his own tastes. Space, showered "with moving color," dammed up "with crowding details," "the essence of history, which lies in the chemical regeneration of each of its moments" and communicated "with the forcefulness of suggestion"[18] —these remarks of Pasternak on the character and texture of the epic canvas tell us of his own way of representing history.

Pasternak's images are so saturated with the general atmosphere of reality that in his poems it is impossible to differentiate the "primary" from the "secondary," to extract the basic line of the story, or distinguish it from the "background" against which the action develops. The "background" itself is as active as it can be, and quite often turns out to be the foreground of the poem. In the fates of the heroes chance has a providential character and takes on a central significance in the development of the narrative. (Later this will occur in the novel *Doctor Zhivago*.) Thus in *Spektorsky* the sudden meetings and discoveries of the heroes, fragments and snatches of phrases, deliberately unmotivated, grasped "in flight," "unawares," as if by the will of chance—all these play an important role in the delineation of the intelligentsia who react in different ways to the revolutionary events and are scattered about the world along the paths and crossroads of history. In the movement of the plot everything is entangled and intertwined; an immediate sequel to a story about events on a grand historical scale may be found in some everyday episode, in an unexpected encounter with some insignificant person, or it may be realized by means of an interior or a landscape.

Pasternak is more apt to tell us what the weather was like at some historical moment or other than to recount in consecutive order the course of what has happened. He reveals the content of an event

---

[18]"Gorky and Soviet Writers. Unpublished Correspondence," *Literaturnoye nasledstvo* [*Literary Heritage*] , 70 (Moscow, 1963), 304-5.

through areas which touch or border upon it, through the atmosphere shrouding it, accompanying it or prefiguring it in the manner of a prelude. In illuminating the most varied processes and phenomena Pasternak is inclined to circumlocutions and prefaces which, at closer range, turn out to be the story of what matters most to him; often the poet's gaze "wanders," only to focus not on the object the poem speaks about, but on its prehistory, its genesis or its larger context. He likes to talk about the "center" in terms of the "edges," to define a thing through its boundaries with neighboring things; in verses about the city he will draw the suburb and will date a poem about the first of May "April 30."

> How I love it in the first days,
> When the Christmas tree is only talked about!

In his lyrics of 1930's-1950's when the epic yearnings disappeared from his verse to seek an outlet in prose, this feature of Pasternak's artistic vision is especially noticeable. Thus, the lyrical cycle "Waves," which opens the book *Second Birth* (1932), is constructed entirely like an introduction to the theme, but as this introduction unfolds, it becomes clear that it is itself the real theme. The poet tells here what he wants to write about, and his intention itself, his promise, turns into a story about life flowing in waves into the future, a life incompletely realized, hiding within itself new possibilities and intentions resembling those schemes which inspire the poet and which are also only half-expressed and roll into the future. The form of the introduction proves thus to be extraordinarily capacious and meaningful, and in harmony with the idea of the living historical and poetic development that is at its core.

In Pasternak's next books— *On Early Trains, Earthly Space, When the Weather Clears*—we again observe the extremely original way in which his poetry tunes in to historical reality. Direct responses to events are rare here. And most important, the works of ·Pasternak which offer such comments, as, for example, several poems about the Second World War ("A Terrible Tale," "The Conqueror"), are noticeably inferior in artistic quality to the poems on the same subject written, not in the rhetorical-publicistic manner, but in the landscape-painting or intimate-lyrical key long characteristic of him ("The Gates," "Winter Is Coming"). It is noteworthy that the best poems of this kind often sound like introductions or prefaces to the future and communicate the state of an epoch through imperceptible movements of nature and the poet's soul, through domestic details of everyday experience.

This conception of art and of its relation to its model, reality, is so organic for Pasternak's vision that we find analogous notions even in his translations. His work as a translator makes up a special chapter in his literary biography. But the distinctive features of his poetry appear in this subsidiary field as well. Pasternak the translator strives above all to recreate the spirit of the original, neglecting details and literal accuracy. Like living reality, a work of genius needs not a literal but a commensurate transposition—one that, ideally, is inspired by the original, and is in consonance with it but is effective in "its own unrepeatibility." In Pasternak's view a translator should not make a mould of the object which he is copying; rather he is duty-bound to convey its poetic force, thus transforming the copy into an original creation that can live on an equal footing with the original, though in another linguistic system.

It is not difficult to see that Pasternak's ideas on the art of translation are very similar to his ideas on art. The poet-translator, he argues in the preface to his translation of *Hamlet*, strives "most of all, for that conscious freedom without which one cannot come near great things." Comparing his work with that of other translators, Pasternak notes: "We do not compete with anyone in individual lines, but we argue with whole constructions; in implementing them, we enter, along with fidelity to the general original, into an ever greater subordination to our own system of speech. ..."[19] "The relationship between the original and the translation should be like the relationship between the premise and the conclusion, the trunk and the bark. A translation should come from an author who has experienced the impact of the original long in advance of his labors. It should be the fruit of the original and its historical corollary" ("Notes of a Translator").

Pasternak nurtured his best translations for years, preparing himself for them by the very process of his inner development. In a certain sense they are even autobiographical.

His translation of *Hamlet* appeared in a separate edition in 1941, marking the beginning of a series of translations of Shakespeare's tragedies. But as early as a 1923 poem we encounter an idea which he was to implement in his translations: "Oh! all of Shakespeare lies, perhaps merely in Hamlet chatting casually with the ghost." "To chat casually," that is, to speak with ease, in everyday language, about the most lofty themes is, as we know, Pasternak's habit. He had other

---

[19]Boris Pasternak, "A New Translation of Shakespeare's *Othello*," *Literary Gazette*, December 9, 1944.

qualities as well which made him akin to Shakespeare's realism, freedom and vividness. Thus, the "impact of the original" (of course, not always a direct one, but often complicated and refracted through the various phenomena of world culture) began long in advance of Pasternak's actual work on Shakespeare's tragedies and in some measure coincided with his own interests and intentions. This is why Shakespeare took such deep root in Pasternak's poetic soil and why the translating work, visibly influenced by tastes, preferences, and proclivities of Pasternak the poet, influenced in its turn his original creations. This is reflected, for example, in the famous poem "Hamlet" and in some qualities of Pasternak's prose, as well as in the unfinished sketch for a drama, "The Blind Beauty," which he began in the last year of his life. In this close, yet at the same time extremely free, contact with Shakespeare, whose greatness and strength Pasternak strove to convey "in its own unrepeatability," he realized in practice his assertion that "translations are not a way of becoming acquainted with individual works, but a medium in the age-old intercourse of cultures and peoples."

III

If in Pasternak's poetry of the period of revolutions and of the 1920s his landscapes took on the characteristics of the historical process and were filled with the noise and murmur of trees holding meetings, in his later lyrics it is rather history that imitates nature. The processes of growth and maturation, striking in their results and yet hidden and imperceptible like grass growing or the seasons changing, predominate in these poems ("Grass and Stones," "After the Storm"). This is likened not only with the evolution of his style, but with a change in his stance as a poet, as well as with fundamental changes around him which reveal new aspects to him. Pasternak is increasingly concerned with moral phenomena, matters that dwell not in the foreground of life, but in its depth and are expressed quietly, unobtrusively, in everyday customs, in the simple events of national and personal life which constitute the very core of history.

"Life without pomp and circumstance" always attracted him. But from the 1930's on, when pomp attained the character of an operative norm and a binding doctrine, Pasternak was even more apt to favor subjects that appeared to lie on the periphery of social life, but were saturated with latent historical significance (see, for example, the poem "On Early Trains"). As he declared in a speech in February

1936, he adjudged "everything bombastically highflown and rhetorical groundless, useless and sometimes even morally suspect." The poet now feels especially drawn to provincial Russian country roads, little houses, docks and ferries, to unsophisticated feelings and humble laboring people. Nature itself seeks correspondences in these settings: fragrant tobacco is compared to a stoker at rest, spring dons a quilted jacket and finds itself a friend in the cattle yard. Prosaisms, colloquial turns of phrase which loomed large in his earlier poetry, now acquire an additional, ethical motivation by underlining the author's democratic sympathies and his distaste for the grand, pretentious phrase.

In the same period Pasternak's views on the individual's fate and calling and on his place in history crystallize and find embodiment in his lyrics. Human personality comes to the fore as the bearer of high moral values. Since for Pasternak the common and the extraordinary are closely linked, every person is potentially a genius, and genius is simple and unobtrusive, emphasis is placed here on an unconspicuous personality living not for show but possessing a rich internal life and performing the feats of voluntary sacrifice in the name of the triumph of life in the fuller, broader sense—of history, of universal existence. The individual personality possesses an absolute significance—not in hostility to or alienation from life, but in unity and confluence with it. In a letter to the poet Kaisyn Kuliyev (November 25, 1948), Pasternak expounds his view of the fate of the individual person and the mission of talent in the following way:

"What is amazing is that innate talent is the childish model of the universe, placed in your heart from your youngest years, an elementary school text on comprehending the world from within in its best and most astonishing aspect. Talent teaches honesty and courage because it reveals what a fabulous contribution honesty makes to the drmatic design of existence. A gifted person knows how much life gains by full and proper illumination and how much it loses in semidarkness. Self-interest urges such a person to be proud and to strive for truth. This profitable and fortunate position in life can also be a tragedy; that is secondary."

In Pasternak's late verses the poet's attitude to the world appears to us in a rather different perspective from his earlier work. The theme of moral service predominates although Pasternak does not cease to affirm the perceptive power of poetry, its capacity to capture a living picture of reality. (The moral element in the artistic perception of the world was always essential to him.) If at one time the image "poetry as a sponge" held a central place in his aesthetics, now, without replacing the older one, another motif predominates: "The aim of creation is giving of the self."[20] At the same time, towards the end of Pasternak's life, there emerges and sounds with full force the awareness of having fulfilled one's historical destiny. This explains, in part, the extraordinarily bright tonality of his late verse and, despite tragic notes in some poems, the dominant feeling of trust in the future.

The idea of "a high calling" which accompanies an individual appears in Pasternak as early as in "Lieutenant Schmidt," where the moral ideal is projected through the medium of the poem's hero. Schmidt sacrifices himself, performing a feat of historical renewal and accepting his tragic fate as his due. From this poem we may trace the path to the late Pasternak, especially to the cycle "Poems of Doctor Zhivago."

The religious philosophical content of this cycle helps us understand Pasternak's statement on Shakespeare's *Hamlet* which he was translating at that time:

> ...Hamlet denies himself in order to do the will of the one who sent him. *Hamlet* is not a drama about the lack of character, but a drama of duty and self-renunciation. ... By the will of chance Hamlet is chosen judge of his own time and servant of the time to come. *Hamlet* is a drama of high destiny, of an ordained feat, of a predestination. ("Notes to Translations of Shakespeare's Tragedies")

The poem "Hamlet" serves as an introduction to Pasternak's poems with an evangelical theme. The poems about Christ are made up of everyday episodes, set forth in the vernacular; at the same time they are sacred parables, speaking of the road to Calvary and the image of the Saviour. They are filled with Pasternak's awareness of his own plight as a writer, his possible and imminent death, and in the broad sense, of the lot of each one of us, inasmuch as the features and events of the Epiphany are recreated in the tonality of the subjective experience, in the homely materials of universal history. Surprising as it may seem, these evangelical verses become at the same time the story of our epoch and, in particular, of the last years and days of Pasternak's own life. Christ still lives today—and today for the nth time he endures the joy, the miracle and the passion of His destiny.

> The skies with their whole leaden weight
> Lay pressing on the roof-tops' line:

[20][From a late Pasternak poem whose last two lines conclude this essay. — Ed.]

Like foxes fawning over him
The Pharisees sought for a sign.

And when the temple's darkened powers
Gave him for judgment to the crowd,
As once they had praised him fervently
So now their curses rang out loud.

The mob that thronged outside the gates
Kept gazing in expectantly
And, waiting for the end to come,
Shoved back and forth impatiently. ....[21]

Pasternak builds his New Testament scenes by blending the miraculous and the humdrum, the exceptional and the workaday, the supernatural and the ordinary. The prosiness of some of the details and the everyday quality of the proceedings serve to authenticate the miracle of which the poem tells and lend the events of sacred history an emphatically contemporary and personal stamp. The author adheres strictly to the canonical story and reproduces it at time with textual precision, but in the language and the psychological and social detail he takes bold liberties which are taken, however, not in order to violate the canvas of the legend, but to make it more exact and tangible. He approaches this theme in roughly the same way as Breughel and Rembrandt did in their time. With the naivete of eyewitness testimony the old masters clothed the evangelical stories in the dress of their contemporaries and projected the action against the background of their native landscapes. Likewise Pasternak surrounds the Birth of Christ, the Mother of God and the infant Jesus with the snow and the drifts of the Russian winter and frames these figures with such vivid painterly detail that the entire poem acquires the look of a scene drawn from nature ("The Christmas Star"). As a result the Biblical text in Pasternak's version appears as the most contemporary, actual reality. His poems on evangelical themes leave us with the feeling that the sacred mystery has endured to this very day.

The poetry and prose of the late Pasternak unexpectedly shift his vision to a different realm — that of philosophical and metaphysical thought which his earlier verse appeared not to enter. The phenomenological surface of history and nature which had always been the object of his close attention suddenly yields to a search for fundamentals, to divining ultimate ends and first causes. Actually, the

[21][Quoted from Pasternak, *In the Interlude. Poems 1945-1960*, translated by Henry Kamen (London: Oxford University Press, 1962), p. 85 — Ed.]

philosophical substance and fullness of his poetry has simply grown
over the years, and become more apparent. The questions which had
always agitated him — those of the meaning of existence, the destiny
of man and the essence of the world — move to the foreground toward
the end of his path and are given a succinct formulation.

> I want to find the essence of
> All things, each part,
> In work, in groping for a way,
> In turmoiled heart.
>
> To touch the core of days now gone,
> Past never known,
> To know the roots, foundation, cause,
> To touch the bone.[22]

The urge to "know the roots" of life characterizes all of Pasternak's work. His salient trait is the spirituality of his poetic vision.
Speaking in the words of *Safe Conduct*, his work was long marked by
"that unfathomable spirituality without which there can be no originality which opens up at any vantage point, in any direction, without
which poetry is only a misunderstanding, temporarily unexplained."
In many of Pasternak's works from the most widely different periods
of his life, we can sense the persistent desire "to dig down to the
very essence," to the roots, and in telling about some thing or other
not only to show it as it is but also to reveal its primordial nature.

> My friend, you ask, who orders
> The speech of God's fool to burn?
> It was in the nature of lindens, in the nature of stoves,
> In the nature of summer to burn.

He does not say "it was a hot summer," but it was "in the nature
of summer to burn" — that is a poetic turn more typical of Pasternak.
This concern with essences, with the nature of things, places the
poet in an ambiguous position vis-à-vis Impressionism, whose traces
we can find in his work, especially in the early period. Critics often
assigned him to that department. In fact, he is akin to the Impressionists in the purity of his sensations, in his heightened receptivity.
Some of his images are reminiscent of the canvases of Monet and
Renoir, Pissarro and Vuillard. Like these painters, he strives to
seize instantaneous impressions of objects and, hiding away his
previous knowledge of the world, to show it just as it appears to him

---

[22][Quoted from Vladimir Markov and Merrill Sparks, *Modern Russian Poetry*
(New York: Bobbs-Merrill Co., Inc., 1967), p. 613. — Ed.]

at a given moment. Here, for example, is a sketch executed in the manner of the Impressionists:

> Plates clattered in the hands of the bartender.
> Counting castors, the butler yawned.
> At the height of a candlestick, on the river
> The fireflies swarmed.
>
> They hung down like a sparkling string draped
> From riverside streets. It struck three.
> With a napkin the butler tried to scrape
> Some wax from the bronze to make it clean.

The lights on the shore, their reflections in the water, the waiter on board ship—the poet captures everything at a single glance, concerned only with encompassing the picture that has suddenly arisen before him and to fix it in this position, once sighted "at the height of a candlestick."

But Impressionism, as a rule, deals with the sensually perceptible surface of an object and not with its essence. Drowning in a sea of colors and smells, it eschews all a priori, preconceived knowledge of an object, shuns concepts and ideas that might muddy the immediacy and purity of perception. Interest in truth, in absolute values and first principles is alien to Impressionism, totally immersed as it is in the flow of impressions coming from *this* and only *this* nature. That is why impressionism enriched art essentially in the realm of concretely sensual representation—in conveying nature as something visible, but not intellectually apprehended.

It is curious that the young Pasternak, visibly passing beyond the confines of Impressionistic nations, coins such a formula for art "as the *Impressionism of the eternal*" ("A Black Goblet," 1916). In this formula he combines his taste for the immediate perception of life, the pure brushstroke of color, the plein air, with his predilection for seeking universal principles and absolute categories. Similarly, in his poetic images he tries to unite sensation and essence, the moment and eternity, and writes of "a storm instantaneous forever," thus lending a picture grasped in a moment an immutable, absolute meaning. He invests the "moment," favored by the Impressionists, with so great a significance that it is no longer a matter of the fleeting and singular, but of the permanent and eternal.

> This moment lasted an instant
> But it could have eclipsed eternity.

While the Impressionist deliberately confines himself to the question "How is this thing perceived at a given moment?," Pasternak goes further and wants to know what it is. Pasternak examines it, penetrates into its core, and often constructs an image in the form of a definition of the object's characteristic attributes, giving not only his first impression of it but also its essential conception. No wonder some of his poems bear the title "Definition" ("Definition of Poetry," "Definition of the Soul" etc.), and a number of other poems follow outwardly the same pattern which makes one think of a textbook or a dictionary.

> Poetry, I will swear
> By you, and finish hoarsely:
> You are not the bearing of the honeyvoiced,
> You are summer in a third-class seat,
> You are a suburb, and not a refrain.

Pasternak is not afraid of such propositions. He eagerly deduces the "formulas" of what he depicts, computes and analyzes properties and ingredients:

> We were in Georgia. Let us multiply
> Need by tenderness, hell by heaven,
> Turn a greenhouse into a base supporting glacier,
> And we will get this country.

> And we will understand in what subtle doses,
> Into the mixture with earth and heaven,
> Go success and labor and duty and air
> So that man should turn out as he does here.

But even as he inquires into the essences and at times ventures into the most abstract realms, he always deals in images and thus remains integral and concrete. All of his "definitions" resemble logical constructions only externally; in fact, they rest upon a picture of life, which lies at the core of the poem. In a programmatic poem cited earlier, "I want to find the essence...," Pasternak expresses his desire to write verses "on the properties of passion," to reveal its "law" and "principle." How does he imagine this work that would explore the essence of an object?

> I would plan verses like a park,
> Their veins meanwhile
> Trembling, lindens would bloom in them,
> File after file.

> I'd bring the breath of roses, mint
> Into this verse

> And meadows, sedge and haying, with
> The thunder's curse.
>
> So once Chopin put this alive
> Miracle of
> Folwarks, park, groves and graves into
> Etudes we love.[23]

Pasternak's verses are poetry of the proximate and the concrete. He paints only what he sees himself. But what he has seen has an expanding significance and some of the details are transferable to a larger plane. The objects around us become the embodiment of goodness, love, beauty and of other exalted conceptions. Uniting the concrete and the abstract, the singular and the universal, the temporal and the eternal, Pasternak creates, as it were, an ideal representation of a real person or fact. "My beauty, all your bearing, all your essence is to my liking," he says to his beloved and through her "bearing" reveals her "essence"—the universal laws of the beautiful.

> To you Polyclitus prayed.
> Your laws were issued long ago.
> Your laws lie in the distant years.
> And I have long known you.

He compares her to the future ("Measuring the silence with your steps, you enter like the future"), and sees in her the embodiment of the "foundations" of life.

> Loving some's a heavy cross,
> But you are lovely, plain and free,
> And equal to the key to life
> Is the secret of your grace to me.

Life, in line with Pasternak's world-view, brings "the taste of great principles" into each of its manifestations. And in its presence the most insignificant objects become more ideal, shining with an inner light. A single rest in pine woods gives occasion for a generalization:

> And so, immortal for a time,
> With the pines we too are sainted
> And from illness and epidemics
> And from death emancipated.

To be called "immortal" was once the prerogative of gods. But here ordinary people, coming into contact with eternal nature, be-

---

[23][*Ibid.*, p. 615.—Ed.]

come immortal, for immortality, according to Pasternak, suffuses the world ("our daily immortality") and is only a synonym or another name for life.

Intensity of poetic thought becomes noticeable in Pasternak from the 1930's on. In his earlier works this quality was harder to discover, and the pithiness of his images at times was mistaken for a formal affectation. With the years Pasternak becomes more intelligible and, as a natural consequence, this aspect of his poetry appears more distinctly. But Pasternak's growing intelligibility is itself, in no small measure, due to the development of his thought which achieves a finer order and an ever keener awareness of its organizing, dominant role in his verse.

In the poet's early work philosophical ideas do not protrude; they are hidden entirely by the picture through which they are projected. Rarely in these poems do we encounter direct ratiocination coming from the author himself, the flow of thought is entrusted to nature, apprehending itself. Moreover, the author's idea is obscured by the abundance of seemingly fortuitous impressions and associations and further complicated by his desire to take all the interacting factors of life into account and to connect them in a fine mesh of metaphor. The early Pasternak is too consistent in his receptivity to life to be clear, and although, as we have noted, his speech is natural and easy, it is the naturalness of chaos bursting forth, a chaos that is in need of disentanglement in order to become totally intelligible.

But the destiny of Pasternak's world and the naturalness of his language could not remain forever behind the locked door of "unintelligibility." For a long time he had yearned for so full a merger of the "fathomless spirituality" of images with "the unheard-of-simplicity" of their verbal expression that the reader would master them without any effort, like a truth requiring no clarification.

The hero of one of Pasternak's poems, who fought in the Second World War, dreams of a play he will write after getting out of the hospital:

> There in a provincial's language
> He will set in order and clarity
> The unimaginable course
> Of a fantastic life.

"A provincial's language," that is, everyday, living language, free from literary cliches, was Pasternak's old ideal. But the concern for "order and clarity" is a new element in his conception of art.

Pasternak achieves harmonious order and clarity largely because in his late work the self ceases to play a subordinate role in relation to his own perceptions, and because it departs from the extreme degree of metaphoric concentration which was characteristic of his earlier verses. He makes a stricter selection among his impressions and, limiting nature's willfulness, frequently projects "pure" feelings and reflections, not translated into metaphoric language. While in Pasternak's earlier work the process of comprehending life was, so to speak, a continuous flow and it was impossible to separate his first glance at the world from his final conclusions about it, later we can discern clearly the "theme" of poetic cognition which, as it grasps things, does not dissolve in them totally but preserves its independence and brings order to the movement of the images.

Accessibility and "universal intelligibility" of poetic speech did not come easily to an artist with a fully crystallized view of life and a distinctive way of writing. Sometimes the demand for simplicity entailed the risk of impoverishing his imagery and producing too direct and declarative a solution to a problem. At other times in the process of reorienting himself, Pasternak wrote poems which were avowedly inferior to his potential. Thus, in the mid-thirties, when the poet was striving with special determination to renew his system, several poems appeared ("Close to my heart is the stubborness..." and others), of which he declared at the time (not, without self-deprecation, of course), that he was forced "to write badly," "to write like a shoemaker," until he got accustomed to the shift. In this case, the situation was complicated by the novelty and lack of concreteness of the subject which he approached somewhat abstractly, in a journalistic manner. As Pasternak said as the time in his speech "On Modesty and Boldness" (February, 1936), he had to execute "a flight from position to position...in a space where the air was thinned by journalism and abstractions, with little in it of imagery and of the concrete."

No wonder that greater concreteness, and at the same time spirituality of the pictorial design, becomes for the late Pasternak the decisive condition of creative mastery. A picture throbbing with thought fills the poem, free from metaphorical glut but not inferior to the earlier works in depictive power, in fact, surpassing them in frank, striking wealth of content. It is precisely in religio-philosophical verse that Pasternak achieves now his greatest success; he is much less effective in the hortatory-publicistic sort of writing or in sketches of everyday life or landscape-painting that are not anchored in a philosophical idea. For him artistic perfection is measured now by the graphic, manifest significance of what is said. One of Pasternak's best and last poems "In the Hospital" is a case-in-point. In this poem everyday detail serves as attestation of eternity; both landscape and human soul are illuminated here by the touch of God....

Having achieved the simplicity he desired, Pasternak also preserved the most valuable of his original gifts—the integral perception and representation of the world. Yet if in the past the barriers between phenomena, between human beings and nature, the temporal and the eternal, had been overcome mainly with the help of the metaphor that shifted objects and characteristics from place to place and brought a Babel of images, in the later poems the metaphor, while continuing to play an important linking role, is no longer the mediator between things. Their unity is vouchsafed now by the breadth and clarity of the poet's view of the world, that spiritual upsurge of feeling and thought before which all barriers fall and life appears as a great whole where "nothing can be lost," where human beings live and die in the embrace of the universal, and the wind

> Sways the cottage and the forest,
> Not each pine separately,
> But all the wood completely
> And all the limitless distance.

Not only are the interconnectedness of things and the poet's communion with the world realized in Pasternak's late works in more direct forms than hitherto, but "the universe itself is simpler than some sly fellows imagine." It is built on the supremacy of a few simple elementary truths which anyone can understand—the earth, love, bread, the sky. Sometimes a poem rests entirely on the affirmation of one such cornerstone of human existence. At the same time everyday life looms in the Pasternak lyric as large as ever, this time without the complicating allegories which were obligatory in his early poems, but with the straightforward meanings of objects, habits and occupations. The poetry of life's prose which always inspired him acquires now special resonance.

Over the half-century during which he wrote Pasternak underwent many changes. But to some ideas, principles and predilections he remained faithful all his life. One of these deep convictions was that true art is always larger than itself for it bears witness to the meaningfulness of being, the grandeur of life and the immeasurable value of existence. This act of bearing witness can dispense with profound symbols or allegories: the presence of greatness reveals itself in the genuine vividness of a story, in the heightened receptivity and poetic inspiration of the artist, awestruck and possessed by the miracle of authentic reality, who always speaks of one thing only—the significant presence of the actual, of life as it is, even if the ostensible subject is merely how the snow falls or a forest rustles.

"Poetry," Pasternak has said, "will always remain that glorified height, far higher than any Alps, which lies about in the grass, under our feet so that we only need to bend down to see it and gather it up from the ground. ..." What is most exalted for Pasternak proves in the end to be what is the most simple—life, all-pervasive, all-embracing. Consequently, whatever facet of the theme of the artist's mission or destiny he tackles, all of Pasternak's philosophical reflections, moral injunctions and poetic tenets come to a single simple and lofty piece of wisdom:

> But be alive, that's all that matters
> Alive and living—to the end.[24]

---

[24][*Ibid.*, p. 617.—Ed.]

Boris Pasternak

by Fyodor Stepun

I

The Revolution of 1905 had a positive impact upon the upper tier of Russian culture or, to use the Marxist lingo, upon its super-structure. Suddenly there emerged poets, writers, literary scholars, and critics of an entirely new cast of mind who, in spite of widely differing endowments, came together in a still insufficiently studied and appreciated movement known as Russian Symbolism. Not all those who proclaimed themselves Symbolists had an equal right to do so if what is meant by "Symbolism" is not only a search for new forms and new literary devices but also a concept of art as the revelation of the invisible rather than a reflection of the visible world. This, the only legitimate definition of Symbolism, was most persuasively championed by Vyacheslav Ivanov[1] in his theory of religious sym-bolism. From Ivanov's vantage point Valery Bryusov[2] could not have been termed a Symbolist, neither spiritually nor stylistically. This is clearly, if indirectly, demonstrated by the fact that his ablest disciple Gumilyov was the first to challenge the Symbolist vague-ness in the futile hope to enhance the "craftlike" status of the "guild" art[3] by playing down its spiritual, notably its religious, thrust.

My schematic outline of early-twentieth-century Russian litera-ture would be incomplete without a mention of the disparate strands in literature, painting, and, in general, culture bracketed together

"Boris Pasternak" by Fyodor Stepun. An abridged version of the essay "B. L. Pasternak" which first appeared in *Novy zhurnal (The New Review)*, 56 (March, 1959), pp. 187-206. Reprinted by permission of the publisher. Translated by Victor Erlich.

[1][Vyacheslav Ivanov (1866-1949), one of the major figures in Russian Symbolism, a critic, philosopher, and poet.—Ed.]

[2][See "Pasternak's Poetry" in this volume.—Ed.]

[3][Reference to the "Guild of Poets," a short-lived Acmeist group founded in 1912 by Nikolay Gumilyov. See "Language and Reality in the Early Pasternak," foot-note 5, in this volume.—Ed.]

under the "Futurist" label. The common denominator of these currents was an unequivocal repudiation of the past. Actually, what the Futurists hated with a passion was not so much the past as the present which emerged from it. This hatred is reflected in the title ,of their best-known manifesto, "A Slap in the Face of Public Taste" [1912]. Since the past as epitomized by Symbolists was implicated in heaven and eternity, heaven was dubbed by the Futurists a cow's udder, and stars—the title of the first collection of V. Ivanov's verse was *By the Stars*—abscesses on that udder. The Symbolist urge to transform the world became at the hands of the Futurists a determination to make it ugly, to deesthetize it. Realizing that meaning restricts the range of possible sound combinations, some Futurists anticipated the Dadaists[4] in producing sonorous nonsense verse—e.g., "Belamotokyoy" (Kruchonykh),[5]—which, however, they did not consider esthetically meaningless.

A salient trait of Futurism was its ambition to conquer the street. Sporting long yellow blouses and wearing heavy makeup or paint on their faces, Futurists of various kinds and denominations haunted the Moscow streets and literary gatherings. The prewar lecture halls were invaded time and again by Mayakovsky's Jericho-like trumpets and by the red glow of the impudent Vadim Shershenevich's batlike ears.[6] In Moscow these antics were widely deplored not only by the "philistines" but also by the socially committed writers. Yet the Futurist excesses were not simply meaningless noises. They grew out of a keen anticipation of the Revolution that was to be not so much a social reconstruction as a demolition of traditional culture. The Bolsheviks sensed this and rewarded the Futurists by entrusting the building of the new, postrevolutionary culture not to the old Bolshevik Maxim Gorky, but to the young Mayakovsky whose poetry they did not understand and whom they found totally uncongenial.[7] Against the backdrop of the Futurist movement—strident, gaudy, impudent and yet essentially prophetic—there emerged only three truly talented and significant figures, of whom, to my mind, only

[4][Dadaism was a radical avant-garde movement, launched in Zurich, in 1916, by the poet Tzvetan Tzara.—Ed.]

[5][Aleksey Krunchonykh (1886-   ), one of the most active Russian Futurist manifesto writers, and an eccentric if resourceful minor poet.—Ed.]

[6][For Shershenevich see "Life as Ecstasy and Sacrifice," in this volume, footnote 6—Ed.]

[7][This is not entirely accurate. The Bolshevik leadership availed itself of Mayakovsky's propagandistic zeal but did *not* put him in charge of the "new, postrevolutionary culture."—Ed.]

Mayakovsky could be termed a true Futurist. Khlebnikov, whom Gleb Struve calls "father of Futurism,"[8] was nothing of the kind. Nor can Sergey Esenin[9] be considered a Futurist.

With which of the above trends can we associate Boris Pasternak? Pasternak scholars tend to classify him as a Futurist, more specifically a Cubo-Futurist,[10] which seems at least partly justified by the reference in his autobiography *I Remember* to "my" Futurist period. Some critics labeled Pasternak an Acmeist,[11] perhaps because of his warm appreciation of Anna Akhmatova's poetry.

All labels, especially in art, are precarious and controversial. No writer worthy of the name can be encompassed by them. Pasternak would have certainly eluded definition had he not provided in *Safe Conduct, Dr. Zhivago*, and *I Remember* a pithy yet incisive statement about his work and his views on art, a statement which clearly associated him with Symbolism and the tenets of critical and Romantic idealism that underlie it.

"To know the word is to render it unrecognizable," said the famous neo-Kantian philosopher Heinrich Rickert. And here is Pasternak speaking about the origins of art: "We cease to recognize reality. It appears to us in some new category.... We try to give it a name. The result is art."[12] The fact that Rickert speaks about knowledge and Pasternak about poetry should not blind us to an affinity between these two statements: knowledge referred to by Rickert rests upon Kant's transcendental esthetics. Likewise Pasternak builds into his definition of art a Kantian concept of "category." Let us emphasize at this point the idea casually broached by Pasternak, notably that the category, within which the world suddenly rendered unrecognizable confronts the poet, appears to us not as a state of mind but as a state of the world. This notion is closely related to Kant's teaching that the world which appears to the naive human consciousness as reality independent of man is actually our own creation—a shap-

---

[8][Gleb Struve, Professor Emeritus of Russian Literature at Berkeley, is one of the leading authorities on modern Russian poetry.—Ed.]

[9][See "Words and Things in Pasternak," footnote 9, in this volume.—Ed.]

[10][The most important grouping in Russian Futurism. The term "Cubo-Futurism" points up the close cooperation between "Futurist" poets—e.g., V. Khlebnikov and V. Mayakovsky—and "Cubist" painters such as N. Goncharova or M. Larionov. —Ed.]

[11][See above, footnote 3.—Ed.]

[12][*Safe Conduct* (London: Lindsay Drummond Ltd., 1945), p. 80. I substituted "category" for "form."—Ed.]

ing of the world by the forms of time and space, of causality and eternity—inherent in human consciousness.

This world-shaping consciousness, however, is not the consciousness of an individual but of a man with a capital M, labelled in Kant the "transcendental subject," in Fichte the absolute "I," in Hegel the absolute spirit and in Pasternak the image of Man which is greater than man. It is this image that prevails in art. "In art," says Pasternak, "the man is silent and the image speaks."[13] But this is only part of the story. As the man who shapes the world through the medium of the "forms" inherent in his consciousness perceives these forms as properties of the world, so, too, the poet sees each metaphor not as his own invention but as a discovery of a truth latent in the world. These views of Pasternak are a nearly literal echo of the V. Ivanov's already mentioned theory of religious symbolism. The objectifying tendency of Pasternakian esthetics is evident in his insistence on the independent role of language in poetic creation. In a moment of inspiration, writes Pasternak, "the relation of the forces that determine artistic creation, is reversed. The dominant thing is no longer the state of mind the artist seeks, as it were, to express but the language in which he wants to express it. Language, the home and receptacle of beauty and meaning, itself begins to think and speak for man."[14] The idea of turning language into some independent creative entity gripped, as early as one hundred years ago, the noted German linguist Wilhelm von Humboldt and the late Romantic poets Hölderin and Novalis. Vyacheslav Ivanov translated Novalis's "Hymns to the Night" and Andrey Bely, for whom Pasternak had high regard, was passionately concerned with problems of poetic language, sensing, not unlike Pasternak, its creative power.

The above sketchy observations on Pasternak's poetics were not intended to suggest his disciplelike indebtedness to either the idealistic philosophy which dominated the Marburg University at the time of his sojourn there or, for that matter, to the romantic ambience of Symbolism. I merely wanted to indicate the intellectual climate which helped shape Pasternak's moral vision.

Let me add that Pasternak's philosophical and atmospheric affinity for the Symbolists is indirectly indicated by the fact that when

---

[13]*Ibid.*, pp. 73-74.—Ed.]

[14][Boris Pasternak, *Doctor Zhivago*, translated by Max Hayward and Manya Harari, (New York: Random House Inc., Pantheon Books, 1958). This and subsequent translations are reprinted here with the permission of the publisher.—Ed.]

in the third part of his *Safe Conduct* he draws the portrait of his young contemporaries roaming despondently the Moscow boulevards, he identifies the force that kept them afloat as the art of Aleksandr Blok, the leading poet of Russian Symbolism, and of Andrey Bely, author of a voluminous work on Symbolism and, without any doubt, its most remarkable prose writer, as well as the art of Skryabin, whose association with Symbolism is attested to by Vyacheslav Ivanov, and, finally, of the most popular actress of the era, Vera Komissarzhevskaya,[15] who, rather than portraying on stage visible reality, strove to embody the invisible.

By positing Pasternak's innermost bond with Symbolism I do not mean to call into question his association, to be exact, the association of pre-1940 Pasternak, whom the older poet was to repudiate in *I Remember*, with the Futurist movement. The real question is: Which of the truly significant Futurist poets did Pasternak find congenial? It goes without saying that, in contradistinction to Mayakovsky, he had never had any use for the Futurist street, for the noisy hangers-on whom, as Pasternak once shrewdly observed, Mayakovsky tolerated out of fear of loneliness.

The residual affinity between Khlebnikov and Pasternak or, for that matter, Khlebnikov's influence on Pasternak, duly acknowledged by Gleb Struve, seems incontestable. But I would be prepared to argue that Khlebnikov, whose soul was an inchoate chaos lighted up now and then by some otherworldly glow, was not a Futurist. A poet who has no firm roots in the past cannot be a herald or a builder of the future. Nor can Sergey Esenin, who clearly was rooted in the past, be termed a true Futurist. A congenitally mischievous and chronically intoxicated revolutionary populist with Slavophile leanings, dreaming about a revolutionary leader in the guise of a peasant tsar, he was essentially an archaic maverick in the Futurist camp.

Among the major poets of the era only Vladimir Mayakovsky was a true Futurist, for he alone articulated in his verse the attitudes which gave rise to European Futurism—the urge to politicize art and to transform it into a social force. Let us not forget that the creator of Italian Futurism, Marinetti, whose Jesuit training did not prevent him from becoming an ardent chauvinist, in 1914 called vociferously for Italy's declaring war on Austria and in 1919 enthusiastically joined the Fascist movement, and that German Futurism

---

[15][Vera Komissarzhevskaya (1864-1910) was a famous Russian dramatic actress. In 1904 she founded her own theater in Petersburg.—Ed.]

as represented by the editor of a well-known journal *Die Aktion,* Franz Pfemfert,[16] visibly gravitated toward Communism. What had to be strenuously propagated in Italy and Germany had ever since Radishchev[17] been fully evident to Russian artists. For all the idiosyncratic brilliance of his poetic talent and style, Mayakovsky was essentially a throwback to the confessional-political tradition in Russian literature, the tradition of Radishchev and Gorky. No wonder that when still a high school student he joined the Russian Social-Democratic Party and promptly found himself on its Bolshevik wing. To be sure, he was never a consistent Marxist, but he was a revolutionary from early on. He reminded Pasternak of "a composite figure of a young small-town revolutionary terrorist in a Dostoevsky novel."[18] With Mayakovsky the Futurist, the Bolshevik tribune, and the political propagandist, Pasternak had nothing in common.

In *I Remember* he writes: "the later Mayakovsky beginning with "Mystery—Bouffe" is inaccessible to me...I remain indifferent to these clumsily versified sermons...set forth so artificially, so confusedly and so devoid of humor. This Mayakovsky is in my view worthless, that is, nonexistent. And the remarkable thing is that it is this worthless, nonexistent Mayakovsky that has come to be accepted as revolutionary...Mayakovsky was beginning to be propagated compulsorily, like potatoes in the reign of Catherine the Great."[19] Repudiating Mayakovsky the Futurist, the tribune, Pasternak loved passionately the early Mayakovsky, not yet distorted by Futurist politicization. With this Mayakovsky, and with a number of his poetic contemporaries, Pasternak shared a quest and a discovery of new poetic modes that pointed beyond the Symbolist achievement. The most accurate label for these innovations is Expressionism, which at the beginning of the twentieth century became the dominant artistic style throughout Europe. The essential trait of Expressionism is emotional turbulence and frenzy which interferes with portraying the world in its primordial natural givenness. The Expressionist poet projects images of the world in sway of that human passion, images seemingly displaced in space and time and, more importantly, metaphorically linked with one another, chaotic and

[16][Franz Pfemfert (1879-1954) was a left-wing German Expressionist.—Ed.]

[17][Alexander Radishchev (1749-1802), an eighteenth-century writer and publicist, was one of Russia's first political dissenters.—Ed.]

[18]["Avtobiograficheski ocherk" ("Autobiographical Sketch"), *Sochineniya (Works),* II, 40.—Ed.]

[19][*I Remember,* pp. 98-99, 101.—Ed.]

"made strange." (Shklovsky)[20] This is reflected in the external devices characteristic of Expressionism—repudiation of traditional
syntax, of logical coherence, and of the need for a visualizable
image.
The style of European Expressionism loomed large in the early-
twentieth-century Russian poetry. Those were the contrivances and
excesses which as early as in 1928 earned Pasternak the stern censure
of Vladimir Weidlé.[21] Yet in the same essay the critic acknowledged
"the poet's individual uniqueness." It is this uniqueness that is at
the center of the article by the distinguished Slavist Roman Jakobson. Having drawn a parallel between Mayakovsky's and Pasternak's
artistic devices, Jakobson concludes that Mayakovsky's poetry thrives
on the striking metaphor, i.e., a juxtaposition of images on the basis
of similarity and contrast. Pasternak's poetry, on the other hand,
though not immune to the metaphor, abounds, in Jakobson's words,
"in metonymic sequences." To simplify though, I trust, not to distort Jakobson's interesting observation one might say that in Pasternak the range of associations is virtually boundless since it is not
restricted by the principle of similarity and contrast. In Pasternak
all images interact and intertwine in a kind of roll call; they echo
each other in the sanctuary of his soul. Jakobson notes that at the
first glance the associative downpour of Pasternak's verse may appear to drown out the poet's own "I." Actually, he argues, Pasternak's
most bizarre images are metonymic companions, if not reflections,
of the poet's self.
These poetic devices are informed, it seems to me, by a definable
poetic world view—a *sui generis* pantheism. There is a pantheism
that dissolves personality within a divinely impersonal universe.
We encounter it in the young Tolstoy. Pasternak's stance is the reverse. He lends human shape to life's faceless phenomena, and since
man is created in God's image, one could say that he deifies everything that lives. His pantheism has no truck with Buddhism. In
fact, if Christianity is compatible with pantheism, Pasternak's pantheism can be termed Christian.

[20][Viktor Shklovsky (1890-   ), a leading Russian Formalist critic. One of his
major contributions to Russian modernist esthetics was the notion of "making it
strange" *("ostranenie")*, of "defamiliarizing" the familiar as the principal function
of art, most notably of imaginative literature.—Ed.]
[21][See V. Weidlé, "The Poetry and Prose of Boris Pasternak," in Davie and Livingstone, eds., *Pasternak: Modern Judgments* (London: McMillan, 1969), pp. 108-125.
—Ed.]

Pasternak feels a special affinity for trees. In his work they are living creatures endowed with freedom of movement. "The old park ...came right up to the shed, stirring the doctor's memories."[22] "The trees, like white ghosts, crowded into the road as if waving goodbye to the white night which had seen so much. ... The birches at the gate make way for the approaching procession. Storm runs up the stairs to the porch. Horses and the gusts of wind sing 'Eternal Memory.'"

This process of personification and humanization draws into its orbit not only natural phenomena but also the protagonist's states of mind. Thus in *Safe Conduct* we are told that the narrator's fellow passenger on the train is his own silence. The same page features a still more bizarre turn of phrase: the standard impressionist description of a morning in the city suddenly ushers in a typically Pasternakian image. Life's fresh pithiness crosses the road, takes the poet by the hand and leads him down the sidewalk. Thus both the silence and the pithiness become living beings with whom the poet enters into a complex human relationship. The tale about the assistance rendered the poet by life's fresh pithiness is capped by the admission that his "brotherhood with a huge summer sky" was undeserved and that he was yet to earn the morning's trust.[23]

In speaking of Pasternak one cannot afford to ignore the remarkable musicality of his verbal gift. This is not simply a matter of vocalic chimes or consonantal whispers such as one can encounter, say, in Balmont.[24] Pasternak's music is a more complex phenomenon. In his autobiography he avers that in spite of a high regard for Andrey Bely, he steered clear of his seminar devoted to the study of the Russian iambic verse since he has "been of the opinion that the music of the word is not an acoustic phenomenon and does not consist of the euphony of vowels and consonants taken by themselves but of the interrelationship between the meaning and the sound of the words."[25] At the very heart of the sound Pasternak could hear silence.

Silence you are the best of all I have heard.

Often the silence would beget a "hiss of anguish which did not

[22][*Doctor Zhivago*, p. 444. The subsequent images are drawn from other portions of the novel and two poems of Yury Zhivago.—Ed.]
[23][B. Pasternak, *Sochineniya (Works)*, II, p. 238.—Ed.]
[24][Konstantin Balmont (1867-1943), a prolific and mellifluous Symbolist poet. —Ed.]
[25][*I Remember*, p. 62.—Ed.]

originate in myself." Coming upon the poet from behind, it frightened him and moved him to pity. It threatened to put brakes on reality and implored him to make common cause with the living air which in the meantime managed to get far ahead of him.

This anguished plea for the living air lends Pasternak poetry its remarkably bracing, bright, and life-affirming quality which suggested to Anna Akhmatova the apt line "he is awarded a kind of age-long childhood."[26] The same point is made by the title of Marina Tsvetaeva's essay about Pasternak, "A Downpour of Light."[27]

II

One has to concede that the letter of the editorial board of *Novy Mir* justified its refusal to publish *Doctor Zhivago* in what was by Soviet standards a rather decorous manner. The letter attests to a careful perusal of the novel. Neither Pasternak's talent nor his seriousness is called into question. Moreover, the letter dispenses with crude political attacks and personal abuse. In its analysis and evaluation of *Doctor Zhivago*, the editorial board clearly endeavored to produce an impression of objectivity.

Yet this civilized manner should not blind us to a fundamental misapprehension of the novel that underlies the *Novy Mir* statement. The misreading begins with equating Yury Andreyevich Zhivago with Pasternak, an equation which is illegitimate if only because Boris Pasternak's formative period was a far cry from the childhood of the orphaned Zhivago. Likewise, in his autobiography Pasternak makes a fleeting reference to a friend by the name of Samarin whose fate closely coincided with that of Pasternak's hero — a seeming warning against confusing the former with the latter: "At the beginning of NEP[28] he returned to Moscow from Siberia where he had spent a long time carried hither and thither during the Civil War. He had grown much more simple and more understanding. He had swollen up from starvation and become covered with lice during his journey. He fell ill with typhus at the time when the epidemic was on the wane and died."[29]

[26][See Anna Akhmatova, "Boris Pasternak," Davie and Livingstone, eds., *Pasternak*, p. 153.—Ed.]

[27][*Ibid.*, p. 42.—Ed.]

[28][This abbreviation stands for New Economic Policy which was adopted by the Bolshevik government in the wake of the Civil War and which entailed a partial revival of private enterprise.—Ed.]

[29][*I Remember*, p. 75.—Ed.]

The editorial board describes Zhivago as an inveterate philistine who, it is true, at first welcomes the Revolution in a few resounding phrases but, having realized that it would be materially disadvantageous to him, decides to take off for Siberia where he can more easily forage for food, in total disregard of the fact that Moscow is in dire need of physicians. Having become embroiled against his will in the Revolution he hates, this individualistic *intelligent* returns to Moscow hungry and lice-ridden, and dies in a Moscow streetcar as pointlessly as he lived, in total isolation from his countrymen, in a blind and haughty repudiation of the historical events he witnessed.

The above, needless to say, is a crude caricature. What is the actual spiritual makeup of Pasternak's hero?

In any genuine work of literary art its tenor and the spiritual ambience of its characters are closely bound up with the narrative manner: the form in which *Doctor Zhivago* is cast differs significantly from the traditional nineteenth- or twentieth-century Russian, or, for that matter, European novel. This is why many a foreign reader and some Russian readers who have not experienced Symbolism (e.g., Bely's *St. Petersburg*) have found Pasternak's imagery diffuse and elusive. In some sense this is unquestionably so. The proposition becomes dubious as soon as this "diffuseness" is construed as an artistic flaw. It goes without saying that the main characters in *Doctor Zhivago* lack the Tolstoyan tridimensionality which Chekhov, Bunin, and especially Aleksey Tolstoy managed to preserve. However, the absence of this quality in *Doctor Zhivago* stems not from Pasternak's alleged creative inadequacy but from the exigencies of the style in which the novel was conceived and executed. It is noteworthy that the "diffuseness of imagery" decried by Pasternak's critics characterizes only the novel's chief protagonists; its secondary characters are drawn very vividly indeed. Suffice it to mention the stationmaster Fufyrkin, his affected wife, and the carriage in which she comes to fetch him, while he, strolling down the road, admires the crease in his pants, the fierce artisan Khudolaev chastising the Tatar boy Yusupka, and the masterfully drawn attorney Komarovsky. Neither Zhivago nor Lara has been vouchsafed so graphic a portrayal. Yet if we do not see them as clearly as Anna Karenina or Vronsky, we apprehend them fully, we vibrate along with their feelings, we hear their heartbeats, we breathe the air they breathe. Such scenes as the conversation between Strelnikov and Zhivago on the eve of the former's suicide or Lara's suddenly confronting, in her late husband's former room, the coffin of

Yury Zhivago are so overwhelming in their emotional impact as to call to mind the best passages in Dostoevsky. Nor is this potency particularly surprising. Apprehension is not always a matter of sensuous contemplation. We cannot apprehend human faces, bodies or movements without actually seeing them, but a soul can be intuited in darkness, in a penumbra of love and death.

Outside of the relative dearth of vivid detail, *Doctor Zhivago* differs from the classical Russian novel in that the connections between the characters are at times rather tenuous. There is something fortuitous about their meetings and interrelationships. Some of them vanish from the stage as if they were diving into the depths of life that seethes around them only to surface in what seems to be a providential encounter. Zhivago's half-brother appears in the novel on only a few occasions, each time without any warning, in order to assist Yury Andreyevich in an hour of need. However, each "accidental" meeting, lacking as it does any logical or psychological motivation, is perceived not as a matter of chance but as an act of fate or a manifestation of a higher concern. After all, chance is nothing less than the atheistic pseudonym for a miracle.

This essentially non-psychological perspective on human relationships is one of the novel's most striking characteristics. Antipov's leaving Lara, his transformation into the uncannily compelling Strelnikov, Zhivago's feelings toward his wife and Lara—all these defy explanation. The psychological cause-and-effect scheme is not applicable to the novel's main characters. Their experiences cannot be accounted in terms of the lives they live in the reader's full view. A relevant interpretation would have to be sought beyond the limits of the visible, which requires from the reader a special intuition. Ordinary, "realistic" love scenes are conspicuously absent here. There is only the mystique and the music of love, its song—sorrowful or triumphant. This mystique and music resound in Lara's meditations over Zhivago's coffin:

> Oh what a love it was, utterly free, unique, like nothing else on earth! Their thoughts were like people's songs. ... They loved each other because everything around them willed it, the trees and the clouds and the sky over their heads and the earth under their feet. Perhaps, their surrounding world, the strangers they met in the street...the wide expanses they saw on their walks, the rooms in which they lived or met, took more delight in their love than they themselves did. ... Never, never, even in their moments of richest and wildest happiness

were they unaware of a sublime joy in the total design of the universe, a feeling that they themselves were a part of that whole.[30]

It could be argued that the transnaturalistic and transpsychological structure and style of *Doctor Zhivago* deprived the novel of the qualities essential to a major epic work. But, clearly, it is precisely this structure and style that enabled Pasternak to lift his narrative to a higher realm by informing it with original and deeply personal meditations about the world's destiny, the tragedy of human existence, the nature and mission of art. Even those who find the novel murky and somewhat chaotic must admit that its chaos is illuminated time and again by the heat lightnings of the spirit. The philosophy which pervades the novel blends with the music of Pasternak's poetic art that reaches its peak in the metonymic descriptions of nature whose elements here are not picturesque actualities, as is the case with Chekhov or Bunin, but man's cosmic interlocutors: "Grief had sharpened Yury Andreyevich's senses and quickened his perception a hundredfold. ... The winter evening was alive with sympathy like a friendly witness. It was as if there had never been such a dusk before and night were falling now for the first time in order to console him in his loneliness and bereavement, as if the valley were not always girded by a panorama of wooded hills, on the horizon, but the trees had only taken up their places now, rising out of the ground in order to comfort him with their presence."[31]

All I have said thus far about Zhivago blends for me into a kind of religious symphony resounding from some transcendental heights over the bloody madness of the man-made world. This madness has been the subject of innumerable volumes but none of these terrible books filled me with such anguish and despair as did *Doctor Zhivago*. This is due in large measure to the fact that in Pasternak the events of the Bolshevik Revolution unfold under the skies filled with unearthly music. No less important, it seems to me, is that in *Doctor Zhivago* the revolutionary events are described by an observer who is uncommonly keen and who lacks any and all ideological preconceptions. Had Pasternak thought in political terms, the picture of the Revolution he drew would have been more meaningful and thus less terrifying. The upheaval would have been construed either as a retribution for the crimes of the Tsarist regime or

---

[30][*Doctor Zhivago*, p. 501.—Ed.]
[31][*Ibid.*, p. 451.—Ed.]

as a warning to the world—beware! this is what socialism is really like!—or, finally, as an inevitably dark prelude to the luminous realm of socialism through the growth of Russia's imperial power. Yet Pasternak dispenses with all this. Absent is even the Blokian music of the Revolution and Christ marching at its head.[32] True, there are a few sparse words in *Doctor Zhivago* that seem to celebrate the Bolshevik coup: talking to his father-in-law, Yury Andreyevich urges him to 'have a look' at the broadsheet he had just pulled out of his pocket, and he talks to himself: "What splendid surgery! You take a knife and with one masterful stroke you cut out all the old stinking ulcers, quite simply, without any nonsense, you take the old monster of injustice, which has been accustomed for centuries to being bowed and scraped to and curtsied to, and you sentence it to death."[33] To be sure, this is a *sui-generis* acceptance of the Revolution, but these half audibly muttered meanderings stop short of a political or social approval. The most positive aspect of the Revolution turns out to be its artistically potent thrust which reminds Pasternak of Pushkin's "blazing directness." What the poet admires in the revolutionary gesture is that like all "strokes of genius," it is "so misplaced and unkindly."

The further course of the Revolution effectively destroys this initial would-be acceptance without turning Zhivago, however, either into a counterrevolutionary monarchist or a democrat of liberal or socialist persuasion. In order to interpret Pasternak correctly, it is essential to realize that he shuns and repudiates the Bolsheviks, not as a political movement to which he opposes another movement that claims his allegiance, but as a salient manifestation of the lie in which contemporary society is enmeshed. It is this artistic rejection of Bolshevism that accounts for Zhivago's admitted failure to take notice of the dislodging of the Provisional Government by the Bolsheviks or to see an essential difference between the evil acts of the Reds and the Whites. Pasternak's thoroughly apolitical stance—which can and, perhaps should be queried—rests on the Christian premises of his philosophy of history whose main tenets are formulated with aphoristic pithiness and undogmatic open-endedness chiefly in parts three and four of the novel.

[32][Reference to Alexander Blok's poem of the Revolution, *The Twelve* (1918) whose finale features Jesus Christ marching—or rather floating—at the head of twelve Red militiamen. "The music of the Revolution" is a phrase which occurs in Blok's 1918 essay "The Intelligentsia and the Revolution."—Ed.]

[33][*Doctor Zhivago*, p. 194.—Ed.]

According to Pasternak, even nonbelievers cannot help but realize that history, in the true sense of the word, began along with Christianity in that "new mode of existence and new kind of communion which we call the Kingdom of God" and within which — this is Pasternak's central message — there are no people in the heathen sense, there are only personalities. Now "personality" does not always mean a single human individual; it could also be a people, not simply a people, though, but a "converted, transformed one." What matters, explains Doctor Zhivago, is precisely "the transformation rather than fidelity to old principles."

Pasternak's conception of personality is quite distinctive. He views it as immortal not because of the doctrine of resurrection but on the grounds that its very birth is an emergence and a resurrection out of the boundless realm of the impersonal and the separate, an entrance into history created by persons. Pasternak inquires: what is man?, and answers thus: the real human being — i.e., a person of the new, Christian era — is one who lives in others. The human soul is what grows in others, what lives on after a person's death. It is thus that immortality is achieved. To label this form of immortality memory is to Pasternak inadequate, possibly even wrong. "And what does it matter," Zhivago says to Anna Ivanovna, "if later on it is called your memory? This will be you — the you that enters the future and becomes a part of it."

The editorial board of *Novy Mir* unequivocally accused Pasternak of individualism. Conversely, his foreign admirers congratulate him on having dared to pit the principle of individualism against that of Bolshevik collectivism. This terminology, which reflects, to be sure, a certain philosophical position, betrays a fundamental misperception of Pasternak's moral stance.

The Latin word *"individuum"* designates something indivisible, a self-enclosed entity, lacking, to use modern existentialist phraseology, the gift of communication. The etymology of the term is quite consonant with the psychological and sociological implications of "individualism." If an individualist is not necessarily an egoist, he is always a more or less self-centered and separate being. To Pasternak an individualist is essentially soulless because a man's soul is "man in others" while an individualist is a man in himself. To use Pasternak's language, a man in himself is necessarily a faceless man, since the mystery of personality stems from Christianity and a Christian lives by the love of his neighbor. In order to safeguard their interests, individualists can easily band together in collectives where everyone, however, operates as an equivalent of any other member of the collective and where, in defending others, everyone actually defends only himself. What makes the present international situation impossible of resolution is precisely the fact that Western European individualism is no more than a reverse side of Bolshevik collectivism.

Only in the light of this philosophical stance can one fully understand Pasternak's attitude toward Bolshevism. He spurns the Bolsheviks because he sees their historical role as a repudiation, indeed as a mockery, of history. No one, says Pasternak, makes history. One cannot see it any more than one can watch grass growing. History is made not in the clamor of mass scenes, or at a fanatic's behest; it ripens in the secret recesses of individual and collective persons yearning for "spiritual bliss." Wars and revolutions are often likened here to such natural phenomena as storm or sickness. At best they are yeast of history rather than history itself. What can be properly called "history" is the apprehension of these phenomena by the spirit of personal creativity.

The philosophy of history which I have derived from *Doctor Zhivago* is quite reminiscent of Berdyayev's[34] historiosophic schemes with their distinction between the two planes, history and metahistory. For Berdyayev, as for Pasternak, the empirical vehicle of metahistory is the person in which the historical process unfolds. There is nothing in Berdyayev that is higher than personality— which is sound Christian theology since only the person is promised resurrection. Though Pasternak does not approach the ultimate truths of Christianity or the substance of its dogma, their mute presence in *Doctor Zhivago* is unmistakable. The beautiful poems of Yury Zhivago—spiritually aglow and yet firmly anchored in sensory and human detail—are eloquent testimony to Pasternak's supraphilosophical and supraesthetic commitment to Christianity.

As indicated above, Pasternak's alleged individualism has drawn both praise and blame. By the same token, while some commend him as a staunch Russian *intelligent,* others, mainly Soviet critics, term him contemptuously an *intelligent* outcast, alienated from the people. One can forgive a Western European for calling Pasternak a typical *intelligent,* but coming from a Russian such designation is inexplicable. To the Russian ear an "apolitical *intelligent"* is a contradiction in terms, since the entire Russian revolution was in the

[34][Nikolay Berdyayev (1874-1948) was an influential publicist, philosopher, and lay theologian. — Ed.]

main the creation of Russian intelligentsia whom some 80 years ago Annenkov[35] described as a kind of "revolutionary order."

In neither of Pasternak's autobiographies is there any suggestion of an affinity for that order. I cannot think of another Russian who walked in such a somnambulist trance past all the turmoils and sores of modern Russian society. (It is significant that the seventy-name index to the recent German translation of *Safe Conduct* does not contain a single political figure with the partial exception of Maxim Gorky, who is mentioned, however, in conjunction with a portrait of his that Pasternak's father was about to paint.) Pasternak was raised among poets, writers, painters and musicians, miles away from the turbulent social and factional strife of the early-twentieth-century Russia. It was thus that he was able to maintain throughout a keen, unimpaired vision and that the Bolsheviks did not succeed in forcing upon it their ideological blinkers. This, to be sure, was his greatest offense vis-à-vis the Soviet government and the Russian Communist Party.

Among many striking statements about art scattered across the pages of *Doctor Zhivago* one finds this perhaps central insight: art is always, incessantly engaged in two things: it ineluctably meditates about death and ineluctably creates thus a new life. I am speaking of genuine, great art—that which is called the Revelation of St. John and that which serves as a sequel to it.

Without raising the question about the distance between the revelation of St. John and *Doctor Zhivago* one can safely say that this novel is a genuine, indeed a great, achievement. It is to Pasternak's everlasting credit that in Bolshevism's global elan, in all that chaos and clatter, in all that frenzied political activism and messianic utopianism, he was able to hear the voice of death and to glimpse a mute face of grief over the desecration of man's most precious, God-given treasure, his likeness to God—the core of the mystery of human personality.

Throughout the fateful decades of his sojourn in the Soviet Union Pasternak managed to remain the keeper of this mystery, and in his novel he bears witness to his life-long dedication. Therein lies the greatness of the service he has rendered Russia and of the service which through his good offices Russia has rendered the world.

---

[35][Pavel Annenkov (1813-87), an intimate of Gogol and Turgenev, a shrewd and knowledgeable litterateur. His memoirs are an important source of information about Russian literary life at mid-century.—Ed.]

Doctor Zhivago:
As from a Lost Culture

by Stuart Hampshire

That *Doctor Zhivago* is one of the great novels of the last fifty years, and the most important work of literature that has appeared since the war, seems to me certain, even when every allowance has been made for the circumstances of its appearance and the effect that this may have upon one's judgment.

The immediate enthusiasm with which it has been received here is not in the least surprising and is no ground for suspicion. This enthusiasm is, I think, quite unconnected with politics in the narrow sense and with Communism, or with any sentimental sympathy with the author's frustrations. The explanation is that, at first reading, a Western European is immediately reminded of all that is best in his own past, of the great tradition of full statement, which he had come to think no contemporary writer could now resume, because the extremes of violence and social change had made any real imaginative reconstruction of the recent past, any whole picture, seem impossible. We have come to take it for granted that the most serious art of our time must be fragmented art and indirect statement. There has for a long time seemed no possibility that anyone should have survived who, in the exercise of his genius, retained all the literary ambitions and philosophical culture of the last century. That is has happened is an extraordinary accident. It is as if in the general devastation one lane of communication with the past has been kept clear and open. Perhaps only a long isolation in a cultural desert could have produced this result, this slow maturing of a work that is independent of any distracting contemporary influences. The fact remains that part of the immediate excitement of the Western reader is a sense of escape and of nostalgia, of a return to the real or imaginary Golden Age when absolute assurance and uncontrived and confident gestures were still possible.

"*Doctor Zhivago*: As from a Lost Culture" by Stuart Hampshire. From *Encounter* (November, 1958), pp. 3-5. Reprinted by permission of the author.

Doctor Zhivago is unlikely to have any great influence on the writing of novels in France, Britian, or America: it is too far away from the main stream and it has been too little affected by the experiments of the last thirty years. It really does seem to come from a lost culture, to be just coeval perhaps with Thomas Mann's *Buddenbrooks*, but certainly not with Faulkner and Sartre. This free, naive, as opposed to sentimental, writing is probably not something that can be imitated or further developed, because the confidence in a complete philosophy, tested by revolution and violence, of which the naivete is an expression, is probably everywhere lacking in the West. Pasternak is after all looking back in this novel and leaving his testimony, proved by his experience and final. Since his experience includes the Communist revolution, the looking back is not mere looking back. He has come to terms in his own mind with that way of life which has the most plausible and widely advertised claim to represent the future. In contrast with this, all the writers of the West are in an uncertain, waiting condition, becalmed in a recognized interregnum, not knowing the worst and therefore incapable of any tested, unqualified statement. It is not surprising, therefore, that they turn to satire or sentimental mannerism, to expressions either of despair or of uncertainty. The whole sum of our experience in forty years of violence cannot yet be calculated.

The difficulty that this novel presents, after a first reading, is the difficulty that any carefully composed and long meditated work of art presents. It is naive art, in Schiller's special sense of the word,[1] but far more naive, in the ordinary sense, in its composition. The other difficulty is of course the language. The English translation, as English, is certainly better than we are used to in translations from Russian, although the familiar jolts of incongruity do sometimes occur. It allows one to guess that the vocabulary of the original is rich and elaborate, particularly in descriptions of nature and in the dialogues of the poor. But not knowing the original is evidently an enormous loss, which cannot be mitigated. The whole book is informed by an intense feeling for everything that is distinctively Russian, by a characteristic kind of mystical patriotism, which is quite unlike the patriotism of the French or the English; the feeling of Russian

[1][Reference to Friedrich Schiller's famous treatise on *Naive and Sentimental Poetry*. The distinction as explicated by René Wellek in his *A History of Modern Criticism* is one between "poetry...written with an eye on the object, a fundamentally realistic, objective art...and poetry [which] is reflective, self-conscious, personal and above all of an age in which the poet is in conflict with his environment and is divided within himself." — Ed.]

landscape and Russian talk are evidently conveyed also in nuances of diction that will have deep associations for any Russian. The endless talk and the endless landscape are as much part of the substance of the novel as the revolution itself, as being the constantly changing background of the central story of love and separation. The vastness of the land, the snow, the episodes of calm and natural beauty after scenes of great violence and misery, are part of the story, which is arranged with a musical sense of fitness in the changes of mood. The whole truth about the experience of these years is to be built up gradually, and, partly for this reason, the first fifty pages of the novel are confused by the lack of a firm narrative. The reader is required to accept a series of impressions, not yet intelligibly related to each other, and a set of unexplained characters who are not clearly identified in his mind until much later. Pasternak does not even attempt the well-known virtues of the storyteller's art. He is writing a philosophical novel, a testimony of thought and experience, and not any kind of novel of character or of the fate of individuals. The villain is an abstract sketch of bourgeois corruption, and the story of his relations with the heroine is mere melodrama.

For this and other reasons any comparison between Pasternak and Tolstoy, either in intention or in effect, appears absurd from the very first page. One thinks of the swift, decisive beginning of *Anna Karenina*, the wonderful clarity and depth of the characters, and the impression left of the whole span of their lives lived in their natural circumstances. Not one of the characters in *Doctor Zhivago*, not even Zhivago himself, is endowed with this rounded naturalness nor are their lives steadily unfolded before the reader. The novel moves forward in short paragraphs and in short episodes, which are all related by strings of coincidence to the central figure; he and the heroine, Lara, together carry the whole weight of the story, as the picture is formed of the old society collapsing and of the new one forming in confusion and terror. If any single literary influence is to be mentioned, it seems to me that the most prominent is Shakespeare. The use of the wild dialogue of the characters of the underplot, the short scenes that somehow, as in *Antony and Cleopatra*, suggest the great events across great distances, and above all, in the suggestion of signs of the supernatural in the natural order. Pasternak's Russia can contain witches and metaphysical fools alongside images of ideal love escaping from corruption, in which the personalities and idiosyncrasies of the lovers and of the villain play no part. There is something Shakespearean, which I cannot now state clearly, in the sudden blending of the imagery and the philosophical reflections, in the affinities found between thought and natural appearances.

It would be very gross and very dishonest to interpret this novel as primarily a condemnation of Soviet Communism. About the author's intentions no mistake is possible, since, like Proust, he clearly explains his philosophy in all its divisions, of aesthetics, politics, and personal morality, both directly and in words attributed to his characters. The Soviet State is indeed condemned as a degeneration from the revolution, which was the moment of liberty and of the assertion of the forces of life. The revolution itself is represented as one of the few great events of human history, comparable with the overthrow of Roman power as the ancient world ended. The old regime is shown as corrupting personal life as deeply, if less violently, than the Soviet fanaticism that succeeds it. But ultimately political action and organisation are incidental to the most serious interests of men and women, which are to be found in the sources of art and religion. These sources of renewal have been discovered, whenever a man achieves some heightened sense of his own part in the processes of life that makes his own death seem not a final waste. Men arrive at this deliverance and rest, when they have succeeded in communicating perfectly with one other person, giving the testimony of their own experience, either in love or in a work of art. The inconsolable people—Doctor Zhivago's wife and Lara's husband—are those who have never perfectly achieved this. This sense of the overwhelming need to communicate one's own individual experience, to add something distinctive to the always growing sum of the evidences of life, is the most moving theme of the book. The political cruelties, the crimes and errors of the Soviet system, are not made into grounds for final pessimism, and are certainly not the grounds for hopes of counter-revolution or of salvation from the West.

There are several long passages that read like a memory of the early writings of Hegel, particularly two in which Pasternak repeats Hegel's account of the historical role of Christianity in creating the modern man, who need no longer be either master or slave. For him Russia, the country in which people "talk as only Russians talk," is plainly the leading nation of this century, and staying at home and somehow keeping alive the radical tradition of the Russian intelligentsia, he has written a work of universal significance, which offers hope and encouragement. The vindication of the freedom of art, and of private life lived on the appropriate human scale, does not appear in this novel as the conventional and now frigid liberalism of the West. There is no suggestion of nervous fence-building, of the shrill, defensive note of those who live within a stockade, trying not to notice the movements outside, by which they know that their fate is being decided.

Written in proud isolation, *Doctor Zhivago* will, I think, always be read as one of the most profound descriptions of love in the whole range of modern literature.

A Testimony and a Challenge —
Pasternak's *Doctor Zhivago*

by Victor Erlich

The long-heralded appearance in English of Boris Pasternak's *Doctor Zhivago* is a cultural event of the first order.[1] Its significance is enhanced by the fact that this, a major novel by Russia's greatest living poet, has not as yet been allowed to appear in the Soviet Union...

Pasternak's narrative spans four fateful decades of modern Russian history—from the Revolution of 1905 through World War I, the 1917 upheaval, the civil war and NEP down to the purges of the 1930's, the Nazi invasion of Russia and its aftermath. It ranges far and wide over Russia's vast expanse, drawing into its orbit the intellectual and the peasant, the "activist" and the uncommitted, the big city and the God-forsaken hamlet, and last but certainly not least, the Russian landscape, evoked here with that mixture of reverence and an uncanny acuteness of perception which is so unmistakably Pasternak's. And yet, as Chiaromonte has already suggested in his admirable article, the parallel with *War and Peace* argued by some Western critics, should not be pushed too hard.[2] An epic artist *par excellence*, Tolstoy delighted in, and excelled at, rendering the solid, tridimensional *texture* of human existence. Pasternak's novel, for all the wealth of physical and social detail which it contains, is not "objective reality" but inner experience, the state of mind, the individual's affective response to the outside world. The "merely" lyrical is transcended here, but never wholly submerged. An introspective epic, *Doctor Zhivago* seeks to embody the ultimate meaning of Russia's turbulent years within several individual destinies which, in the course of the

"A Testimony and a Challenge—Pasternak's *Doctor Zhivago*" by Victor Erlich. A slightly abridged version of a review which first appeared in *Problems of Communism* (Washington, D. C.: United States Information Agency, November-December, 1958), pp. 46-49.

[1] Boris Pasternak, *Doctor Zhivago*, translated from the Russian by Max Hayward and Manya Harari (New York: Pantheon, 1958).

[2] See N. Chiaromonte, "Pasternak's Message," Davie and Livingstone, eds., *Pasternak*, pp. 235-36.

events described, become inexorably and fatefully intertwined — those of the chief protagonist, of Lara who is to become the great love of his life, and her husband Antipov-Strelnikov, the hero and the victim of the Revolution. This bulky novel-chronicle is above all a poetic biography of one individual, Yury Andreyevich Zhivago, a physician, a poet and a thinker. The structural and emotional focus of the narrative is provided by Zhivago's unremitting efforts to maintain his personal identity under mounting outside pressures and by the ever-sharpening conflict, as one of the characters puts it, between the Communist style and his own.

This incompatibility does not become immediately apparent. For one thing, Yury Zhivago, a son of the upper-class intelligentsia, is too keenly aware of the evils of prerevolutionary Russia, too strongly imbued with a sense of justice, to be a nostalgic apologist for the *status quo*. When in the summer of 1917 he returns from the front to Moscow, he seems only too eager to come to terms with the new realities. He is harshly critical of his own milieu, its unnecessary luxuries, its excessive sophistication, its self-indulgence. The March Revolution appears to him as a "new birth," a prodigious release of pent-up popular energies, a beginning of freer and more creative life, and he speaks of this "stupendous spectacle" in images throbbing with lyrical excitement:

> Mother Russia is on the move, she can't stand still, she's restless and she can't find rest, she's talking and she can't stop. And it isn't as if only people were talking. Stars and trees meet and converse, flowers talk philosophy at night, stone houses hold meetings.[3]

A few months later, the October Revolution elicits from Zhivago these words of unqualified admiration:

> This fearlessness, this way of seeing the thing through to the end, has a familiar national look about it. It has something of Pushkin's uncompromising clarity and of Tolstoy's unwavering faithfulness to the facts.[4]

The poet in Zhivago is carried away by the sheer sweep of Lenin's grand design. The procrastinating *intelligent* is fascinated by the categorical language of the Bolshevik decrees, by the surgical decisiveness of the break with the old.

But this fascination is soon to give way to disenchantment with, and estrangement from, the methods, slogans and doctrines of the new regime. About a year later, having left Moscow for the Urals in

---

[3]*Doctor Zhivago*, p. 146.
[4]*Ibid.*, p. 195.

futile quest of a more viable existence for himself and his family, Zhivago reacts with frank irritation to the clichés mouthed by a local busybody labeling Marxism a scientific, objective theory of reality:

> Marxism a science?...I don't know a movement more self-centered and further removed from the facts than Marxism....as for the men in power, they are so anxious to establish the myth of their infallibility that they do their utmost to ignore the truth. Politics doesn't appeal to me. I don't like people who don't care about the truth.[5]

But it is in a subsequent conversation with Lara that Zhivago speaks his mind most effectively:

> ...In all this time something definite should have been achieved. But it turns out that those who inspired the revolution aren't at home in anything except change and turmoil; they aren't happy with anything that's on less than a world scale. For them, transitional periods, worlds in the making, are an end in themselves. They aren't trained for anything else, they don't know anything except that. And do you know why these never-ending preparations are so futile? It's because these men haven't any real capacities, they are incompetent. Man is born to live, not to prepare for life.[6]

Needless to say, this instinctive revulsion from the "professional-revolutionary" mentality does not make of Zhivago an active "counter-revolutionary." Indeed, he tries his best to steer clear of either camp, to avoid taking sides in the savage civil war raging around him. But the position of noncommitment proves literally impossible to maintain. Zhivago is kidnapped by a Red Partisan unit, in dire need of a physician. An episode which occurs during this period of near-captivity epitomizes his predicament. Unwittingly, Yury Andreyevich finds himself on the firing line. The Whites launch a suprise attack on his detachment. As he lies alongside the Red guerilla, Zhivago is overcome by the "ambiguity of his feelings"—a mixture of personal loyalty to "his" unit and of admiration for the desperate courage of young White volunteers advancing recklessly across an open field. Yet "to look on inactively while the mortal struggle raged all around was impossible, it was beyond human strength" (p. 334). He was being shot at. He had to shoot back or at least pretend to do so. In deference to the "rules of the game," Zhivago grabs the rifle relinquished by a fallen comrade and starts firing steadily—at a tree in front of him.

[5]*Ibid.*, pp. 258-59.
[6]*Ibid.*, pp. 296-97.

In the process he happens to hit one of the assailants whom he later in secret nurses back to health.

As the White armies begin to melt away, Zhivago manages to escape. He retraces his steps back to the Siberian town which had become his second home only to learn that his family, dislodged by the civil war and subsequently forced into emigration, is lost to him forever. But Lara is still there, waiting patiently for the miracle of his return.

There ensues what is perhaps the most moving section of the novel and one of the most beautifully orchestrated love duets in all of Russian fiction. Amidst the unspeakable brutality of the civil strife, of the chaos and disarray, these two richly endowed human beings succeed in salvaging, indeed in exalting, such untimely and timeless values as the poetry of love and the love of poetry. It is as if the very violence of the social upheavals lent their feelings a special intensity and depth, by stripping them of all that is superficial and trivial, by "laying them bare." Lara remarks:

> The whole human way of life has been destroyed and ruined. All that's left is the naked human soul stripped to the last shred. ...You and I are like Adam and Eve, the first two people on earth who at the beginning of the world had nothing to cover themselves with—and now at the end of it we are just as naked and homeless. ...[7]

This precarious interlude was much too beautiful to last. A cunning lawyer who had played a sinister role in Yury's as well as in Lara's childhood, whisks Lara away under the pretext of rescuing her. Zhivago wearily makes his way back to Moscow—to find the intelligentsia of the capital falling prey increasingly to a "political mystique," the hard-won ability to justify and eulogize one's own enslavement. (In a memorable scene, Zhivago explodes when his erstwhile friend, Professor Dudorov, declares with apparent sincerity that prison reeducated him and helped him mature.) What follows inexorably is utter loneliness, rapid deterioration, and after a brief recovery of creative powers, a fatal stroke in a crowded Moscow streetcar, in 1929.

But the destiny of Zhivago is not consummated thus. The epilogue adds a significant postscript to what may appear at the surface as a story of ¡defeat and failure. This time the narrative focus is provided by Zhivago's two friends, Gordon and Dudorov, whose addiction to official clichés had been severely tested in the 1930's by the "inhuman cruelty of Yezhov's terror." In their first conversation, which takes

---

[7]*Ibid.*, pp. 402-3.

place in 1943, World War II with all its horrors characteristically appears to them as an end of a nightmare, a partial relief from the "magical power of the dead letter." In the final scene of the novel, set a few years after the liberation, we see these aging professors poring over a slender volume which embodies Zhivago's literary heritage. (Twenty-five exquisite samples of Zhivago's love and devotional poetry are appended to the novel. They deserve a separate treatment.) The air of the peaceful summer evening is redolent with the yearning for freedom, for a better life which, they feel, is bound to come after the terrible exertions of the war and the still more terrible prewar ordeal. "And the book they held seemed to confirm and encourage their feeling." (p. 519)

Is not this the posthumous vindication, the ultimate triumph of Dr. Zhivago? By lending support and sustenance, twenty years after his death, to the overwhelming desire for freedom which animates his countrymen, this gentle, seemingly ineffectual "outsider" emerges as a history-making force.

The phrase is used here advisedly. For to Pasternak making history is a matter of vanquishing death rather than of manipulating life; it is a disinterested act of individual creation rather than a brutal projection of organized will.

It has been said that the central philosophical theme of *Doctor Zhivago* is the dichotomy of History and Nature.[8] It would be more accurate to say that Pasternak tends to conceive of the historical process by analogy with nature, more specifically, with the "vegetable world." Not unlike Tolstoy, he juxtaposes the "sound and fury" of recorded public events with what he sees as real history—a process of slow, imperceptible, organic transformation. "Nobody makes history, one cannot see history, just as one cannot see the growing of the grass."

But if the *rhythm* of history is viewed here as akin to that of nature, the *meaning* of each historical epoch is derived from its major creative achievement, its deepest spiritual ferment. In Pasternak's philosophy of history the vision of a poet, awe-struck by the mystery and the beauty of the world, joins hands with a *sui generis* Christian personalism, reminiscent of Dostoevsky and Berdyaev.[9] "What is history?" reflects Zhivago's uncle, a defrocked priest turned lay religious philosopher. "It is the centuries of systematic explorations

[8]See Alberto Moravia, "Un adolescent aux cheveux gris" ("An Adolescent with Gray Hair"), *Preuves* (June, 1958), pp. 3-7.

[9][See Fyodor Stepun, "Boris Pasternak," footnote 34, in this volume.—Ed.]

of the riddle of death, with a view to overcoming death" (p. 10). Since the advent of Christ, he continues, the moving force of each historical advance has been a certain spiritual elan, which encompasses the ideas of a free personality and of life as sacrifice. It is in behalf of this elan that Lara's friend, a woman-mystic Sima, can calmly dismiss the official rhetoric about "peoples and leaders" as a throwback to the pre-Christian era, with its nomadic tribes and its patriarchs. It is in behalf of this thoroughly un-Soviet hierarchy of values that Yury and Lara can serenely ignore the Communist ethos, with its idolatry of politics, and its notion of culture as a weapon. Defiantly Lara proclaims over the corpse of her lover:

> The riddle of life, the riddle of death, the enchantment of genius, the enchantment of unadorned beauty—yes, yes, these things were ours. But the small worries of practical life—things like the reshaping of the planet—these things, no thank you, they are not for us.[10]

That a book of such moral depth and such enduring beauty—a book full of tragedy and yet life-affirming, breathing (as Pasternak says of his hero) the spirit of freedom and detachment—could have emerged from the Soviet Union is a tribute to the creative integrity of a man who for many years now has stood almost alone in saving the honor of Russian poetry. More broadly, it is a truly historic event, in the Pasternakian sense of the word. The act of conceiving and composing a novel such as *Doctor Zhivago* in what must have been some of the darkest hours of the Stalinist inquisition is a magnificent triumph of the spirit over the brute force of circumstances.

---

[10]*Doctor Zhivago*, p. 502.

Doctor Zhivago:
Liebestod of
the Russian Intelligentsia

by Robert Louis Jackson

At times I have a dim presentiment of an immense danger
which threatens all culture. The great wave which will wash
us from the surface of the earth will carry off more than
that one which washed away powdered wigs and shirt-
frills. It is true that to those who perished then it seemed
that with them the whole of civilization was perishing.

SIENKIEWICZ's *Without Dogma*

She died or vanished nobody knows where, forgotten under
some nameless number on one of those lists that afterwards
got lost, in one of the innumerable mixed or women's
concentration camps in the north.

PASTERNAK's *Doctor Zhivago*

Life is without beginning and without end.

BLOK's *Retribution*

Doctor Zhivago and its author share with the great tradition of
Russian literature an exceptional forthrightness, a moral fervor and
a deep sense of responsibility before Russian life. Many of the philosophical, religious and mythopoetic motifs of the novel are part of the
tapestry of Russian literature and thought. The problem of the individual facing the invincible laws of historical development—ex-

"*Doctor Zhivago: Liebestod* of the Russian Intelligentsia" (originally titled "*Dr.
Zhivago* and the Living Tradition"), by Robert Louis Jackson. From *The Slavic
and East European Journal*, New Series, 4 (XVIII) (1960), 103-18. Copyright © 1960
by the Board of Regents of the University of Wisconsin System. The article appears
with minor stylistic changes. It is reprinted by permission of the publisher.

plored in all its tragic essence by Pushkin in his narrative poem
"The Bronze Horseman," resolved in part in Tolstoy's *War and Peace*
through a philosophy of reconciliation with reality—is explored
again by Pasternak in the somber and protesting tones of Pushkin's
poem; yet like Pushkin, Pasternak acknowledges the historical inevitability of the power crushing his hero.

The problem of the fatal cleavage between the masses of people
and the intelligentsia; the question of the apocalyptic and the nihilistic
as elements in the Russian nature; the conception of a family, the
Zhivagos, experiencing in its separate links the retribution of history
and milieu; the mystical apprehension of Russia and the dramatization
of its destiny in religious terms and symbolism—all this, entering
into *Doctor Zhivago*, defines Pasternak as a writer in the tradition
of Dostoevsky, the philosopher Vladimir Soloviev, the poet
Alexander Blok and other Russian writers and thinkers of the late
nineteenth and early twentieth centuries.[1]

Pasternak's *Dr. Zhivago* is a work which stands in close relation
to Tolstoy's epic *War and Peace*. At the center of each work, and de-
termining its structure, is a violent historical event embracing the life
of Russian society. Both the war of 1812, in *War and Peace*, and the
revolution and civil war of 1917-21, in *Dr. Zhivago*, are viewed as
central events in a vast tidal movement of happenings the "causes"
of which cannot be ascertained in conventional historical terms.
"It's petty to rummage about for the causes of Cyclopean events,"
observes Zhivago in his prophetic speech at the duck dinner in
Moscow. "There aren't any."[2] Both Tolstoy and Pasternak depict
the individual as essentially powerless in the great tidal movements
of history. But in *War and Peace* this powerlessness of the individual
is tragic only when it is unrecognized or denied by the individual;
in *Dr. Zhivago* it is unconditionally tragic.

The different historical character of the events of 1812 and 1917
gives shape to Tolstoy and Pasternak's radically different approach to
the individual and to the individual's relation to history and people.
In his subscription prospectus to his journal *Time* (*Vremya*), 1860,
Dostoevsky called attention to the essentially centripetal character
of the war of 1812. "After the reform [of Peter the Great] there was
only one single case of unity between it [the people] and us, the

---

[1] For a discussion of the relation of *Doctor Zhivago* to Chekhov and Ibsen, see my
essay, "The Symbol of the Wild Duck in *Dr. Zhivago*," *Comparative Literature*, Vol.
XV, no. 1 (Winter, 1963), pp. 39-45.

[2] All citations are from the Russian edition published in the United States; Boris
Pasternak, *Doktor Zhivago* (Ann Arbor: The University of Michigan Press, 1958).

educated class—[the patriotic war of] 1812, and we saw how the people gave account of themselves."[3] In *War and Peace* Tolstoy apprehended 1812 in just this way; he emphasizes the national-patriotic character of the war and places in the forefront of his work, as the embodiment of his moral values, not the individual "hero," but the Russian people. War is intrinsically evil in Tolstoy's view, but it provides a corrective to the individual's egoistic strivings; through contact with the elemental-primal force of the people—its unpretentious patriotism, its instinctive self-sacrifice, its modest heroism —the individual is elevated, ennobled; the way is opened for moral-spiritual regeneration, for a reconciliation with one's own destiny, with nature, with life. "The great thing is to live in harmony," remarks the peasant Platon Karataev, whom Tolstoy in *War and Peace* calls an "unfathomable, rounded, eternal personification of the spirit of simplicity and truth...of everything Russian, kindly and round." Tolstoy's protagonists, Prince Andrey and Pierre Bezukhov, are continually upsetting the "harmony" of Karataev's universe. Yet the rebellious elements represented by both Andrey and Pierre are always defined in the magnetic field of 1812; the ideological center of this field is the people, its heroism, its moral superiority, its unassuming example.

The revolution of 1917, unlike the national war of 1812, released violently centrifugal forces which blew apart the entire structure of Russian society. Pasternak has depicted this explosion at the moment the parts of this once integral society are being scattered, but at a moment when the memories of the old world are still intact. Zhivago, in his impromptu address before his friends gathered at the duck dinner observes:

> I too think that Russia is fated to become the first socialist kingdom since the beginning of the world. When this comes to pass, it will stun us for a long time, and, when we come to our senses, we shall have lost half our memories forever. We shall have forgotten what came first and what followed, and we shall not be looking for explanations of the unprecedented events. The new order will surround us and be as natural as a forest on the horizon or clouds overhead. It will encircle us on all sides. There will be nothing else.   (Part VI, ch. 4)

The desolation caused by the exploding revolution is depicted in a figurative as well as literal sense in the "Conclusion" of the novel when, half stunned by his experiences, Zhivago works his way across

[3]Dostoevskii, *Stat'i* [Articles], *Polnoe sobranie khudozhestvennykh proizvedenii [Complete Works]* , XII (Moscow, 1930), 498.

an exhausted countryside. Pasternak carries his epic through World War II when the "action of the forces directly rooted in the nature of the upheaval ceased."

"This is the Last Judgment on earth, my good Sir," Strelnikov (Lara's husband) remarks to Zhivago, "a time for creatures from the Apocalypse with swords, for winged beasts, and not for fully sympathetic and loyal doctors." The revolution is a judgment of an entire way of life. "The doctor saw life without illusions. The fact that it was under sentence stared him in the face. He regarded himself and his milieu as doomed. ... He realized that he was a pigmy before the monstrous machine of the future."

When Zhivago complains that "history hasn't consulted me," that "I have to put up with whatever happens, so why shouldn't I ignore facts"—he is affirming more than his helplessness; he is acknowledging the complete divergence of his personal interests and those of the Revolution; the machine of history is out of control and is rushing blindly into the future. "Is there a reality in Russia today?" Zhivago asks his father-in-law. "In my opinion, it has been so frightened that it is in hiding."

Zhivago increasingly withdraws into himself and into the circle of his family existence. Formerly, he observes, he used to love "everybody," but now "I love only you and father." The search for the family, the hearth, the vanished center, is a constant one in *Doctor Zhivago*. "What could be worth more than peaceful family life and work?" Zhivago asks. "The rest isn't in our hands." But even the family is not in Zhivago's hands. The war broke down not only trains and food supplies, but also the "foundations of family life, the moral structure of consciousness."

War and Peace concludes on a note of family happiness; the world of the Zhivago comes to an end on a poignant note of awareness that this happiness is a chimera. "We keep bustling about hastily so as not to see that this isn't life, but a stage set, that it isn't real, only 'pretend,' as children say," Lara remarks ("Return to Varykino"). The joy of Varykino is a tragic one; like Ivan Karamazov's love for the "precious graveyard" of Europe, it is built on a love for that which is dying—an entire way of life, an entire world. "What disrupted your family life if you loved each other so much?" Zhivago asks Lara, who replies:

> Ah, how difficult it is to answer that. I'll tell you about it now. But how strange. How is it that I, a weak woman, should explain to you, such a wise person, what is happening now to life in general, to human

life in Russia, and why families get broken up, including yours and mine. Ah, as though it were a matter of people, of being alike or different in temperament, of loving or not loving. Everything that has been evolved, brought to working form, everything relating to normal everyday living, to the human abode and to order, all this has crumbled in the upheaval of all society and in its reconstruction. The whole human reality has been upturned and destroyed. All that remains is the isolated, alienated, unapplied strength of the naked soul stripped to the last shred; and nothing has changed for this soul, because at all times it has been cold, trembling and reaching out to its nearest neighbor, just as naked and lonely as itself. You and I are like Adam and Eve, the first two people on earth who at the beginning of the world had nothing to hide, and we are now at the end of it, just as naked and homeless. And we are the last remembrance of all that immeasurable greatness which has been created in the world in all the thousands of years before them and us, and it is in the memory of those vanished marvels that we breathe and love and weep, hold one another and cling to one another. (Part XIII, ch. 13.)

The world that is mourned in this *Liebestod* of the Russian intelligentsia, finds its most lofty expression in Russian literature in Tolstoy's *War and Peace.* "We go on endlessly rereading *War and Peace*, [Pushkin's] *Eugene Onegin* and all the poems," Zhivago writes in his notebook during his initial stay in Varykino—that final effort of the Zhivago family to reestablish the pattern of its home life. Zhivago finds in Pushkin's writings a "paean to honest labor, duty, the habits of everyday life!" He cites approvingly lines from Pushkin's "Travels of Onegin": "My ideal now is a housewife/ My desires—tranquility/ And a big bowl of cabbage soup."

Not suprisingly does the Zhivago family steep itself in *War and Peace* and *Eugene Onegin*. For the world of these works—with its moral rectitude, its sancitity of marriage and the hearth, its established customs and traditions—is the lost center of *Doctor Zhivago*. Of this world, of its unique and almost anomalous position in Russian life, Dostoevsky speaks at the conclusion of his novel, *The Raw Youth*. The mentor of Arkady Dolgoruky writes to his former pupil:

> Pushkin selected the subjects for his future novels from the "traditions of a Russian family", and, believe me, everything beautiful we have had so far is to be found therein. At least everything that has been brought to some sort of perfection. I don't say this because I am accepting unconditionally the truth and justness of this beauty; but here, for example, there were completely worked out forms of honor and duty which, except in the nobility, have never existed in Russia even

in the most rudimentary shape. I speak as a calm man seeking calm. Whether that honor was a good thing, and whether that duty was a true one, is a secondary question; but what is more important to me is precisely the finality of these forms and the existence of at least some sort of order, and not prescribed, but at last developed from within. Good heavens, what really matters most of all is to have at last any sort of order of our own! All hopes for the future and, so to speak, tranquillity of outlook, lie in our having something at last built up, instead of this everlasting destruction, instead of chips flying in all directions, instead of rubbish and disorder which has led to nothing for two hundred years.   (Part III, ch. xiii)

The problem of Russian culture posed here is the dichotomy between the perfect "forms," "beauty," and "order" created by the educated classes, and the formlessness and "disorder" surging below. "There are no foundations to our society," Dostoevsky wrote in some notes to *The Raw Youth*, "no principles of conduct that have been lived through, because there have been none in *life* even. A colossal eruption and all is crumbling, falling, being negated, as though it had not even existed. And not only externally, as in the West, but *internally, morally.*"

The crisis of Russian culture in *Doctor Zhivago*—of "everything that has been evolved, brought to working form, everything relating to normal everyday living, to the human abode and to order"—is depicted against a background of chaos and disorder rising from below. The confrontation of the eloquent Senator's son Ginz with the soldier—deserters in *Doctor Zhivago* is not only a meeting of two revolutions—the bourgeois-democratic February Revolution and the October Bolshevik Revolution—but a symbolic encounter between two Russias: the one taking its provenience in the nineteenth century "nests of gentlefolk," the world of the Rostov family *(War and Peace)* with its recognized forms of honor, duty, and virtue, and the other in the inchoate and centrifugal material of the Russian masses. The ominous, sullen challenge of these masses is hinted at in *War and Peace* when the serfs on Princess Marya Bolkonskaya's estate at Bogucharovo—at the time the French armies were moving on Moscow—refuse to assist in her departure. The obdurate peasants are mastered single-handedly by the young Count Nikolay Rostov, who declined to await armed help in bringing the peasants to order. The little fires of Bogucharovo became the conflagration of 1917. The place of the masterful Nikolay Rostov is filled by his modern counterpart Ginz, with his "sense of honor cultivated through generations, a city-bred sense of honor, imbued with a sense of self-sacrifice, and out of place here," with his foolhardy bravery, his eloquent phrases, his class-rooted underevaluation of the people. "The people, he says, are like children, and so forth, and he thinks that all this is a child's game. Galyullin entreats with him: don't arouse the beast, he says, leave him to us."

Ginz is killed when he singlehandedly tries to deal with the soldier-deserters; he is killed by Pamfil Palykh, a soldier of the tsarist army "with an inborn class instinct." This soldier, who is later disclosed as a cruel degenerate ("The Forest Brotherhood"), is characterized as a type by Pasternak:

> In those first days [of the revolution]people like the soldier Pamfil Palykh were regarded as rare finds by ecstatic left-wing intellectuals and were greatly valued; without any encouragement these people hated with a terrible and savage hatred intellectuals, gentry, and officers. Their inhumanity seemed a miracle of class consciousness, their barbarity a model of proletarian firmness and revolutionary instinct. Such was the fame that Pamfil had acquired. He was held in the highest esteem by the partisan chiefs and Party leaders.
>
> (Part XI, ch. 9.)

The tragically absurd Ginz and the wild "beast" Pamfil: it is between these two extreme antitheses that Pasternak places his hero Zhivago. Zhivago is of course sympathetic with Ginz, as he is later with the cadets at whom he must fire in the forest skirmish—those "heroically dying children" who belonged to families "close to him in spirit, education, moral make-up and values." But Pasternak underlines their fatal eloquence, their false adherence to form and divorce from realities. The Russian intellectual, in Pasternak's portrayal, is incapable of playing any vital role in the Revolution. "Make it snappy, Yura! Put on your coat and let's go," cries Zhivago's uncle, Nikolay Nikolaevich, bursting in to announce the street fighting on the eve of the October seizure of power. "'You've got to see it. This is history. This happens but once in a life-time.' But he himself went on talking for a couple of hours."

But it is the people—the "beast"—that has risen to challenge the privileges of the ruling classes that causes Pasternak to recoil. Nowhere is Pasternak's rejection of Tolstoy's idealized image of the "people" more strongly felt than in those pages of *Doctor Zhivago* devoted to Zhivago's enforced stay with the partisans. The ordeal of Zhivago, his eighteen months' captivity, is a completely antipathetic experience; it could stand, in its essentials, in sharp polemical contrast to Pierre Bezukhov's experiences as a Russian prisoner of war during the French retreat. Pierre's experiences on the battlefield of Borodino fill him with an admiration for the soldiers and arouse in him a desire to "enter into this communal life completely, to become imbued with that which makes them what they are. But how cast off all this superfluous, devilish burden of my outer self?" The possibility is offered Pierre. His semidelirious experiences in deserted Moscow (when, in his desire to kill Napoleon and save the world from the "antichrist," he himself falls prey to Tolstoy's heresy of individualism) are followed by his experiences as a Russian prisoner of war. Here, enduring hardships with other Russians, Pierre meets Platon Karataev, who comes to embody for him the ideal in harmonious orientation to man's fate. Pierre "learned that just as there is no condition in the world in which man can be happy and completely free, so there is no condition in which he need be completely unhappy and lack freedom."

In contrast to Pierre, Zhivago sharply experiences his captivity (in which he actually enjoyed considerable freedom of movement) as "unfreedom"; far from entering into the communal life of the brotherhood and divesting himself of his "outer self," Zhivago retreats more deeply within himself in hostile recoil from the life around him. He finds no Karataev in the brotherhood to give meaning to his condition, to rationalize it. All that Zhivago has to console him are the maddening homilies and political pep talk of the dope-fiend leader of the partisans, Livery (Liberius), who imagines that Zhivago is depressed because of a lack of faith in the triumph of the Red forces. Livery finally drives Zhivago to exclaim with almost Dostoevskian "underground" malice:

> Try to understand, try to understand, once and for all, that all this means nothing to me. "Jupiter," "never panic," "whoever says A must say B," "the Moor has done his work, the Moor can go"—all these vulgar commonplaces, all these expressions mean nothing to me. I will say A but I won't say B—even if you break me up and pound me to pieces. I admit that you are the shining lights and liberators of Russia, that without you everything would be lost, sunk in misery and ignorance, and still I don't give a whit for you and spit on you, I don't like you, and may you all go to the devil.   (Part XI, ch. 5.)

Zhivago, who cannot kill the enemy cadets in whom he recognizes people like himself, is driven by Livery to murderous thoughts: "Oh, how I hate him! As God is my witness, I'll kill him some day.... Lord, Lord! And that loathesome, insensate animal is still orating and won't let up! Oh, some day I'll lose control of myself and kill him, I'll kill him."

The episode "The Forest Brotherhood," with its accent on civil war, the atrocities committed by both Reds and Whites, on the internal struggles and purges among the partisans, on the degenerates Pamfil Palykh and Livery, brings to a high point the impression of chaos and irrationality closing in on Zhivago. The isolation of Zhivago here, broken only by his escape to Yuryatin and then to Varykino for the last time with Lara, portends his final absolute isolation and destruction. To the rising chaos around him Zhivago opposes the perfectly developed forms of his culture—his poetry—in an effort to come to grips with this chaos, to divine its meaning, to define himself, Lara, Russia, life. His poetry enters the future as a force in the rebirth of Russia, but he himself perishes in his earthly alienation, unable to participate in the renewal that his poetry itself portends. Zhivago's mother is defined as a "gentle dreamer." The tragedy of Zhivago, though linked with the tragedy of the middle classes and the Russian intelligentsia, is essentially that of the dreamer, the poet whose world—for all his desire to participate in it as a "socially useful" being—was not so much the real world as the *forêt de symboles* of Baudelaire's poem. Lara, at the funeral of Zhivago, defines his relation, as well as her own, to the world:

> The riddle of life, the riddle of death, the enchantment of genius, the enchantment of unadorned beauty, this, if you please, this was ours. But petty world squabbles like reconstructing the earth, these things, no thank you, they are not for us.   (Part XV, ch. 16.)

If Zhivago, in Pasternak's conception, bears within him the seed of Russia's creative future, it is Lara, "charged...with all the imaginable femininity in the world," who is the maternal embodiment of Russian life in its ferment, the *Ewig-weibliche,* the Margaret of Pasternak's own *chorus mysticus* drawing forward his sinking hero, his abortive Faust, sustaining him in his last flowering.

Lara was the "indictment of the age," Strelnikov remarks; it is the wronged Lara that is identified with the revolution in all its aspects. The abyss into which Lara fears she is sinking, in the early days of her relationship with the corrupt lawyer Komarovsky, is the abyss of Russian life opened up by misery and oppression. It is symbolic that Lara succumbs to the assault of Komarovsky, that her "purity" is defiled and that she is subject to the mysterious "spell" of Komarovsky—confidante of Zhivago's father, the dissolute, guilt-ridden representative of old bourgeois Russia. "Now she has become his slave for life. How has he subjugated her?" Komarovsky—who lives in a part of Moscow that resembles St. Petersburg—never loses his power over the girl from Moscow.

Tolstoy's heroine, Natasha Rostova, this living Tolstoyan embodiment of instinctive, spontaneous Muscovite Russia, is also the object of a concerted assault by the Petersburg element in Russian life —by the Kuragins; she is also carried away into a "strange, senseless world...a world in which it was impossible to know what was good or bad." Natasha, falling in love with Anatole Kuragin, feels that he is her "master" and that she is his "slave, yes, his slave!... I told you, I have no will." But the assault of the Petersburg Kuragins on the Rostov family is turned back. This victory of the Rostovs— this preservation of the purity and honor of Natasha—is not an accidental element in *War and Peace*, but an integral part, on the ideological plane of Tolstoy's epic, of the victory of Russia in 1812. It is a reflection of the triumph of the primal Moscow element over Petersburg with its show and artificiality, of the Russian people over Napoleon. The preservation of the purity of Natasha is the prelude to that final triumph of the maternal element in the Epilogue—the family life of Natasha. The defiling of Lara's purity, on the other hand, portends the disintegration of the whole fabric of Russian life and of its central unit—the family. Lara, dominated by the child-hating Komarovsky, abandons Tanya, her daughter by Zhivago. It is significant that the area of Lara's greatest failure— the family and motherhood—should be the area of Natasha Rostova's greatest triumph.

"The whole development of the world tends to the importance of the individual," Kierkegaard wrote in his *Journal* in 1847; "that, and nothing else, is the principle of Christianity." The individual is at the center of Pasternak's universe, the humanism of the individual—in the sense that Kierkegaard understood it—as opposed to the benevolent humanism of an ideology, social system, state. The people, the masses, far from being a source of creativity to Kierkegaard's "individual," is a central antagonist of him. Kierkegaard wrote in his *Journal* in 1847:

> "The masses"; that is really the aim of the polemic. ... I wish to make people aware, so that they do not squander and dissipate their lives. ...I wish to make men aware of their own ruin. And if they will not listen to good then I will compel them through evil. Understand me, or at least do not misunderstand me. I do not mean that I am going to strike them (alas, one cannot strike the masses); I mean to make them strike me. And in that way I all the same compel them through evil. For if they once strike me they will be made aware of their position, and I shall have won an absolute victory.... The reformer who, as it is said, fights against a powerful man (a pope, an emperor, an in-

dividual man) must aim at bringing about the fall of the powerful; but the man who, with more justice, takes arms against the masses, from whom comes all corruption, must see to it that he himself falls.

Zhivago, like Kierkegaard's man who takes arms against the masses, is marked out for sacrifice; but here, in Pasternak's design, lies his paradoxical victory. "You are a mockery of that world," Komarovsky observes to Zhivago, "an offense to it." The remark, however, applies not so much to a wilful effort on Zhivago's part to mock communism, as to what Zhivago symbolizes in his inevitable choice of isolation, in his inability and unwillingness to come to terms with the revolutionary camp (or any camp), in his clear insistence on living out in his own person his conception of Christianity. The defeat of Zhivago—in the light of his own meditations and those of his uncle on Christianity—is for Pasternak a moral triumph; at the basis of this triumph lie the "chief components of modern man, without which he is unthinkable, namely, the idea of free personality and the idea of life as sacrifice."

"In life it is more necessary to lose than to gain," Pasternak observes in his autobiographical sketch *I Remember*. "A seed will germinate only if it dies." This idea is at the basis of Dostoevsky's *The Brothers Karamazov*. Dostoevsky took the epigraph for his novel from the Gospel of St. John: "Verily, verily, I say unto you, Except a corn of wheat fall into the ground and die, it abideth alone: but if it die it bringeth forth much fruit." The violent, earthly Karamazov force in Fyodor Karamazov plunges into the ground, but is reborn and redirected in Alyosha (Dmitry already at the end of his trial feels within him a "new man" and predicts that Ivan will "surpass us all"). Central to Dostoevsky's novel is the Russian philosopher Fyodorov's idea that the sons must resurrect the fathers.

A variation on this theme may be found in Alexander Blok's beautiful, though unfinished, poem "Retribution"; here, against the background of the late 1870's and the *mal de siécle* of the 1900's, the poet traces the degeneration and ultimate resurrection of a family line. In a preface to his poem, Blok wrote that he conceived it

in the form of concentric circles which grew narrower and narrower, until the smallest circle, compressed to its limit, begins again to live its own independent life, to break open and spread out against the surrounding milieu and, in its turn, to act upon the periphery. ... The theme consists in showing the development of the links of a unified chain making up a family line. Separate offspring of each generation develop to their appointed limit and then are swallowed up anew by the surrounding milieu; but in each offspring there ripens and is made something new and something more enduring, at the price of endless losses, personal tragedies, failures in life, falls, etc. ... There was a man—and then was not; there remains trashy, flabby flesh and a rotting little soul. But the seed is cast forth, and in the next youngling there grows something new, more stubborn and in the last youngling this new and stubborn thing begins, at last, tangibly to act upon the surrounding environment; in this way a generation, which has experienced the retribution of history, of milieu, of the epoch, begins in its turn to create retribution; the last youngling is already capable of snarling and giving forth leonine growls; he is ready to grasp with his little manly hand the wheel which moves the history of mankind. And perhaps he will in some way grasp at it. ... What more is there to say? I don't know. ... I can only say that this whole conception took shape under the pressure of a growing hatred in me for various theories of progress.[4]

Pasternak's *Doctor Zhivago,* of course, took shape under similar pressures of hatred for various "theories of progress." Blok's conception of his poem is suggestive of a basic creative idea underlying *Doctor Zhivago:* the portrayal of the Russian revolution—the painful drama of Russian progress—in terms of an organic life process in which continuity is not lost, but retranslated in new links of life. Yury Zhivago is at the center of Pasternak's work; but at its outermost limits—and these are the limits of the epoch depicted—are two other Zhivagos: Yury's father, on the one hand, and his daughter Tanya, on the other. In a religious-ethical sense, the dramas of these three generations constitute a single completed cycle—a cycle of sin, suffering, and redemption.

"Who is being buried?" asked the passers-by as they made their way for the funeral procession of Zhivago's mother. "Zhivago," they were told. The juxtaposition of the words "buried" and "Zhivago" (Zhivago is derived from the Russian word "to live"), and the ascendancy given to the latter, on the opening page of Pasternak's work, establishes the basic theme of death and resurrection in *Doctor Zhivago.*

The opening chapter "Five O'Clock Express" has three high points: The death of Zhivago's mother (the introduction of the theme of resurrection); the remarks of Yury's uncle Nikolay Nikolaevich defining love of one's neighbor, the idea of free personality, and the idea of sacrifice as basic attributes of modern man; and the

[4]Aleksandr Blok, *Sochineniya v dvukh tomakh* [Works in Two Volumes] (Moscow, 1955), I, 478-79.

suicide of Zhivago's father (the "Five O'Clock Express" is delayed when Yury's wealthy father throws himself off the train). Not the theme of resurrection, but that of damnation is hinted at in connection with the death of his father; old Zhivago in his life has negated the basic attributes of modern man: he has abandoned two families and devoted himself to the accumulation of material goods; and in the manner of his death he has violated the very spirit of life. "He can wait, he'll have to have patience," thinks young Zhivago as he postpones saying prayers for his father whose suicide takes place in the episode that follows.

Zhivago does not assume the financial burdens of his father, but he bears the stigma of the "bourgeois." He perishes, swallowed up by the surrounding Revolution. But the poetry of Zhivago survives, and it is Tanya—the fruit of Zhivago and Lara—who painfully inherits the new world. Tanya Bezocheredeva (Tanya Out-Of-Turn) is "fatherless"; a laundry girl, she is no longer linked to the bourgeois past; her "terrible story" links her with the rebirth of Russia, of which she is a part. "It's the same type, you see it all over Russia," Dudorov observes of Tanya's face. In Tanya the alienation of Yury Zhivago has been overcome in actuality; it is for Tanya that the "portents of freedom"—of which Pasternak speaks at the end of his work—should have most meaning. Pasternak's drama of death and resurrection completes its cycle in her.

The death of old Russia and the rebirth of a new Russia, in Pasternak's creative design, essentially are a part of the mystery of all death and birth—the mystery Zhivago contemplates after the birth of his son:

> Raised higher towards the ceiling than ordinary mortals usually are, Tonya lay in the cloud of her spent pain, as though smoking from exhaustion. Tonya dominated in the middle of the ward the way a barque might stand out in a bay—a barque that had just moored and been unloaded, after having completed a voyage across the sea of death to the continent of life with new souls immigrating from nobody knows where. One such soul had just been landed and the ship now lay at anchor, resting, its flanks unburdened, empty. The whole of her was resting—her overstrained masts, and planking, and her oblivion, her vanished memory of the place where she had been recently, the crossing and the landing. And since nobody had explored the country under whose flag she was registered, no one knew the language in which to speak to her.   (Part IV, ch. 5.)

In *Doctor Zhivago*, Pasternak completes the cycle of his own "Retribution," but without sacrificing what he feels to be the truth

of his generation, a truth that illuminates the tragedy of the prerevolutionary Russian intelligentsia.

To many of the young generation of Soviet Russians, brought up
on the heroes and martyrs of the revolution, seeking new heroes,
and emulating old ones, who can utter Gogol's mighty word "Forward!" Zhivago indeed may seem an incomprehensible, if not completely alien figure as he stands alone in the fiery twilight of his
generation. To others of the young generation the word "hero"
will have a more tragic ring. And they may yet recall the poet Blok
who observed in his poem "Retribution" of the gentry family that
experienced woe from both people and tsar:

> All this may seem
> Ridiculous and old-fashioned to us,
> But really, only a boor
> Can mock Russian life.
> It is always between two fires,
> Not everyone can become a hero,
> And the best poeple—we will not conceal it—
> Are often impotent before it
> So unexpectedly severe it is,
> And full of eternal changes;
> Like a spring river it
> Suddenly is ready to move,
> To pile up floes of ice
> And in its path to crush
> The guilty, as well as the innocent,
> Those without rank, as well as those with rank.[5]

---

[5]*Ibid.*, I. 493-94.

The Poems of *Doctor Zhivago*

by Dimitri Obolensky

> It is more important in life to lose than to acquire. Unless the seed dies it bears no fruit. PASTERNAK[1]

The poems factitiously ascribed to Yury Zhivago constitute the seventeenth, and last, chapter of Pasternak's novel *Doctor Zhivago*.[2] Their relevance to the plot of the novel and to its hero's personality is repeatedly stressed by the author: we are told that Zhivago, already in his student days, wrote poetry distinguished by "vigour and originality."[3] Much later, during the last days of his life with Lara at Varykino, he is shown composing several of the actual poems printed in the last chapter of the novel.[4] After his parting from Lara, he wrote poetry inspired by her.[5] And after Zhivago's return to Moscow in 1922, his poems were privately printed and sold in the bookshops of the city.[6] The purpose of this essay is to demonstrate and explain the connection between "the poems of Yury Zhivago" and the rest of the novel. It will, in particular, be suggested that the three basic themes of this

"The Poems of Doctor Zhivago" by Dimitri Obolensky. Reprinted from *Slavonic and East European Review*, 40, no. 94 (June 1961), 123-35, by permission of the author and Cambridge University Press.

[1]*An Essay in Autobiography,* London, 1959, p. 85.

[2]This numeration shows that the poems should be regarded not as an appendix to, but as an integral part of the novel. In the English translation of *Doctor Zhivago* (by Max Hayward and Manya Harari, London, 1958) the poems are printed separately at the end, outside the numbered chapters. The correct numeration—and the essential link between the poems and the rest of the book—are preserved in the French translation of the novel (Paris, 1958). Pasternak himself has emphasized this link by describing *Doctor Zhivago* as "a novel in prose with a section in verse" *(An Essay in Autobiography,* p. 119).

[3]*Doctor Zhivago* (Ann Arbor, Mich.: University of Michigan Press, 1959), p. 66; English translation, p. 68—The Russian original and the English translation will subsequently be referred to as *D.Zh.* and *E.T.* respectively.

[4]*D.Zh.,* pp. 447-53; *E.T.,* pp. 391-5.

[5]*D.Zh.,* p. 464-5; *E.T.,* p. 405-6.

[6]*D.Zh.,* p. 486; *E.T.,* p. 424.

sequence of poems — nature, love, and the author's views on the meaning and purpose of life — occupy an equally central position in the book as a whole; that the themes of nature and of human love are treated in these poems in conformity with a poetic outlook which has always been typical of Pasternak's work; and that the author's reflections on the fundamental problems of human existence, which are scattered throughout the novel and often woven into its very texture, are clarified and completed in this cycle of twenty-five poems.

The treatment of nature in these poems is a counterpart of Pasternak's conception of the town as the symbol of the life and destiny of modern man. His use of urban scenery and of imagery derived from urban life is a feature often encountered in his poetry, and one which stems in part from his early association with the Russian Futurist movement. In the same vein Zhivago, rejecting "pastoral simplicity in art" as a form of literary fraud, states his belief that "the living language of our time is urban."[7] In *Doctor Zhivago* the modern town is not only a storehouse of imagery, but a basic theme: "the incessant, uninterrupted rustle and movement of the town outside our doors and windows is a huge, immeasurable overture to life for each of us."[8] And the city of Moscow, whose agony in 1917 filled Yury Zhivago with such pity, is termed in the epilogue of the novel "the principal heroine of the long tale."[9] Several of Zhivago's poems have the life of a modern town as their background. In a symbolical sense, this, in Pasternak's own view, may be said of "Hamlet," the opening, and in some respects the key-poem, of the sequence.[10] "Summer in the Town" evokes a typically Pasternakian picture of the morning heat drying the puddles in the streets after the night rain. In "White Night" the poet sketches the wide panorama of St. Petersburg viewed from the top of a "skyscraper"; but in this poem

[7] *D.Zh.*, p. 500; *E.T.*, p. 436.
[8] *D.Zh.*, p. 501; *E.T.*, p. 436.
[9] *D.Zh.*, p. 530, cf. *E.T.*, p. 463.
[10] *D.Zh.*, p. 501; *E.T.*, pp. 436-7. The connection between the poem "Hamlet" and the modern town, hinted at in the novel, appears somewhat obscure. It may, however, become clearer if it is realized that the poem refers to Hamlet's soliloquy "To be, or not to be," and that this soliloquy was interpreted by Pasternak in these terms: "The bitter and disorderly beauty of the monologue in which Hamlet's perplexities crowd and overtake each other and remain unsolved recalls the sudden chords, abruptly cut off, tried out on the organ before the opening of a requiem." ("Translating Shakespeare," in B. Pasternak, *I Remember*, p. 131; the original in *Literaturnaya Moskva*, I, Moscow, 1956). These words strikingly recall the "huge, immeasurable overture to life for each of us" which in *Doctor Zhivago* is represented by the modern town.

the urban vistas significantly shade off into a distant rural landscape: "out there, far off" (*vdali*) extends the countryside, with its forests and nightingales; and this relation between town and country is expressed more clearly still in the poem "The Earth": here the streets and the houses of Moscow in the spring are contrasted with the distant horizon (*dal'*) "weeping in mist" and with the bitter-smelling dung of the countryside; and the poet's task is to bridge the gap between town and country, so that "beyond the limits of the town the earth should not feel lonely." Few writers have been as successful as Pasternak in bridging this gap: he is at once an urban poet, with a profound awareness of the part played by the town in shaping the consciousness and inspiring the art of modern man, and a highly accomplished poet of nature, who in one of his last poems could justly write of himself: 'I have made the whole world weep over the beauty of my native land.'[11] Pasternak's lyric poetry abounds in descriptions of the Russian countryside, marvellously evocative and exciting, in which nature is generally depicted in a state of movement and flux. Spring, which reveals the creative power latent in the universe, is understandably one of his favorite themes; and it is not suprising to find that most of the poems of the *Zhivago* cycle which describe nature are concerned with spring: these include "March," "In Holy Week," "White Night," and "Spring Floods." In the last two the advent of spring is heralded by the "thundering" and "raging" of a nightingale's song. This singing is often in Pasternak's poetry the expression of the ecstatic beauty and creative power of life: in a poem written in 1917 he defined poetry as "a duel of two nightingales." In the poem "Spring Floods" the nightingale conjures up the image of Nightingale the Robber, a fantastic monster, half bird, half man, whose whistle kills human beings and makes the earth tremble, and the same creature is associated with the nightingale in an earlier part of the novel.[12] Nature in Pasternak's poetry frequently participates in man's inner life: this is especially true of flowers and trees, which can associate themselves even with his spiritual acts: in the poem "In Holy Week" the trees, standing "like worshippers at a service," take part in the ritual burial of Christ; similarly, when Zhivago's dead body is lying in its coffin, the flowers which fill the room make up for the absence of a religious ceremony by "taking the place of the singing and the psalms" and by "seeming to be accomplishing a ritual."[13] The poems of Yury Zhivago, no less than the novel as a whole, with its incom-

---

[11] "The Nobel Prize": *Poeziya (Izbrannoe)*, Frankfurt/ Main, 1960, p. 408.

[12] *D.Zh.*, p. 295, *E. T.*, p. 260.

[13] *D.Zh.*, pp. 504-5; *E.T.*, p. 440.

parable descriptions of the Russian countryside, show how successful the author has been in his attempt "to make sense of the earth's wild enchantment and to call each thing by its right name."[14]

The acuity of vision and passionate intensity which Pasternak has brought to his descriptions of nature appear likewise in his treatment of human love. *Doctor Zhivago* contains what is surely one of the most moving and profound accounts of the mutual love of a man and woman in contemporary literature; and it is not surprising to find this theme much in evidence in Zhivago's poems. Of particular significance is "Winter Night," remarkable for its combination of passion and restraint, for its musical texture — in which the dominant sound is the vowel *e* (e.g., *Svecha gorela na stole, svecha gorela*) — and for its close connection with the plot and the structure of the novel. The poem, which describes in impressionistic terms a lovers' meeting in a room at night, is dominated by the recurrent refrain "the candle burned on the table, the candle burned." This burning candle is one of the symbolical centers of meaning round which *Doctor Zhivago* is constructed; it is one of the book's focal points, at which the destinies of the characters mysteriously intersect. The flame of this candle is first seen by Zhivago when, at the age of eighteen, he is driving with his future wife through the streets of Moscow to a Christmas party. The candle is burning in a room in which Lara, who will become the love of his life, is sitting with her future husband. At that moment the poem which foreboded his destiny began to form in his mind; but he got no further than the words, "the candle burned on the table, the candle burned."[15] It was some ten years later, during his life with Lara at Varykino, that the final version of the poem came to him.[16] And the fateful flame of that candle, with which Zhivago's destiny is so closely bound up, is evoked once again at the end of the novel: by an astonishing coincidence, Lara on her return to Moscow revisits the house she knew so well as a young girl, and finds Zhivago lying in his coffin in the very room where she had sat on the first Christmas night: she can remember nothing of that scene, except the burning candle.[17] That room in Moscow, with its "astonishing associations,"[18] is a striking example of those mysterious coincidences which abound in the novel, and which Pasternak deliberately uses to illustrate the impact of supernatural forces upon man's destiny

---

[14]*D.Zh.*, p. 76; *E.T.*, p. 76.
[15]*D.Zh.*, pp. 81-2; *E.T.*, p. 81.
[16]*D.Zh.*, p. 447; *E.T.*, p. 391.
[17]*D.Zh.*, p. 511; *E.T.*, p. 446.
[18]*D.Zh.*, p. 508; *E.T.*, p. 443.

on earth.[19] Speaking to Lara of his relationship with her husband, Zhivago quotes the words from *Romeo and Juliet*, "one writ with me in sour misfortune's book," which he renders somewhat freely as "we are in the same line on the book of Fate."[20] All those characters in the novel who were "written" in this book together with Zhivago—with the significant exception of his wife Tonya—find their way at different times to that room in Moscow where "the candle burned." The room is thus a fitting symbol of the "crossed destinies" evoked by the author in "Winter Night."

The same characteristic bend of passion and restraint appears in the other love poems of the cycle. In "Explanation" the author shows that love can be an uncontrollable and destructive force:

> Take your hand off my breast.
> We are high-tension cables.
> Look out, or unawares
> We shall again be thrown together.[21]

Yet the intensity of the poet's passion is always controlled by a deep-seated reticence which prevents him from dwelling on the physical aspect of love. In "Winter Night," for instance, a poem aglow with sexual passion, the poet's beloved is not even described: we are merely given a glimpse of her hands, her feet, her shoes, and her dress. In part, no doubt, this is a conscious device: Pasternak has often tended in his love poetry to present his lovers metonymically, in terms of separate parts of their bodies and, as it were, in pieces; in this way he achieves greater precision and concentration.[22] But his restraint in describing love scenes stems in the main from a specific attitude he adopts towards his art. In a particularly revealing passage of the

[19]This is clearly suggested by such expressions as "it's as if it were all predestined" (*D.Zh.*, p. 411; *E.T.*, p. 360); "a coincidence sent down from above" (*D.Zh.*, p. 509; cf. *E.T.*, pp. 443-4); "predestination" (*D.Zh.*, p. 511; cf. *E.T.*, p. 446).

[20]In all of the most penetrating essays on *Doctor Zhivago* yet written, Professor Stuart Hampshire suggests that the presence in the novel of signs of supernatural may be due to the influence of Shakespeare (*Encounter*, 62, London, November 1958, p. 4). [Professor Hampshire's essay is reprinted in this volume.]

[21][This, and the subsequent translations of the Zhivago poems cited here were provided by the author in the footnotes, (In the text of "The Poems of Doctor Zhivago" as it appears in *Slavonic and East European Review* all the citations are in Russian.)—Ed.]

[22]This has been shown by N. A. Nilsson to be the case in Pasternak's early poem "Oars at Rest": "Life as Ecstasy and Sacrifice" [which is reprinted in this volume] (*Scando-Slavica*, 5, Copenhagen, 1959, pp. 180-3). The same may be said of "Do not touch," another poem written by Pasternak in 1917.

novel he describes Zhivago's attempts to write about Lara after their separation:

> The reason for this correcting and rewriting was his search for strength and exactness of expression, but it also corresponded to the promptings of an inward reticence which forbade him to expose his personal experiences and the real events in his past with too much freedom. ... As a result, the steaming heat of reality was driven out of his poems and so far from their becoming morbid and devitalized, there appeared in them a broad peace of reconciliation which lifted the particular to the level of the universal and accessible to all.[23]

Union and separation are the principal themes of the love story related in the novel. Zhivago and Lara are several times brought together, and parted, by circumstances outside their control. And the highest and most intense phrase of their love—their last days together at Varykino—is immediately followed by their final separation, which is seen to be the result both of the tragic upheaval of their native land and of Zhivago's deliberate will. Union and separation are likewise the two poles of Zhivago's love poetry. In "Autumn" the two lovers, despite their awareness of the fact that their love is a disintegrating force which will end by destroying them, are irresistibly drawn together. In "Explanation," on the other hand, the violent attraction and the most religious reverence which the poet feels for his beloved are eclipsed in the long run by the even stronger force that pulls them apart—"the passion to break away." "Parting" describes the feelings and behavior of a man, left alone after the departure of the woman he loves, as he returns to the house where they had lived together. The poem bears a striking resemblance to the scene in which Zhivago re-enters the house at Varykino after Lara has left him for ever. We see the same picture of the disorder created by her sudden departure, the same poignantly familiar household objects that remind him of her recent presence and cause him to break down in a fit of weeping; and in both cases the memory of his beloved brings up in the man's mind a picture of the waves of the sea, breaking on the shore; this image dominates Zhivago's thoughts of the absent Lara: "This is how I'll trace your image. I'll trace it on paper as the sea, after a fearful storm has churned it up to

---

[23]*D.Zh.*, p. 465' *E.T.*, p. 405. This reticence of Pasternak, part natural and part contrived, has been well described by Victor Zorza: "[Pasternak] manages to record the Revolution without once describing any of its major actions, just as he manages to weave into it the story of a most passionate love between a man and a woman, with hardly the mention of a caress between them." (*The Manchester Guardian*, 4 September 1958.)

its foundations, leaves the traces of the strongest, furthest-reaching wave on the shore. ...This is how you were cast up in my life, my love, my pride, this is how I'll write of you."[24] And the same image appears in the poem:

> She was as near and dear to him
> In every feature
> As the shores are close to the sea
> In every breaker.[25]

The frightening awareness that human love can be a powerfully destructive force is combined in Zhivago's poetry with admiration for the loved one, which becomes at times a quasi-religious reverence. In "August," a strangely prophetic poem in which the author dreams that he is dead and that his beloved is making her way through a wood to a country cemetery to attend his funeral, she appears as a heroine of a great spiritual battle: the poet addresses her as "a woman who hurls a challenge to the abyss of humiliations," and he exclaims: "I am your battle-field." This admiration is balanced, in Zhivago's love poetry, by a profound pity for the woman he loves. This feeling is poignantly expressed in the poem "Meeting"; and it is always present in Zhivago's love for Lara. She arouses pity in him on the first two occasions on which he sees her—when she appears to him helplessly dominated by her evil genius Komarovsky,[26] and again when she unsuccessfuly tries to shoot the latter.[27] Much later, during their last days together at Varykino, Zhivago, recalling the former incident, tells Lara that he fell in love with her on that occasion and that his love for her was already then imbued with an overwhelming pity.[28]

Another poem, which undoubtedly refers to Lara, provides by its allegorical significance a connecting link between Zhivago's love poetry and Pasternak's philosophy of life. Entitled "A Fairy Tale" (*Skazka*), it tells a story of a horseman of ancient times, riding to battle across the steppe; hearing a distant cry for help, he makes his way through a forest and encounters a dragon coiled round a captive maiden, who has been surrendered to the monster as tribute by the local people. The horseman raises his eyes to heaven in silent prayer and does battle with the dragon. The nameless horseman is St. George,

[24]*D.Zh.*, p. 464; *E.T.*, pp. 404-5.
[25]*D.Zh.*, p. 551; *E.T.*, p. 489.
[26]*D.Zh.*, pp. 61-2; *E.T.*, p. 64.
[27]*D.Zh.*, pp. 85-6; *E.T.*, pp. 84-5.
[28]*D.Zh.*, p. 437; *E.T.*, pp. 382-3.

as the author himself explains in a passage of the novel which describes how Zhivago wrote this poem.[29] The story is clearly inspired by the oral religious poems of medieval Russia. The setting of this poem, part medieval, part legendary, is suggested by several archaic terms in the first few stanzas, by its heroic atmosphere, and by its opening words: "in olden days, once upon a time, in a land of fairy-tale."[30] The medieval poems about St. George, highly popular in Russia, exist in two main variants: the first describes the saint's sufferings at the hands of the Emperor Diocletian, his miraculous escape from prison and his journey through Holy Russia, where he seeks to establish the Christian faith; the second relates how he saved a young princess from the attacks of a dragon. "A Fairy Tale" combines features from both versions; but the highly original conclusion of Zhivago's poem is Pasternak's own. He makes the curtain fall on the scene of battle between St. George and the dragon before the first blow is struck; when it rises again, centuries have passed, the dragon lies dead on the ground, and the human protagonists, the horseman and the maiden, are suspended between life and death: the former, knocked down in battle with the monster, is still unconscious, the maiden is in a trance. The issue of the battle for the maiden's salvation, which has lasted for centuries, is thus still in doubt:

> But their hearts are beating.
> Now he, now she
> Struggles to awake
> And falls back to sleep.

Thus does an ancient legend, itself a symbol of the fight between Christianity and paganism, turn into allegory. An allegory of what? The author himself raises the question in the poem: referring to the maiden, he asks: "Who is she? A princess? The daughter of the earth?" But the question remains unanswered, and we must conclude that Pasternak was loathe to give his poem any single, over-simplified interpretation.[31] In one sense, the maiden in the poem is undoubtedly Lara, and in at least one passage of the novel Zhivago imagines the

---

[29] *D.Zh.*, p. 452; *E.T.*, p. 395.

[30] The Old Church Slavonic "Vo vremya ono" has, moreover, strong ecclesiastical associations which underline the connection between the theme of the poem and the so-called spiritual verses. The expression "in a land of fairy-tale" seems to suggest, in the context of the novel, at once a fairy story and an allegory of reality.

[31] Notwithstanding the efforts of some critics, as ingenious as they are misguided, to discover in *Doctor Zhivago* a collection of hieroglyphic, though decipherable, riddles, it cannot be too often stressed that the characters and situations in the novel may be regarded as symbolic only in a deeper and more poetic sense of the word.

hostile forces which are conspiring to separate him from his beloved in the guise of "a dragon who...lusted after Lara."[32] But the captive maiden, on another plane, is surely to be equated with Russia.[33] To this double symbolism of the maiden corresponds a two-fold interpretation of the dragon, which may be identified both with Komarovsky, Lara's evil genius, who appears to Zhivago early in the novel to be holding her captive,[34] and with the forces of evil unleashed by the war and the revolution, which were devouring his native land. It is significant that Lara herself, speaking of these events to Zhivago, and using the archaic language of Russian heroic poetry, stated that it was then that injustice (*nepravda*) came into the land of Russia.[35]

It is however, in the figure of St. George, the horseman who battles with the dragon, that the symbolical significance of this poem can most clearly be seen. The ideals of heroism and sacrifice which he embodies link the theme of "A Fairy Tale" with that of "Hamlet," the opening, and the most strikingly original, poem of the cycle. In St. George, as in the actor who plays the part of Hamlet and who, coming out onto the stage, peers prophetically into the future, there is doubtless much of Zhivago himself.[36] The significance of the poem "Hamlet" becomes clearer in the light of Pasternak's interpretation of Shakespeare's tragedy. In his remarkable essay on the problems of translating Shakespeare, he wrote: "From the moment of the ghost's appearance, Hamlet gives up his will in order to "do the will of him that sent him." *Hamlet* is not a drama of weakness, but of duty and self-denial. ...Chance has allotted Hamlet the role of judge of his own time and servant of the future. *Hamlet* is the drama of a high destiny, of a life devoted and preordained to a heroic task."[37] This interpretation of Hamlet's character explains why the Hamlet of Pasternak's poem, in praying to his father that the cup might pass from him, speaks with the words of Christ at Gethsemane: for Hamlet, like Christ, has been sent by his Father, and both of them—together with the Poet who stands behind them—follow alone their path of sacrifice. The Poet, like they, surrounded by falsehood and

---

[32]*D.Zh.*, p. 451; *E.T.*, p. 394. In another passage a waterfall evokes the image "of the dragon...of these parts, who levied tribute and preyed upon the countryside" (*D.Zh.*, p. 243; *E.T.*, p. 215; cf. *D.Zh.*, pp. 466-7; *E.T.*, p. 407).

[33]*D.Zh.*, pp. 401-2; *E. T.*, pp. 351-2.

[34]*D.Zh.*, p. 62; *E.T.*, p. 64.

[35]*D.Zh.*, p. 414; *E.T.*, p. 363.

[36]It may be pointed out that Yury Zhivago's first name, is a Russian form of the name George.

[37]"Translating Shakespeare," *op.cit.*, pp. 130-1.

Pharisaism, must accept with dignity and humility the task for which he has been sent into the world: he must live his life obedient to his calling and, if necessary, offer it so that others may live by his poetry and his example.[38]

This view of the poet as a sacrificial figure exemplifies a fundamental belief of Pasternak, and one that is central to his novel as a whole and to the Zhivago poems in particular: the belief that suffering, voluntarily accepted on behalf of others, and the sacrificial surrender of self, are the true purpose of man's life on earth. In the poem "The Wedding Party" (*Svad'ba*) he writes:

> And life itself is only an instant,
> Only the dissolving
> Of ourselves in all others
> As though in gift to them.

And in "Daybreak" he says, referring to his fellow-men:

> I am conquered by them all
> And this is my only victory.

Here the sacrificial theme is given an explicitly Christian connotation: for the subject of this poem is the author's personal conversation to Christianity after an experience in which he is reborn to life and begins to see the surrounding world with new eyes.

The religious poems in *Doctor Zhivago* are notable for their concern with death and resurrection, for their approximation to the narrative of the Gospels, and for their connection with the liturgy of the Orthodox Church. Death and Resurrection are contrasted in these poems not metaphysically, but liturgically: the ontological gulf between them is viewed in terms of a liturgical time-sequence—the interval between the night of Good Friday, during which the Church takes part in the ritual burial of Christ, and Easter night. The poem "In Holy Week," which describes the Burial Service on Friday night, starts by suggesting that Christ's death and His Resurrection are separated by an immeasurable gulf:

> It is still the dark of night
> And still so early in the world
> ...And dawn and warmth
> Are a thousand years away.

Yet the gulf will be bridged in the liturgy of Easter night, for:

---

[38] See the excellent commentary on this poem by N. A. Nilsson: "Life as Ecstasy and Sacrifice."

> Death can be vanquished
> Through the travail of the Resurrection.

The same idea is expressed in the second of the two poems on Mary Magdalene, in which Mary herself bridges in her soul the gulf between the Crucifixion and the Resurrection by growing to understand how inadequate was her former, possessive and exclusive, love of Christ:

> But such three days will pass
> And they will push me down into such emptiness
> That in that fearful interval
> I shall grow up to the Resurrection.

The key to the mystery of death's defeat by the Risen Christ is to be found in the events that took place between Good Friday and Easter night: this idea, expressed in the poems "In Holy Week" and "Mary Magdalene," is touched upon in an important passage of the novel, in which Zhivago, plunged in a delirium induced by typhus, dreams that he is writing a poem:

> The subject of his poem was neither the entombment, nor the resurrection but the days between. ... Near him, touching him, were hell, corruption, dissolution, death; yet equally near him were the spring and Mary Magdalene and life.—And it was time to awake. Time to awake and to get up. Time to arise, time for the resurrection.[39]

The themes of death and resurrection recur in most of the religious poems of the Zhivago cycle. The majority are concerned with the events of Holy Week immediately preceding Christ's Passion. A Notable exception is "The Christmas Star," which tells the story of the Nativity in a manner that combines the traits of a fairy-tale, of a child's memories of Christmas, and of a medieval Russian icon. The setting and the landscape, despite a half-hearted attempt at "local color"—camels and cedar trees are mentioned—deliberately evoke the Russian winter. Pasternak's intention was to draw the Nativity scene against the background of contemporary Russia. This is evident in an early passage of the novel, where the young Zhivago thinks of "painting a Russian version of a Dutch Adoration of the Magi with snow in it, and wolves and a dark fir forest."[40] Yet the timelessness of the scene is also suggested by the vision of humanity's future which

---

[39] *D.Zh.*, p. 211; *E.T.*, p. 188.
[40] *D.Zh.*, p. 81; *E.T.*, p. 81. In the same passage Zhivago conceives the thought that the poet Blok "was a manifestation of Christmas in the life and art of modern Russia."

the poem conjures up. Pasternak appears to have attached great importance to "The Christmas Star": it is alluded to twice in the course of the novel, both times in connection with the crucial poem "Winter Night," and is described as one of "the poems which he [Zhivago] remembered best and which had taken the most definite shape in his mind."[41] This subject had clearly been in Pasternak's mind for a long time: in his early autobiography, *Safe Conduct,* published in 1931, there is a passage that foreshadows "The Christmas Star": "There is a special Christmas-tree East, the East of the pre-Raphaelites. There is the presentation of the starry night according to the legend of the worship of the Magi. There is the age-old Christmas relief: the top of a gilded walnut sprinkled with blue candle wax."[42]

The cycle of poems about Christ's Passion opened with "The Miracle," which relates the episode of the barren fig-tree, commemorated in the Orthodox Church on Monday of Holy Week; this is followed by "The Earth," whose last stanza contains a veiled though unmistakable allusion to the Last Supper:

> This is why in early spring
> My friends and I gather together,
> And our evenings are farewells
> And our parties are testaments,
> So that the secret stream of suffering
> May warm the cold of life.

The next poem, "Evil Days," covers the first four days of Holy Week, from the entry into Jerusalem to Christ's appearance before His judges. The two following poems, dealing with Mary Magdalene, identify her with the woman who poured precious ointment upon Christ's head in the house of Simon the leper. This event, commemorated in the liturgy of the Wednesday of Holy Week, inspired one of the famous hymns of the Orthodox Church, composed by the ninth century Byzantine poetess Cassis, which is discussed and quoted in part in Pasternak's novel.[43] The cycle closes with the magnificent "Garden of Gethsemane," in which the author, quoting passages from the Gospels, relates the agony of Christ before the judgment and crucifixion, and affirms that His approaching death is the pledge of life eternal. And in the final stanzas of this poem Pasternak, rein-

---

[41]*D.Zh.*, pp. 81-2, 447; *E.T.*, pp. 81, 391.

[42]*Okhrannaya gramota*, B. Pasternak, *Sochineniya*, v. II, p. 255; Engl. Transl.: *Safe Conduct* in B. Pasternak, *Prose and Poems*, ed. by S. Schimanski, London, 1959, p. 77.

[43]*D.Zh.*, pp. 424-5; *E.T.*, pp. 371-2.

terpreting the Gospel story in the light of his own vision of world history, puts these words into Christ's mouth:

> You see, the course of ages is like a parable,
> And may burst into flames on the way.
> For the sake of the parable's awesome grandeur
> I shall descend into the tomb in voluntary suffering.
>
> I shall descend into the tomb and shall rise again on the third day,
> And, like rafts floated down a river,
> The centuries, like barges in a convoy,
> Shall come floating to Me out of the darkness, to be judged.

It is significant that this, the last poem of the Zhivago sequence, reiterates, on a grander scale and on a universal plane, the theme of "Hamlet," the opening poem of the cycle. Hamlet, who in his solitary agony prays to his Father that the cup may pass from him, is compared to Christ at Gethsemane. And Hamlet, it cannot be doubted, is Zhivago himself. Are we therefore to conclude that Zhivago in some symbolical sense represents Christ? Such a comparison, if it is made to depend on a moral assessment of Zhivago's character and behavior, may well appear absurd and even blasphemous. Zhivago, a vacillating man, capable of concealing the fact that he is a doctor in order to preserve his freedom of action, unfaithful to his wife and later guilty of bigamy, sinking during the last years of his life into a progressive moral and social degradation, scarcely cuts a heroic figure. And yet it cannot be denied that on the symbolical plane which underlies the human story of *Doctor Zhivago* his life of suffering and his death are consciously related by Pasternak to the themes of Calvary and the Resurrection. Curiously enough, the first critics to draw attention to the connection between Zhivago and Christ were a group of Soviet writers who in September 1956 wrote a letter to Pasternak explaining the reasons why the editorial board of the literary monthly *Novyy* Mir had decided not to publish *Doctor Zhivago*.[44] The connection between Zhivago and Christ, implicit throughout the novel, is, they argued, particularly apparent in the cycle of Zhivago's poems. They cited the words spoken by Christ to His disciples in the poem "The Garden of Gethsemane": "The Lord has granted you to live in my time," and compared them to Zhivago's unvoiced thoughts, addressed to his "dear friends," the faithful few who remained his disciples to the end: "The only bright and living

---

[44]This letter, signed by B. Agapov, B. Lavrenev, K. Fedin, K. Simonov, and A. Krivisky, was published in *Literaturnaya Gazeta* on 25 October 1958.

thing about you is that you lived at the same time as myself and knew me."[45]

Though there is some exaggeration in the claim of these Soviet critics that "Zhivago's entire path through life is consistently likened to "the Lord's Passion" in the Gospels, their arguments contain more than a grain of truth. Further evidence to support their view could be adduced from the passage of the poem "The Earth," cited above, in which Zhivago, is a context unmistakably alluding to the Last Supper, writes of his farewell meetings with his "friends." It seems likely that Pasternak's aim in *Doctor Zhivago* was not so much to portray his hero as a Christ-like figure, as to suggest that his life and death acquire their true significance when they are illumined by the reality of Christ's sacrificial death and His Resurrection.[46] Viewed in this light, the life and death of Yury Zhivago appear as a sacrifice, and his loss of everything he holds most dear, save only, at the end, his poetic vision and his spiritual integrity, is a freely accepted surrender of self. And this surrender is shown to be the pledge of his immortality. In an early passage of the novel, Zhivago, reflecting on the meaning of resurrection, suggests that the clearest proof of man's immortality is his capacity to live after his death in other people: "Your soul, your immortality, your life in others." To support his view, he refers to the Book of Revelation: "There will be no death, says St. John."[47] And in the closing lines of the Epilogue, which sums up the meaning of this long, tragic, but in the last resort optimistic book, we see that Zhivago's life has been of this kind, that he continues through his poetry to live in and through others, and that his path through life, though filled with human weakness and riddled with failure, has ended in triumph. More than twenty years after his death, two of his faithful friends, sitting by a window overlooking Moscow, were re-reading a book of his writings:

> They felt a peaceful joy for this holy city and for the whole land and for the survivors among those who had played a part in this story and for their children, and the silent music of happiness filled them and enveloped them and spread far and wide. And it seemed that the book in their hands knew what they were feeling and gave them its support and confirmation.[48]

[45] *D.Zh.*, p. 493; cf. *E.T.*, p. 430.

[46] On this point, see V. Frank, "Four-dimensional Realism" (*Mosty [Bridges]*, Munich, II, 1959, pp. 208-9).

[47] *D.Zh.*, pp. 68-9; *E.T.*, pp. 70-1.

[48] *D.Zh.*, p. 531; *E.T.*, p. 464.

Thus, in the last resort, the story of Yury Zhivago is illumined by the words and example of Christ: "Verily, verily, I say unto you, except a corn of wheat fall into the ground and die, it abideth alone: but if it die, it bringeth forth much fruit."

Pasternak's Last Poetry

by Angela Livingstone

Pasternak's last collected poems, written in the years 1955-59, bear the title *When the Weather Clears*—an optimistic title, with its "when" rather than "if." The poems in the volume* can be divided into two main groups (although some will belong to both groups): poems of personal confession and—the larger group—poems that describe some natural or urban scene. I will speak of the latter first.

In 1923 Marina Tsvetaeva wrote, of Pasternak's relation to *byt*—the common environment of everyday life—that it was to him as the earth is to the foot of someone walking: a moment's contact and a flying off.[1] This simple image sums up much of his earlier poetry. The Pasternak of thirty years later has a different relation to reality. Now all the ordinary things of daily living (the trains and houses, cupboards and Christmas trees, stamp collections, drainpipes), as well as the woods and steppe and lakes, seem the firm, accepted ground to stand upon. So a less imaginative view of walking is appropriate: every step of the walker comes down on the ground.

But he believes now in that ground in a way he did not before. He no longer feels that, as poet, he will transform the given world into something new and intense and extraordinary. Instead, he will go along with it, letting its whole presence work on him, until it yields its own splendid moment, its promise, its own transformation. He no longer seizes, but patiently contemplates, until similes arise as of themselves. Thus, the sunlight's striking through the leaves recalls stained glass windows in a cathedral, with their pictures of saints 'looking into eternity'; warmly, thankfully, he accepts the image, and says:

"Pasternak's Last Poetry" by Angela Livingstone. From *Meanyin Quarterly.* (December 1963), pp. 388-95. Reprinted by permission of the author.

*Poems 1955-1959 (When the Weather Clears). By Boris Pasternak. With English versions by Michael Harari (Collins and Harvill Press, London, 1960), pp. 128. See also Boris Pasternak, *Sochineniya* (Works), Vol. III, pp. 59-110 (University of Michigan Press, 1961).

[1] A rather free translation. See Marina Tsvetaeva: *Proza* (New York, 1953), p. 362.

> World's tabernacle, nature,
> I kneel through your long service.
> A trembling hugs me;
> I cry with happiness.[2]

This is the poem that gives its title to the volume. Many others have a similar pattern: a landscape is transformed by the weather or season so that the thought of some universal change or religious revelation is quickened in it. "Avenue of limes," through imagery evoking the interior of a cathedral, describes a dark walk of trees, blossoming into something marvellous and light. "Autumn forest," similarly constructed, has, not light dispersing darkness, but the wakeful communicative sound of cocks breaking through a sleepy silence: there is such a waking up that the forest itself, opening out, "sees new sights/ Fields, distance and blue skies." In "Ploughing" he asks what has happened to the usual landscape; for, transformed by the season and its work, it seems new, as if the limits were erased from earth and sky and—again an unemphasized suggestion of biblical imagery—as if mountains had been made level and the valley had been swept, and the trees (like people?) had stretched out to their full height. Everything has become clean and clear.

In other poems, though there may be no such definite idea of transfiguration, yet there are often images like that of the sun lighting up small mushrooms in the dark woods, or of the elk that for one precarious moment enchants the grove as it stands there and drinks; or again, the impossibility of walking in the Autumn forest without making a great clatter of leaves "so that everyone knows,"—images which suggest that clarity, meaning, beauty are constantly being created and discovered. Frequent metaphors of book and speech and language add the idea that this is something readable, to be interpreted.

Pasternak does not exactly interpret anything. At his most explicit, he merely says that a better future is coming. In two or three poems he describes a sense of seeing the future. For instance, when the bare trees make the forest seem opened up and spacious, the poet feels he is looking right through time, sees what is to come and rejoices in its certainty and safety ("Fulfilment," "Round the Turning"). And again, in "After the Storm" "everything is alive with the change of weather" and "memories of half a century recede with the passing storm...It is time to give way to the future."

[2]Translations...from *When the Weather Clears*...are partly mine, partly adaptations of Manya Harari's. They do not pretent to convey more than the literal meaning. [See *note on page 166 for their source in the present volume.—Ed.]

The epilogue of the long poem "Bacchanalia," which is seemingly about Pasternak himself, reaffirms the theme of the clarity and purity that must follow the days of confusion and strain. But there sounds also a note of sadness or weakness, as though the poet is remembering that he himself is at an end. It is true that after the Bacchanalia flowers will shed their sweetness from a vase; after the heartless party the plates are washed and everything is forgotten. But the lonely man who couldn't get intoxicated and could only find truth when he recognized the tradition of sacrifice still enacted in "Maria Stuart" and could only find happiness at moments with another isolated person, will also be forgotten and left in the past.

However, Pasternak is sure that he will come into his own for, like Maria Stuart and like the actress who represented her, he has played not to his own age but "to the centuries." The theme of the artist's fame—that he cannot have it in his life and should not seek it (he must hide away, work in secret, be unknown) but that if he works for eternity it will be his (and therefore, in a sense, already is)—this theme, which is thus also that of sacrifice and of faith, runs through much of the poetry in previous volumes, and also through the second group of poems in *When the Weather Clears*.

These poems contain certain conclusions about life and show a final attitude of simple-hearted love and acceptance, as well as a resolution to keep going to the end, "to be alive, only alive, only alive to the end." On the whole they partake of the tone of adopted commonsense and decision, of self-confidence mixed with careful understatement, which is heard in the opening stanza of the poem "Bread":

> With half a century to pile,
>> Unwritten, your conclusions,
>>> By now, if you're not a halfwit,
> You should have lost a few illusions,

It seems Pasternak is determined to be glad, grateful, responsive, and to work on with faith; but—and this is my main point—the poems are often unsatisfying because the determination seems to exceed the force of his feeling about these things. Addressing himself, with something like Chekhov's "one must drill oneself" in mind, he repeats very simple injunctions and morals, such as:

> ...Living a life and not a lie.

or:

> Work; watch;
> Don't waver; work.

or again:

> [You] Grasped the pleasure of study,
> The laws and secrets of success,
> The curse of idleness, the heroism,
> Needed for happiness;

Behind the bright faith lies a dull effort, which is sad, and all the more sad because it is not admitted as sadness. Pasternak does not have a tragic view of life, and he even seems to be carefully avoiding such a view. Part of his insistence on simplicity is the insistence on optimism. He resolutely praises and thanks wherever he can. Just as, in an earlier volume, he says "blagodarstvuyte" (thank you) to nature for being so beautiful, here he says "spasibo" (thank you) to women for having meant much in his life; he writes gratefully of Blok for having been what he was; and he thanks all the people who have written him letters in his time of trouble. If he finds himself risking a tone of despair or regret he immediately overcomes it and turns the poem's course back to the affirmative. Thus "Soul," which is a poem of mourning for friends who have suffered and died, is laconic, almost noncommittal, and ends with a pointing back to life and construction: for, having compared his soul to a vault, a sobbing lyre, a funeral urn, and a morgue, he finally compares it to a mill, that can change dung, lost experience, ruined lives, into the elements of new growth. Life must come forth out of the very substance of death—this is also a main motif in *Doctor Zhivago*. It is a moving poem, and yet it is not strong with the sense of the survived struggle, the endured despair, that its writer must have known. Two other poems about his own unhappy position fail to be moving at all, except if the reader deliberately relates them to the biographical circumstances, but then he is moved by the memory of the man, not by his poem. These are 'God's World' and—a poem not included in the London publication of *When the Weather Clears* but to be found in the Complete Works—"The Nobel Prize." The sadness in the first poem tries to be humorous and succeeds in being trivial. In the second a bewildered grief is expressed...slackly, and it is likewise subordinated to what is here a disturbingly vague faith in a good future:

> Yet, though almost at the grave,
> I believe a time will come
> When the force of malice and meanness
> Will be conquered by the good.

In spite of this example, Pasternak's faith in the possibility of change, his images of freshness and illumination—these are what is

most impressive in the present volume; but this invites comparison
with a similar faith and similar language in the work of his youth,
and if we make this comparison we shall find that the later work
(i.e. both groups of poems I have distinguished) is weaker. Though
Pasternak himself might reject tragedy (to see himself tragically may
well be for him part of the romantic exaltation of the "life of the
poet" which he renounced when he met Mayakovsky), yet something tragic seems to have happened to him as a poet.

His faith in the future does reasonably follow from ideas latent
in his much earlier writings—it is in a way a development of the
same thing—but now the immediacy and the tension—the fight—
has gone out of it. It is more an expounded faith than an urgent
experience.

The poems of *My Sister, Life* (1917) implied a world constantly in
process, in movement; ceaselessly changing and developing. The
images were full of a dynamism and force, as though everything
were straining, rushing forward and colliding, leaning and imping-
ing, one thing on another, more powerfully than our ordinary sight
had supposed. Even leaves at a window did not merely grow there
but—

> There's a pressing and crowding of leaves at the window.

Dawn was not simply a change of light:

> Dawn, like a tick, bit into the bay.

The steppe itself changes, as a train passes through it:

> The steppe is crumbling between step and star[3]

It was as if the poet, unable to pause in his vigilance and with no op-
portunity for reflection, had to capture the essence of one after another unique and amazing image flung up by the continuous process
of change. If February came he straightaway had to answer:

> February! Get ink and weep!...

One sensed some living creative power—its robustness and strength
and pressure—working in nature and identically working in art.

In every moment there is new life: this was then a sensation, which
came upon him as if from outside, and each poem seemed the result
of an intellectual fight to control and form the jagged elements of
intense perceptions, with always a risk of incomprehensibility. But

[3]Adaptation from J. M. Cohen's translation.

now he is not overwhelmed, but more simply says: since something new is always coming, let us trust in the future. To support this trust, he notes all signs of hope and meaning in the world around him, to record them in a poetic form that is chiefly concerned to avoid extravagance. He even explains that he would like to write poetry now, not in the way he once recommended—as casually and generously as a garden scattering its colours of amber and lemon—but with a plan, laying out his verses like a planned garden in which lime-trees grow, one after the other, in rows. All is to be modest and regular.

Now this does describe the poems in the present volume. Instead of the old casual splendour, they do contain rows of rather general and simple abstractions. Abstract words, in the early verse, always dissolved immediately into particular images, but here they are ranged together without concrete detail. There are many lines of this sort that one would like to set against lines from his earlier poetry, to the advantage of the latter. In "After the Storm," for instance, which says that the artist washes all things clean and dyes them so that there come forth, in a transformed state,

> life, reality and past,

these words in their deliberately imprecise attempt to indicate everything at once, recall such an earlier use of the word "life" as:

> My sister is life and today in a flood
> She is shattered in spring rain over all...

The two abstractions in the line:

> In the forest is quietness, silence...

could be contrasted with [lines] from "The Weeping Garden" (1917), with its greater delicacy of alliteration then characteristic of Pasternak:

> The quiet insists. A clearing
> Waits in the distance, awestruck...

Or again, when reading the now typically summarizing lines:

> ...Among the birth,
> Sorrow and death that circle
> Their set ways round the earth.

one may well recall the description of an actual birth in "The Urals" (from *Above the Barriers*, 1917), of a definite grief—in 'The End' (from *My Sister, Life*), and of a particular death—'Death of the Poet' (from *Second Birth*, 1932).

Pasternak stands at a greater distance from the world than before; and the chief stylistic effect (or means) of this distance is, besides the use of abstractions, the device of listing, or enumeration. Nouns are put side by side, their connotations cut short by the comma, and offered to the reader in a kind of silence. The first poem of the volume consists very largely of lists, such as "meadows, sedge and harvest,/ peals of the storm," or "the miracle/ of farms, parks, groves and graves." The unrhetorical, harmonious addition of word to word seems to indicate—without evoking—a bigger harmony that the poems will not deal with; and often it is an attempt to give discreet, unexaggerated praise to all the things of the earth, to get everything in that is worthy, to leave nothing out.

> Road and milestones.
> Trees and ditches.
> We shuffle away
> To look for mushrooms,

But there are also instances where the lists produce no other effect than that of a rather cautious flinging wide of arms and a calling out: look at all the things there are, for all are included and all are good! This thankful all-comprehension is often monotonous and unimaginative as in the poem "In Hospital," where an injured man, in emphatically commonplace and stupid circumstances, suddenly realizes he is to die. The poem's climax is:

> "How perfect are your ways,
> O Lord," he mused, "men, wall,
> Night city, death in the night
> And beds in hospital."

And at its worst it is almost meaningless, as in "God's World":

> Mountains and lakes, islands
> And continents unfold;
> How many reviews, discussions,
> Children, young people, old.

The use of enumeration is a weakness throughout the present volume. It appears as the result of a decision by a great poet of detail, a poet who once confessed:

> I don't know if the question
> Of the after-life is decided,
> But life, like silence
> In Autumn, is full of detail...

to go in for the generalities he then eschewed, the result of his attempt to see things more wholly—not only in the novel, which, as he recognised, was adapted to carrying such a vision, but also in his last poems.

There is one poem—that which opens the collection, and which, as I have noted, contains very many examples of nouns in lists—where Pasternak voices a certain sense of impotence. It begins:

> I want the heart of the matter
> Always, in work,
> The chaos of feelings,
> The quest for a way;

This and the next two stanzas name over the things from which he wishes to obtain the essence: the past, its causes, its roots; fate. . . . They are recorded as if in a column, with much repetition and wholly abstract vocabulary, which continues in:

> Think, feel, love, live

Nothing could be further from an actual capturing and conveying of "the heart of the matter." The poet goes on to express a particular wish for something he feels he cannot achieve:

> If I could muster
> However crude
> A dozen lines
> On the properties of passion,
>
> Its vandalism,
> Pursuits and panics,
> Impromptus,
> Hustling and hands;

Now, in fact, this very task was accomplished, forty years before, almost to the last detail; for there is a poem in *Themes and Variations* (1923) which offers, in one line more than the eight here desired, the "properties of passion," not abstractly, but concretely, and not only including all the elements mentioned above but even placing in particularly prominent positions the very words: pursuit, elbows, palms. I refer to the fifth poem in the cycle "Razryv" (Separation):

> O twine up this downpour, like waves, of cold elbows
> And, like lilies, of satiny powerful-with-weakness palms!
> Hit back, exultation! Out into the open! Seize them—this wild
>   game of catch

> Keeps the keening of forests that choked in the echo of hunting
>   in Calydon
> Where, like a deer, to the clearing, Actaeon, frenzied, chased
>   Atalanta,
> Where loving was made of the depthless azure that hissed in the
>   ears of the horses,
> Kisses were kissed in the baying-forth of pursuit,
> And caresses were all of the peals of the horn and the crackling
>   of trees, hoofs and claws,
> Out! Out to the open, like them!

Rhythms and rhymes, especially the fine complex of multiple al-
literations and variously balanced internal rhymes (all untranslatable) strike the reader before he quite knows what the poem is about.
Here a highly controlled rationality has created a poem which in-
fects with nonrational fervour before it addresses, as it also does, the
more thoughtful intelligence. Lawlessness and sins, pursuits and
chases, breathless impromptus —they are all here, not "in part" but
wholly, indeed exaggeratedly, in these eight and a half brilliant
lines.

Pasternak has not forgotten his previous work, nor does he long
for a lost capacity. He means, as is seen by the next line—"I would
deduce its law"—that what he really thinks he should write about is
not the essence of passion but its law, its principle. He wishes, not to
present it any more, but to indicate and encompass it; not even to
pronounce its "names," but only their "initials," in a poem that is
to be delicate, distant, all-inclusive from a distance. This is his new
ambition. Not that the new kind of poem is to be emptied of images
in favour of philosophical comments: it is to full, he says, of "flower-
scents, fields, harvest and thunder" (and these *are* the subjects of
most of the poems in this book); but all these, I feel he is also saying,
will point carefully and restrainedly to a reality of human fate and
feeling which is beyond Pasternak. The wish—indeed the sense of
compulsion—to be simple and general is accompanied by a loss and
a renunciation.

All critics who have praised Pasternak's early poetry have stressed
above all an extraordinary power of perception, his seeing the world
as if for the first time. In particular, two contemporary poetesses—
Akhmatova and Tsvetaeva, whom I have already quoted—have
spoken enthusiastically of this power and both have said that it is
something childlike. Tsvetaeva even says:

> It is not Pasternak who is an infant, but the world is an infant in him.
> Pasternak himself I would regard as belonging to the very first days of

creation; the first rivers, first dawns, first storms. He is created before Adam.[4]

This seems to be written about an altogether different poet from the author of *When the Weather Clears.* For in this book, although there is certainly something uncorrupted and wholehearted which might be called childlike, yet the child's freshness, the wonder, the strong joy of acclamation of a world just created, is no longer there. Now the poet is seeing the world for the last time. He sees it at a distance —sees more of it than before, but much less of it in sharp detail; he loves it and finds truth and faith in it, but cannot really smell or taste it. He adds it up, recognizes its sum as right and good, and then leaves it: it is not any more his world.

There is a sentence in *Doctor Zhivago* which, though not perhaps relevant to all the points I have mentioned, expresses some of the feelings that may lie behind these poems: the positive expectation of the future, the last look at the world he has loved, the attitude of willingness, readiness to be close to it, and the personal impotence. It is about Yury in the year of the Revolution:

> He understood that he was a pigmy before the hugeness of the future, feared and loved that future and was secretly proud of it, and for the last time, as in farewell, looked with eager eyes of inspiration at the clouds and trees, the people going along the street, and the great Russian city, straining to overcome its misfortunes, and was ready to sacrifice himself to make things better, and could do nothing.[5]

[4]*Op.cit.,* p. 356.
[5]*Doctor Zhivago,* VI, 5.

The End of the Journey

by Vladimir Weidlé

Having read *My Sister, Life,* Marina Tsvetaeva wrote an essay which nearly flew to bits under the impact of her breathless enthusiasm.[1] Yet at some point she observed very sagaciously: "Pasternak is a major poet. Today he is larger than any of his contemporaries; most of them have been, some are, he alone will be. For, to tell the truth, he is not yet: a babbling, a chirping, a tinkle—he is all tomorrow! The choking cry of a baby—and this baby is the world. A choking, a gasping for breath. Pasternak does not speak, he has no time to finish his sentences, he is all bursting as if his breast could not contain it all—a-ah! He does not yet know our words; there is something here that is childishly—paradisically incoherent and totally upsetting. ..." A little later Tsvetaeva adumbrates: "It is not that Pasternak is an infant but that the world is an infant within him. He belongs, I feel, with the first days of creation: the first rivers, the first dawns, the first storms. He is created before Adam."

I will not echo Tsvetaeva in calling those words "helpless gesturing." Everything she says is true. First, that Pasternak is a major poet; this is much more apparent today than it was at the time, but it was true then too if less easy to see. Tsvetaeva is equally right about Pasternak's impetuousity: "He has no time to finish his sentences," "his breast cannot contain it all"—here is indeed one of his salient traits, which found its fullest expression in his early verse but is in evidence in his later periods as well. Equally acute is Tsvetaeva's observation about the childish incoherence, the infantilism—"a babbling, a chirping"—be it that of the poet or of his world. (Ontogenesis repeats philogenesis and Zhenya Luvers looks with the eyes of a savage or a poet at the incomprehensible but shatteringly vivid

"The End of the Journey" by Vladimir Weidlé. First appeared as an introductory essay to Volume 3 of B. Pasternak, *Sochineniya (Works),* pp. vii-xv. Translated by Victor Erlich.

[1][See "Introduction, in this volume p. 3.—Ed.]

spectacle that unfolds in front of her window.) Finally, it is true, indeed downright prophetic, that the poet of *My Sister, Life* "will be, that he is all tomorrow, that, to tell the truth, he is not yet." In Tsvetaeva's essay the theme was sounded briefly and promptly given a different twist. But one would like to assume that, be it for a moment, Tsvetaeva came close to affirming what for us now is unquestionable, notably, that, when all is said and done, this collection of verse in which a poet signaled so forcefully to a fellow poet was much more a promise than a fulfillment.

If *Themes and Variations* differ very slightly from *My Sister, Life,* the poems that followed attest to a search for a new or a renewed poetic style which in many peoples'—and, for all one knows, Pasternak's—opinion was found, at least as far as lyric poetry was concerned, when in 1932 there appeared a collection whose very title seemed to announce a major shift, *Second Birth.*

This view was bolstered by the often quoted lines from the new volume:

> There are in the lives of great poets
> Traits of complete naturalness.
> And having sensed it there, one cannot
> But end in all silence, speechless.
>
> And feeling near to all things, greeting
> In daily life what is to be
> At last one cannot help but falling
> Into an unheard-of simplicity.
>
> But if we do not keep it hidden
> No mercy will be shown us here.
> It's what is needed most—but people
> Do find complexities more clear.[2]

Let us note that the above celebrates naturalness and simplicity not unconditionally but on the assumption that the poet will not lapse into these qualities as into a heresy, risking thereby total dumbness, but will manage to conceal them under the cover of seeming complexity which people comprehend more readily even though they need simplicity more. As suggested by this tedious paraphrase, to proclaim this poem as a return to the tradition, as a new classicism or anything of the sort would be unduly rash. The poet did not go dumb, he did not sacrifice his gift for the sake of that "unheard-of simplicity," inaccessible to people, noble and surpassing, but not at-

[2][Quoted from V. Markov, ed., *Modern Russian Poetry,* p. 603.—Ed.]

tainable through conscious efforts. Perhaps, he should not have invoked at that point naturalness and simplicity. If it cannot be denied that these qualities loom larger in the 1932 collection than in the previous ones, they are merely a by-product of his endeavors and not their direct aim. What he was primarily aiming at was a more conscious control over his chief poetic treasure—a crowd of images generated by his vision, and at transforming these into direct designations of objects. In Pasternak these images always emerged from sensory perceptions and addressed themselves to such perceptions; they were tangible, concrete, *(veshchnye)*, but they always bore witness to something occurring in his inner world. Now they were enjoined to designate elements of external reality or, more exactly, this assignment was given to essentially the same words that were used before, but this time they were to cease acting as images, as metaphors; the lyrical merger or the inner with the outer was brought under control. Imagery was supplanted by representation and the lyrical "I" by "feeling near to all things," by the poet's broadened "experience."

Consequently, the "incoherence" noted by Marina Tsvetaeva was much less apparent in *Second Birth* or in the historical poem *Spektorsky* than it was in Pasternak's early poems. Its volume decreased, in line with an expanded role of narration, description, landscape painting, portraiture, in a word, of a verifiable correspondence with matters accessible not just to poetic but also to "ordinary" experience. Yet Pasternak's language in and of itself did not become more natural or transparent; and this failed to happen because he persisted in equating this language with poetry. In this crucial aspect he remained faithful to Modernism, which captured him in his youth even though he had been moving away from it as he was reaching beyond the purely lyrical toward narration, objectivity, and the epic, ultimately, toward prose. Thus among the poems included in the volume *On Early Trains* (1943), the first two cycles composed in 1936 are closer in this respect to *Second Birth* than to the verses dated early 1941 and forming the cycle "Peredelkino." It is the latter that opens Pasternak's last period—a stage most clearly anticipated by some pages of his prose, notably of "A Tale," and by verses for children, e.g., "The Zoo" and "The Merry-Go-Round." One of the finest instances of this new and truly "unheard-of" simplicity, of this new poetry which Pasternak was vouchsafed toward the end of his life was quite appropriately, and probably at his behest, included in the first volume of his *Selected Works* that was to appear in Moscow in 1957. The title of the poem is "Wintering":

The door opened and from the yard
The air rolled steamily into the kitchen.

The date here too is 1941. The statement in Pasternak's second autobiography *I Remember,* "I do not like my style up to 1940" should be taken quite literally. That year was indeed the turning point; the shift from the old to the new manner occurred in 1940. What was the nature of this shift?

It goes without saying that poetry is inseparable from language; it lives only with it and in it; it is fully embodied in the word. But there is a significant difference between looking at words as words, that is, viewing the whole of which they are constituent parts as a work of art, and approaching them *sub specie* of the total meaning they embody, with some awareness of the speaker responsible for that meaning. There is a difference between listening to words, to their sounds, to the sound of word combinations, seeking to grasp the manifold semantic emanations that crisscross and play on their surface, and listening intently to live speech in order to reach through the words toward the Word they utter. To be sure, no poet or, for that matter, no sensitive reader of poetry can afford to bypass words, to be satisfied with the sense designated by words rather than actually embodied in them. Otherwise, he would fail to distinguish between poetry and colloquial language, between verbal art which makes use of words and ordinary human intercourse. He always listens to words, weighs them, assesses the vividness, the novelty, the "interest" of verbal textures, but in Modernism he does nothing but that; he refuses to *speak* in verse, he insists that poetry is made up of words (Mallarmé),[3] that the poet bears no responsibility for the poem's meaning, and invites the reader to read into it whatever meaning he pleases, claiming that the best, the most unexpected and striking sound combinations are arrived at not deliberately but by chance (Futurists, Surrealists). It is not true that the poet thus leaves the reader out of account; on the contrary, he is only too mindful of the reader. In fact, he looks at himself through the eyes of the reader, or more exactly, through the eyes of an uncommonly sophisticated reader, one fully equipped to distinguish between striking, new, interesting word combinations and stale, hackneyed ones. Essentially, Pasternak never was a Modernist (and neither was Mallarmé or

[3][An allusion, clearly, to an alleged exchange between Mallarmé and Degas. As the latter wondered why he had so much trouble writing verse even though he had so many good ideas, Mallarmé is reported to have replied: "one does not write poems with ideas, my friend; one writes them with words." — Ed.]

Valéry or, for that matter, any genuine poet), but he was affiliated with Modernism, grew under its aegis, and because of the nature of his poetic endowment could be easily mistaken for a Modernist.

Words jostled each other in front of his door, and kept bursting into his room *en masse,* in response to any and all lyrical impulse. Since they would subside into verse reluctantly, and not until some violence was done to their sense, the resultant verbal design was apt to be especially whimsical and intricate. Those were the "affectations," the "twists" and the "rattles" which Pasternak was to repudiate later. This is not to say that back in his early years he sought those qualities, was deliberately reaching for them as did his friends the Imagists. But how could he have been expected to do without what he was urged to admire and what no one around him thought of eschewing?

"In everything I sought not the essence but an extraneous cleverness," he said in *I Remember.* And yet in the same autobiography we find this comment about a search for new means of expression which gripped "Andrey Bely, Khlebnikov and some others": "I could never understand this quest. To my mind, the most remarkable discoveries occur when content filling the artist to the brim allows him no time for reflection and he hastily utters his new word in the old language, scarcely aware of whether it is old or new." The Society for the Study of Verse Rhythm, led by Andrey Bely, elicits the following: "I did not go to his lectures because I have always been of the opinion that the music of the word is not an acoustic phenomenon and does not consist of the euphony of vowels and consonants, taken by themselves, but of the relationship between the meaning and the sound of the words."[4] Pasternak expressed himself still more clearly in speaking of his first collection of verse: "My persistent concern was with the content, my most ardent wish that the poem itself contain something. ...." In the same passage he described the title of his first book *Twin in the Clouds* as "pretentious to the point of stupidity."[5] Consequently, even in the period when such pretentiousness was possible and when Pasternak wrote in "The Black Goblet" that "art demands only that its assignment be executed brilliantly," he did not interpret these "assignments" as purely formal ones and sought "content," correlation of sound with meaning, cared not just about words but about what the words convey. But if so, why does he accuse himself of having striven for extraneous cleverness rather than for substance?

[4][*I Remember,* p. 62.—Ed.]

[5][B. Pasternak, *Sochineniya,* II *(Works),* 32, 31.—Ed.]

It seems to me that the contradiction here is more apparent than real and that Pasternak is not guilty of arbitrarily crediting his youth with a concern of his later years. It stands to reason that he always searched for content or, more exactly, yearned to express, to embody in his verse something he has glimpsed or discovered and did not have to look for. This is stated more profoundly, if in a somewhat confusing language, in the diary of Yuri Zhivago: "I have never seen art as form but rather as a hidden, secret part of content."[6] That part, it is elaborated further, which cannot be reduced to themes, situations, plots; subsequently, the point gets somewhat blurred (since the word "art" is used simultaneously in several senses), but what remains incontestable is that the most important thing about the work of art is neither individual words nor forms, nor the object of representation, but what is conveyed and what could not have been conveyed in any other fashion, "some statement about life," "some idea" (not the most felicitous way of putting it) "which outweighs the importance of all the rest and turns out to be the essence, the soul and the foundation of the depicted." There is little doubt that already in his early period Pasternak sensed this, however vaguely. His overabundant imagery was reaching toward the Word though at times it remained a matter of mere words; it was a short-hand—as Pasternak once called the Shakespearean metaphor—which the very nature of his poetic gift impelled him to adopt. When some years later he turned to epic description and narration, he persisted in his search for the essence and the soul of the depicted, even if at times—e.g., in *Spektorsky*—he was apt to lose his grip on that essence and lapse into pedestrian concreteness. At that second stage of his journey he was free from his youthful temptations but susceptible to others more appropriate to maturity. The goal which still beckoned, or at least shimmered in the distance, has not yet been reached. Here is what he says toward the end of his novel about its hero: "It had been the dream of his life to write with an originality so discreet, so well concealed, as to be unnoticeable in its disguise of current and customary forms; all his life he had struggled for a style so restrained, so unpretentious that the reader or the hearer would fully understand the meaning without realizing how he assimilated it. All his life he had striven for an unostentatious style, and he was dismayed to find how far he still remained from his ideal."[7]

"All his life." These echoing words are more applicable to the

[6][*Doctor Zhivago*, p. 281.—Ed.]

[7][*Ibid.*, p. 440. I have permitted myself to tamper with the translation by substituting "all his life he had striven" for "He had striven constantly."—Ed.]

author of the novel than to its much younger hero. And he uttered them knowing that he had finally found what he was seeking all his life. It is in this restrained, unpretentious style that he couched his expansive tale about Dr. Zhivago, the poems which conclude the novel, and all his other verses written after 1940. This final stage is not discontinuous with the poet's past: he was getting there, however slowly, all his life. Some of what was flawed in the old—a light tinkling of a dispensable jingle—recurs now and then in the new, while the best is fully preserved. There is no less keenness of the eye or fineness of the ear in his late prose than in the early one, in "Wintering" than in "Melchior" or any poem in *My Sister, Life.* The gift for a striking image was not lost either; it was simply brought under control, it was transformed as was Pasternak's entire art—a process that cannot be reduced to increasing selectivity and maturation. This transformation was primarily a matter of a shift from a conspicuous to an inconspicuous style, a shift brought about by repudiation of such conspicuousness, or, to reach a bit deeper, by a refusal to pay attention to the quality which in the past Pasternak was apt to use as a chief criterion in evaluating his own works, notably the dazzle of their verbal texture. The dazzle is not extinguished thereby; it is merely subordinated to the Word that shines through it. At first glance both the verbal and narrative texture of *Doctor Zhivago,* in comparison with that of *Safe Conduct,* appears less tightly woven and less precious. One is likely to have the same first impression in comparing the late Pasternak's best verse—e.g., his marvelous New Testament poems—to the lyrics which secured his early fame. But overcoming Modernism is not a farewell to poetry. Transparence of the texture should not be equated with its deterioration. This texture is at its most precious when in contemplating it we realize that it is not the most precious thing in the work. Words are not jewels.

> They [the Magi] stood in shadow in that cattlestall
> And whispered, lost in awe at what to say,
> When suddenly a hand came from the dark
> And moved them gently from the way.
> He looked around; there, like a guest, afar
> Upon the Virgin gazed the Christmas Star.[8]

When we read these lines, we do not pour diamonds from palm to palm, we merely listen and glimpse in the distance through their light shimmer the world's rainbow: gold, purple, and azure.

[8][Quoted from "Christmas Star," Boris Pasternak, *In the Interlude: Poems, 1945-1960,* translated by Henry Kamer (London: Oxford University Press, 1962), p. 71. —Ed.]

Were one to press the inquiry beyond the consequences of the shift into the essential nature and the sources of this transformation, one would have to admit that there is no direct testimony which would warrant a confident answer. Yet if a poet, a wielder of words, resolves them back into the Word, makes them serve the Word, he must have found something that transcends all words. The only antidote to a religion of art, which cripples art, is religion. It is difficult to imagine that the crisis experienced by Pasternak in 1940 was a crisis of some other, nonreligious order. And there is little reason to assume that in talking to himself Pasternak never called this crisis a miracle.

> But a miracle is a sign—an act of God!
> In days of confusion, at a call unforeseen
> We stand unprepared, before God our Lord.[9]

---

[9][Quoted from "The Miracle" ("The Poems of Doctor Zhivago"), Boris Pasternak, *Poems,* translated by Eugene M. Kayden (Yellow Springs, Ohio: The Antioch Press, 1964), p. 218 — Ed.]

Chronology of Important Dates

1890	February 10: Born in Moscow in the home of Leonid Pasternak and Rose Kaufmann-Pasternak.
1903	Meets the composer Alexander Scryabin and begins a serious study of music, which was to last for six years.
1907	Joins a literary-artistic circle, Serdarda.
1908	Enters Moscow University as a law student. Nearly a year later changes to philosophy.
1912	May 9-August 12. Studies neo-Kantian philosophy under Prof. Hermann Cohen at the University of Marburg. Toward the end of that period abandons philosophy for the sake of poetry.
1913	Passes his state examination at Moscow University. February 10: Gives a lecture on "Symbolism and Immortality" in a Moscow sculptor's studio.
1914	Joins Tsentrifuga (Centrifugue), a Futurist grouping. Meets Mayakovsky. Publication of his first volume of verse, *Twin in the Clouds*.
1914-16	Tutors in the provinces. Travels and works in the Urals and the region of the River Kama.
1917	After the February Revolution returns to Moscow. Publication of his second volume of poetry, *Over the Barriers*.
1918	Works as a librarian in the Commissariat of Education.
1921	His parents and sister emigrate to Germany.
1922	Publication of *My Sister, Life*. Marries Evgenia Lourié (née Muratova), painter.
1923	Publication of a volume of poems, *Themes and Variations*. Birth of his first son, Evgeny.
1924	Publication of the long poem *The Lofty Malady* and of the story "The Childhood of Luvers."

1925   Publication of a collection of four short stories under the title of one of them, "Aerial Ways." (The other three, in addition to "The Childhood of Luvers," were "Il Trotto di Apelle," "Letters from Tula.")

1926   Publication of the narrative poem "The Year 1905."

1927   Publication of the narrative poem "Lieutenant Schmidt."

1931   Divorces his first wife. Journeys to Tbilisi with his future second wife at the invitation of the Georgian poet Paolo Yashvili. Meets another Georgian poet Titian Tibidze. (Both, who soon became his close friends, perished in the purges of the late thirties.) Publication of an unfinished novel in verse, *Spektorsky,* and of the autobiographical work *Safe Conduct.*

1932   Publication of a volume of verse, *Second Birth.* Marries Zinaida Neuhaus. Moves into a house in Peredelkino, a writers' colony near Moscow.

1934   Speaks at the First All-Union Congress of Soviet Writers in Moscow. Publication of the story "Povest," later translated into English as "A Tale" or "The Last Summer."

1935   Goes to Paris as a member of the Soviet delegation to the International Congress of Writers in Defense of Culture.

1936   Speaks "On Modesty and Boldness" at the Congress of Soviet Writers in Minsk.

1938   Birth of his second son, Leonid.

1941   Evacuated along with a number of Moscow writers to Chistopol, a provincial town on the river Kama; by 1943 is back in Peredelkino.

1943   Publication of the volume of poetry *On Early Trains.*

1945   Publication of the volume of verse *Terrestrial Expanse.*

1946   Repeatedly attacked in the course of an official campaign against independent writers and artists, most notably by A. Fadeyev, the First Secretary of the Soviet Writers' Union.

1954   Publication in the miscellany *Literaturnaya Moskva* of his article on translating Shakespeare. Publication in the journal *Znamya (Banner)* of "Ten Poems from a Novel" which were later to appear in *Doctor Zhivago.*

1956   The journal *Novy Mir* refuses to publish *Doctor Zhivago.* A moderately phrased statement of the editorial board terms the novel a repudiation of the October Revolution.

1957   Publication of *Doctor Zhivago* in Italy.

1958   October 23: Is awarded a Nobel Prize in Literature. His immediate reaction is one of "great [though] a lonely joy." October 29: Faced by a press campaign, expulsion from the Soviet Writers' Union and threats of banishment, cables the Swedish Academy: "Considering the meaning this award has been given in the society to which I belong, I must reject this undeserved prize." November 1: Writes to N. Khrushchev; "A departure beyond the borders of my country would for me be equivalent to death." Publication of *Essay in Autobiography* (the title of the 1959 American edition is *I Remember*) outside of Russia.

1959   Publication of his last volume of verse, *When the Weather Clears*, in Paris.

1960   May 30: Dies in Moscow.

Selected Bibliography

Note: There is no mention here of any individual essays in the Davie and Livingstone collection, though many of them are essential to the student of Pasternak. Only works in English are included.

Abel, Lionel. "Boris Pasternak's *Doctor Zhivago*." *Dissent* (Autumn, 1959), pp. 334-41.

Bowra, Maurice C. *The Creative Experiment,* Chapter on Pasternak, pp. 128-58. London: MacMillan, 1949.

Chiaromonte, Nicola. "*Dr. Zhivago* and Modern Sensibility." *Dissent* (Winter, 1959), pp. 35-44.

Cohen, J. M. "The Poetry of Pasternak." *Horizon* (July 1944).

Conquest, Robert. *The Pasternak Affair: Courage of Genius.* London: Collins and Harvill, 1961.

Davie, Donald. *The Poems of Doctor Zhivago.* Manchester University Press, 1965; New York: Barnes and Noble, 1965.

Davie, Donald, and Angela Livingstone, eds. *Pasternak. Modern Judgments.* London: McMillan, 1969.

Gerschenkron, Alexander. "Notes on *Doctor Zhivago.*" *Modern Philology,* 58 Chicago, (February, 1961), iii, 194-200.

Gifford, Henry. *Pasternak.* Cambridge: Cambridge University Press, 1977.

Hayward, Max. "Pasternak's *Dr. Zhivago.*" *Encounter* (May, 1958), pp. 38-48.

Jakobson, Roman. "The Contours of *Safe Conduct*" (translated from the Czech). *Semiotics of Art,* pp. 188-96. Cambridge, Mass.: MIT Press, 1976.

Livingstone, Angela. "Pasternak's Early Prose." *Aumla,* 22 (November, 1964), pp. 249-67.

Lamont, Rosette C. "'As a Gift'...Zhivago the Poet." *PMLA,* 75, no 5 (December, 1960), 621-33.

Markov, V. "Notes on Pasternak's *Dr. Zhivago.*" *Russian Review,* 1 (1959), 14-22.

Mathewson, Rufus. *The Positive Hero in Russian Literature.* 2nd. ed.; chapter on Pasternak, "An Inward Music," pp. 259-78. Stanford, Cal.: Stanford University Press, 1957.

Milosz, Czestaw. "On Pasternak Soberly." In *Books Abroad,* Norman: University of Oklahoma Press, v. 44 (Spring, 1970), pp. 200-209.

Monas, Sidney. "The Revelation of St. Boris: Russian Literature and Individual Autonomy." *Soviet and Chinese Communism: Similarities and Differences,* pp. 255-87. Seattle, Wash.: University of Washington Press, 1967.

Muchnic, Helen. "Pasternak and Yury Zhivago." *From Gorky to Pasternak,* pp. 341-04. New York: Random House, 1961.

Plank, Dale L. *Pasternak's Lyric: A Study of Sound and Imagery.* The Hague: Mouton and Co., 1966.

Poggioli, Renato. "Boris Pasternak." *Partisan Review* (Autumn, 1958), pp. 541-54.

Pomorska, Krystyna. "Music as Theme and Constituent in Pasternak's Poems," in *Slavic Poetics. Essays in Honor of Kiril Taranovsky,* pp. 333-49. The Hague: Mouton and Co., 1973.

————. *Themes and Variations in Pasternak's Poetics.* The Hague: Peter de Ridder Press, 1975.

Struve, Gleb. "Sense and Nonsense About *Dr. Zhivago.*" *Studies in Russian and Polish Literature,* pp. 229-50. The Hague: Mouton and Co., 1962.

Wilson, Edmund. "Doctor Life and His Guardian Angel." *New Yorker,* November 15, 1958, pp. 201-26.

Notes on the Editor and the Contributors

VICTOR ERLICH is Bensinger Professor of Russian Literature at Yale University. His published works include *Russian Formalism, The Double Image, Gogol,* and a number of articles on Russian literature and criticism.

MICHAEL AUCOUTURIER is Professor of Russian Literature at the Sorbonne. His publications include *Pasternak par lui-méme* and articles on Pasternak, Tolstoy, Akhmatova, and Solzhenitsyn. He is also the editor of the Proceedings of the 1975 Symposium on Pasternak in Cerisy-la-Salle.

SIR ISAIAH BERLIN of Oxford's All Souls College is a philosopher-historian. He is the author of *Karl Marx, The Hedgehog and the Fox, Historical Inevitability, Two Concepts of Liberty,* and many articles on European and Russian intellectual history.

STUART HAMPSHIRE, Warden of Wadham College, Oxford University, is the author of *Spinoza, Thought and Action, Freedom of the Mind,* and *Modern Writers and Other Essays.*

ROBERT LOUIS JACKSON is Professor of Russian Literature at Yale University. He is the author of *Dostoevsky's Underground Man in Russian Literature* and *Dostoevsky's Quest for Form* and the editor of *Chekhov: A Collection of Critical Essays* and *Twentieth-Century Interpretations of Crime and Punishment.*

ANGELA LIVINGSTONE teaches Russian Literature at the University of Essex. She has written a number of articles on Pasternak and co-edited with Donald Davie an anthology of Pasternak criticism *Pasternak. Modern Judgments.*

YURY LOTMAN, Professor of Russian Literature at the University of Tartu/ (Estonia), is a literary historian and theoretician. His published works include *The Structure of the Artistic Text, Analysis of the Poetic Text,* and studies of Pushkin, Gogol, and other nineteenth-century Russian writers.

NILS AKE NILSSON, Professor of Russian Literature at the University of Stockholm, has written on Gogol and Petersburg, Ibsen in Russia, Chekhov, and modern Russian poetry, most notably Russian Imagism. He is the editor of a quarterly *Russian Literature.*

DIMITRI OBOLENSKY, of Christ Church, Oxford has written extensively on Russian and Slavic cultural history. He is the author of *Byzantium and the*

Slavs and *Bogomils* (a study in Balkan neo-Manicheanism) and the editor of a bilingual anthology *The Heritage of Russian Verse.*

ANDREY SINYAVSKY, Russian critic and fiction writer, wrote under his own name essays on modern Russian poetry and under the pseudonym Abram Tertz "underground" fiction, notably *The Trial Begins, Fantastic Stories,* and, more recently, studies of Gogol and Pushkin. Sentenced in 1965 to a prison camp for "slandering his country," he was later encouraged to leave Russia. He is now in Paris, teaching Russian literature at the Sorbonne.

FYODOR STEPUN, a philosopher, essayist, and memoir writer, left Russia shortly after the Revolution and until his death, in 1959, lived and lectured in Germany. Among his works are *Fundamental Problems of Theater, The Russian Soul and the Revolution,* and *Encounters.*

YURY TYNYANOV, a literary historian and a historical novelist, was one of the leading theoreticians of the Formalist school of Russian criticism. He is the author of studies in Russian poetry from Pushkin to Pasternak and in general verse theory—most notably, *Archaists and Innovators* and *The Problem of Verse Language*—and of biographical novels such as *Kyukhlya and Pushkin.*

VLADIMIR WEIDLÉ, a literary critic and art historian, left Russia in 1942 and has lived since in Paris. He is the author of *Les Abeilles d'Aristée: essai sur le destin actuel des Lettres et des Arts* (*The Bees of Aristaeus:* An Essay on the Actual Fate of Arts and Letters), *Russia Absent and Present,* and of numerous essays on modern Russian poetry and on general poetics and esthetics.